WINNER TAKES ALL

A BREAKING INTO THE BLACK ELITE NOVEL

SHONETTE CHARLES

Seamare Press LLC

www.seamarepress.com

Seamare Press LLC
PO Box 99095
Raleigh, NC 27624
www.seamarepress.com

Publisher's Note: This is a work of fiction. Names, characters, places, organizations and incidents are a product of the author's imagination. Locales and public names are sometimes used for atmospheric purposes. Any resemblance to actual people, living or dead, or to businesses, organizations, events, institutions, or locales is completely coincidental.

Quantity sales. Special discounts are available on quantity purchases by corporations, associations, and others. For details, contact the address above.

Winner Takes All/ Shonette Charles. -- 1st ed.
ISBN 978-0-9964568-6-9
eBook ISBN: 978-0-9964568-7-6

Library of Congress Control Number: 2017909023

Published in the United States of America by Seamare Press, Raleigh, NC.

Acknowledgments

Thank you to God and everyone that has supported me. Bringing this trilogy to life was an amazing journey. I can't wait to see what the future holds!

ONE

....

Sahara held the white sheath wedding gown with the deep "v" illusion neckline against her body and twirled in front of the oversized gold-leaf mirror in the bridal shop's dressing room. Her shoulder length, curly brown hair was the perfect halo to the contrasting image of the white dress against her smooth copper skin. "Ohhh, this is so pretty! I feel like a princess," she said as she pictured herself at a lavish reception with her real-life knight in shining armor.

Draped across the gold couch like she was the Queen of Sheba, her Soror and Belles & Beaus sister, Tania looked up from the wedding magazine on her lap. "That dress is beautiful, but I hate to tell you this. You and Noah are already married."

Sahara raised one eyebrow. "True. But, there is nothing wrong with a little role play...you know to keep things spicy!"

Donna, the primary reason why they were at the bridal boutique, stepped from behind the curtain of the changing area and walked up the steps to the elevated platform in front of the three massive mirrors. "What do you think?" she asked.

Sahara and Tania looked at their friend and then back at each other. Donna had put a new twist on bridal dress with the antique ivory, strapless jumpsuit with a tulle overskirt trailing behind her that she had on now. "So, do you like it?" Donna asked again as the sunlight caught her hazel eyes causing them to shine even brighter.

"Well...talk about role play. Which one are you—the bride or the groom?" asked Tania with a straight face as she touched her Halle Berry hairdo fixing an invisible hair that was out of place.

Donna rolled her eyes at her best friend since forever. "What do you think, Sahara? Do you like it?"

Always the peacemaker, Sahara could see the hope in Donna's eyes, and she hated to crush it. "Who is the designer? I like it. But, it's not very traditional, is it?"

Donna looked at herself in the mirror and sighed. "Well, I don't think I'm a traditional woman. However, Alton is a traditional kind of guy." She sighed. "Who am I kidding? He'll hate this." She walked down the platform stairs and looked at Sahara. "And, Monique Lhuillier is the designer."

However, before she retreated behind the curtain, something outside the window of the bridal shop caught Donna's eye. She let out a surprised "Ewww!" before striding to the window.

"What is it? What do you see?" asked Tania as she and Sahara hurried to get an eyeful.

Donna moved to the side of the window so that she was out of view of a passerby on the street. "It's Emery."

Sure enough, there was Emery Edmonds in a peach summer shorts suit strolling down the streets of Midtown without a care in the world. "Well, you better get over your dislike of her. You know she and Alton are friends," said Tania as she returned to her perch and flopped back on the gold couch. "Don't forget. She is Sahara's line sister." Tania grinned in Sahara's direction, as Donna grimaced.

Sahara bulged her eyes at Tania. Why did she have to comment about Emery? She knew that Donna didn't like Emery, although Sahara wasn't quite sure why. Truth be told, the first year that Sahara lived in Fairchester, she couldn't stand Emery. But that was mainly because of Rozlyn...or as she liked to refer to her...she whom shall not be named. And, finding out that Emery was engaged to her husband, Noah, when they were in college certainly hadn't helped.

But, they were in a better place now...sort of. They were initiated into Belles & Beaus together so Tania was right. They were line sisters, in a way. They hadn't developed the bond that Sahara had with her sorority line sisters, but she was connected to Emery...and Zora...in a special way now.

Tania continued, "And Sahara, you should tell your girl that Rozlyn Wormley is putting her business out in the street." Tania was also in the Belles & Beaus chapter with Emery so Sahara wasn't sure why informing Emery was only her responsibility.

Donna perked up. "What is she saying?"

Tania swatted her hand at Donna. "Now, you know Rozlyn is messy so don't even worry about it. We got enough on our plates disputing the lies the Republican presidential candidate spreads. Isn't that enough?"

"Now *that* certainly is the truth!" said Sahara as she shook her head in agreement with Tania. And, unfortunately, she knew what it was like to be the recipient of Rozlyn's untruths and deception. There was no need to go there with her latest nonsense.

Tania looked Donna up and down. "Anyway, you have more pressing concerns. Like figuring out why you want to wear pants to your wedding. Is there something we should know? Girl, that's the real gossip." Tania smiled at Donna sweetly.

Sahara tried her best to not laugh. When they moved to Fairchester, she met Donna and Tania the same night that she met Emery—at a Theta Iota Kappa party, of all places. However, Donna and Tania were her girls...her Lambda Upsilon Alpha sorors...wearers of the pink and green...her sisters. They just clicked from day one. Sahara's relationship with Emery didn't even compare.

Donna collapsed into one of the zebra printed occasional chairs and took a sip from her champagne flute, a perk of shopping for wedding dresses in the upscale boutique. Fairchester was small, but it still had its

4

trendy areas, and Midtown was one. Million dollar condominiums, hip restaurants, and stylish stores dotted the high-end area. Sahara used to bring her children, Clarissa and Trevor, to the popular park in the neighborhood.

"I don't know why it bugs me that Emery and Alton are friends. I mean they aren't even close anymore. They just grew up together." Sahara was almost blinded as Donna twirled the two carat, brilliant cut engagement ring on her finger and the sun's rays danced across the symbol of love and loyalty. "I just...I just feel like I'm so in love with Alton that I'm going crazy."

Tania looked up from her magazine. "Crazy, huh? Maybe you should see someone about that."

Donna closed her eyes as a look of exasperation crept on her face. Tania and Donna had been best friends since college, but Sahara knew that Donna's theatrics were sometimes too much for Tania—and Tania's sarcasm sometimes was too much for Donna. "I know that Alton is a meat and potatoes, traditional type of guy. So, why even bother trying on this stupid wedding jumpsuit? I know that he will hate it."

"Well, do you like it? You can't stop being who you are for Alton," said Sahara.

"Can't I?" asked Donna. "I love him, and I want this marriage to work. And, all relationships require compromise."

Compromise sure, but not complete surrender. Sahara wondered how much Donna was "compromising," but she didn't say anything.

Donna downed the remaining champagne then held up her glass. "Isabelle, can I have more, please?"

Isabelle, the boutique's assistant, staggered in with an arm full of dresses and hung them on the rack outside the changing area. Then, she walked over and refreshed Donna's champagne flute. "Let me know if you need anything else."

"Just leave the bottle," said Donna, as Isabelle was about to exit the room.

Isabelle didn't seem surprised by the request and placed the bottle of champagne on the table by the wall. Donna didn't waste any time drinking the contents of the crystal glass before refilling it again. "Alright. Back to the drawing board," She said as she stood up. She flipped through the dresses that Isabelle hung on the rack, selected one, and disappeared behind the curtain of the changing area.

Tania looked up from her magazine. Sahara guessed that with Donna and her drama tucked neatly behind the changing area curtain, Tania felt free to re-engage. "So, are you going to the Belles & Beaus cluster next month? It's in Greensboro, so it's pretty close."

"Yes, I'm going. Emery is too," replied Sahara.

"I was trying to get under Donna's skin before, but you and Emery are becoming good friends, aren't you?"

Sahara shrugged her shoulders. "Like you said...we're

line sisters, right?" Sahara grinned at Tania.

Tania laughed. "You better not let Donna hear you claim her. You know she has a complex about Emery. I don't know what has gotten into her lately." Tania's face became serious. "Anyway, how is Zora doing? When is she due?"

"In November." Zora also was initiated into Belles & Beaus with Sahara and Emery. "She's in her second trimester so she's feeling great right now, but I don't think that she's coming to cluster."

"Well, I'm sure that her plate is full with her little prince and soon-to-be-born princess. And, I heard that Cass took over his family's business, so I'm sure he's super busy."

"I didn't know that. Which one? The stores, the private schools, or construction?" asked Sahara.

"The whole enchilada. I heard the old man retired."

Wow. "That's huge," said Sahara. "But, I thought Cass' mother was the brains behind the operations. Did she retire?"

Tania laughed. "Isn't that always how it is? The men think they have the power, but the women are the real masterminds."

Zora's family was one of the most prominent black families in the area. Her aunt was the president of the local Sphinx chapter, and her father was in The Shield and The Coalition. However, her husband, Cass was the son of Blake Montgomery, one of the richest—and most powerful—men in the state. Between Zora's pedigree in the black community and Cass' connections in the white one—they could be the ultimate high-profile power couple, if Zora wasn't such a homebody.

Donna emerged from the changing area in a beautiful, jaw-dropping gown. Embroidered from head-to-toe in ivory and gold, it skimmed tastefully over all her curves and fit her like a glove. Tania looked at Donna. "I like the dress, and it's definitely a step up from the jumpsuit...." Tania paused for a second. "But, I'm not crazy about the gold."

"I love the dress, but it does seem like it would be more appropriate at a ball or a gala," added Sahara. Donna reminded Sahara of a trophy, especially standing on the platform. *And the Academy Award goes to....*

Donna let out a huge sigh and descended from the platform. She took a swallow from her champagne flute before returning to her zebra print throne. "I guess I do look like a statue." She laughed. "Anyway, did y'all hear what happened at the Sphinx Ball?"

"Something happened at the Sphinx Ball?" asked Sahara. The local Sphinx chapter held a masquerade ball every May, and it was the premier event for Fairchester's black elite. Noah and Sahara attended the past few years as guests of Zora's aunt. Tania was also there at the Belles & Beaus table.

Donna sat up, welcoming the distraction from wedding dress analysis. "Well, Soror Christina told me that there was some mix-up with who was sitting at the Lambda Upsilon Alpha table. Apparently, Trish Owens received official notification from the chapter that she could sit at the table. However, when she arrived, there wasn't a seat for her."

Tania covered her mouth with her hand and gasped, "Oh no!"

"Was it the chapter's fault or an issue on The Sphinx's end?" asked Sahara. She, Donna, and Tania were in the same LUA chapter in Fairchester.

Donna and Tania glanced at each other. "C'mon, you know that it was our fault," said Donna. "Someone in the chapter messed up the count and informed too many people that they could sit at the table."

"Well, that seems like a mistake that anyone could make," said Sahara.

"True. But, it doesn't reflect well on the chapter," added Tania. "And, there have been a bunch of problems lately."

"A bunch of problems?" asked Sahara while raising her eyebrow.

"Yes," said Donna. "Let's be honest. Our community programs are not what they used to be. Sure, we have programs, but some things are just for the sake of doing things and don't have the impact that they could or should on the community. Our fundraisers are not what they used to be. And, don't get me started on sisterly relations." Donna took a sip of champagne. "I don't even know whom half the members are anymore—and I attend everything. It just seems like we need to do a better job of connecting with community...and each other."

"I hear you," said Tania.

"Well, elections are this program year. Soror Elizabeth told me that she was thinking about running for an office," said Sahara. "She's our age and a lot younger than most of the sorors on the executive board. She can bring some fresh ideas."

Donna stood up and walked over to the rack of wedding gowns. "I think a lot of people are considering running for positions. If we get our acts together, maybe the young members can shake things up and take over the chapter. Then, we could really get the chapter on the right foot." She took one of the wedding dresses off the rack and returned behind the curtain.

"Do you think the young sorors can really run the chapter?" asked Sahara. As long as she had been in the Xi Epsilon Omega, older sorors were the ones in charge. And, from knowing the history of the chapter, the older sorors had always been the chapter's leadership.

"I hope so...because we have to do better. Speaking of...," said Tania taking her first sip of champagne. "Would you consider running for a position?"

"Me? Run for an office?" Sahara looked at Tania and tried to get a clue about what she was thinking. "I don't know, Tania. You know I'm relatively new to the chapter. I just got into Belles & Beaus. I don't...."

At that moment, Donna walked out and paraded in front of them. Dressed in a white ball gown with a rhinestone-encrusted bodice, long sleeves, and a cascading tulle skirt, she looked heavenly. Tania was the first to speak. "Oh my goodness! Absolutely gorgeous! Now, THAT is a wedding dress."

Sahara smiled at her friend. "You look beautiful, Donna."

Donna twirled around one more time. "Do you think Alton will like it?"

"Does he have eyes?" asked Tania. "Of course, Alton will like it. No, he'll LOVE you in it. And then, love you out of it." Tania winked as Donna and Sahara laughed.

"Well, that's the reaction I'm going for...so I'll take it," said Donna as she walked away to change out of the dress. "And Sahara...you need to run for president."

"Huh? What?" She thought they were talking about wedding dresses. "Why don't you run for president?" Sahara shot back at Donna. "You are more involved in the chapter than I am."

"I'm running for vice president of programs," Donna said from behind the curtain. "We have 'young sorors' that are willing to run for most of the offices on the executive board. But, we need someone strong to run for president. Tania is on the executive board for Belles & Beaus already, so that leaves you."

So, the young sorors were trying to stage a coup? Since when? And, how did she get pulled into it? "Me?

No, I don't think...," said Sahara.

However, before she could finish, Donna emerged from the changing area in the blouse and jeans she wore into the bridal boutique. "Just think about it. Please? For me? This is our chance to make our chapter strong again."

Sahara finished her glass of champagne. "Well, I guess I have politics in my blood." They all laughed.

"Girl, I'm glad that you said it...because I was thinking it!" said Tania as she stood up.

"Me too!" Donna poured the last drops in the bottle into her champagne flute. "No use in letting good champagne go to waste."

Clearly, that wasn't going to happen under Donna's watch. She had...one, two, three...three glasses of it, not counting the last little drops she just took.

"Are you okay to drive, Donna?" asked Sahara while eyeing the empty champagne bottle.

Donna chuckled. "Girl, I'm good. That little bit of champagne isn't going to affect me. I'm from the country, where we grew up drinking moonshine."

"Alright, Al Capone...," replied Tania as she reapplied her lipstick, and they walked out the dressing room. "Where are you headed now?"

Donna stopped at the front counter to make the arrangements for ordering the wedding dress she selected. "Where else? To the store and then home to cook dinner for my man. I just sent him a text. He's waiting for me at home."

"Is this the dress that you want? It's beautiful," said the black woman at the register. Then, she stopped. "Sahara?"

"Yes?" said Sahara. How did the woman know her name? Wait. Was that.... "Helena! Oh my goodness! I haven't seen you in forever! How is Jasmine?" Helena was a member of Coffee Moms, a playgroup that Sahara would take her children, Clarissa and Trevor, to when they first moved to Fairchester. "What are you doing here?"

"Oh, I work here. Been here for about two years now. What about you?"

"I'm here with my sorors, but I'm now the program coordinator at the Fairchester Economic League," said Sahara. "Yes, that's why I'm not involved in Coffee Moms anymore." Well for that reason and others.

"That sounds pretty important. Good for you. I remember that you wanted to go back to work."

At that time, Sahara did. Unfortunately, she didn't know how good she had it. Now that she was working again, she was over it.

Tania coughed. "Okay...Sahara and Betty Crocker...I'll see you ladies later."

"Well, I should get her measurements so that I can order her dress," said Helena. Donna gave her a look that said she agreed. "But, we should get the girls together sometime."

Jasmine, Helena's daughter, was Clarissa's first friend in town. At first, Sahara tried to keep in touch with Helena after she left Coffee Moms. However, her schedule became busy with LUA activities, trying to get an invitation to the Sphinx Ball, and now she was a member of Belles & Beaus. There was not enough time for everything, as her schedule became busier, and some of their early connections in Fairchester, unfortunately, fell by the wayside.

"We should," said Sahara with a quick smile. She then leaned over and gave Donna an air kiss and said, "I'll give you a call later," as she walked out the bridal shop.

As Sahara got into her car, she thought about their conversation concerning the LUA chapter. Like she said, she'd only been in the chapter a brief time, but even she could see the change. Her friend and neighbor, Meranda was the president at the time the chapter was chartered, so Sahara hated for the chapter to not live up to the standard that Meranda set. She was being facetious about having politics in her blood. However, technically she did. But, run for president? She didn't see it happening.

She glanced at the car next to her at the stoplight. Was that Alton? She thought that he was at home waiting for Donna to cook his dinner. She was only a few blocks from the boutique, and Alton and Donna lived close to the west side. What was he doing all the way over here?

Sahara stared into the car. It looked like Alton, but maybe it wasn't. This guy was a little haggard as he tried to pull himself together as they waited.

When the light turned green, the red Porsche gunned it. Sahara got a glimpse of the license plate as the car sped off.

NDALWYR?

Sahara hoped not, but she did know the license plate. It was Alton. However, the way he was bobbing and weaving through traffic, he was going to need one soon.

TWO

....

"Honey, Davis doesn't have a clue about what is going on," said Rashida.

"Not. At. All," replied Natalie. "Davis thought he was running things, but Charley is really the one pulling the strings."

"Davis is playing checkers, and Charley's playing chess," said Sahara from the backseat of the car.

"Amen," said Tania as she changed lanes.

Ding.

Sahara opened the email that just hit her inbox. *Call for LUA Nominations for....* She exited out the email without a second thought.

As the conversation of the television show *Queen Sugar* moved on from the power moves that Charley was making with Davis' career to the eye candy that was Ralph Angel, Sahara looked out the car window. The four of them decided to carpool to the Belles & Beaus cluster that was being held in Greensboro. Sahara didn't know Rashida and Natalie well. They were initiated into the chapter the same year as Tania. Yet, they had a good time talking and laughing about the television shows they watched, the books they read, and the people they hated during the hour drive to Greensboro.

The trip reminded her of when she was in college, and they would drive to Rhode Island for Greek parties. And, it was just how she liked road trips—short and sweet. As Tania pulled up to the campus of North Carolina Union, the ladies were still chatting and giggling like coeds.

The campus, dating back to the 1800s, looked idyllic with its green landscape and ivy covered brick buildings. Gladys Knight, Maynard Jackson, Ronald McNair, and Taraji P. Henson were just a few of the celebrated African Americans that attended the fine institution as undergraduates. Noah, Emery, and several of their friends were also alumni. Yet, although the school boasted an enrollment of more than ten thousand students, the campus was half deserted since it was the beginning of August, and the students had not returned to campus for the fall semester.

The Belles & Beaus mothers drove into the parking lot, which was already filled with cars adorned with the organization's decals and license plates. Then, they joined the scattering of members making the trek from the parking lot, past the new science tower with its modern design and huge glass windows, to the box-like building that was the Institute of Journalism, where the Belles & Beaus cluster was being held.

As they approached the front doors, one of the mothers in front of them fell as she walked up the stairs. "Are you okay?" said everyone as they rushed to her aid.

"Yes, yes. I'm alright," she said as she stood up and brushed off her skirt unable to hide her embarrassment. "I'm not sure what happened. One minute, I was walking. The next, I was on the ground."

"This looks like your culprit," said Rashida as she used her foot to rock a loose brick on one of the steps back and forth.

"They need to get that fixed before someone breaks her neck," said Natalie to a chorus of "uh huh" and "they do."

Exasperation expressed, everyone continued into the building and followed the signs to the auditorium. The school's maroon and blue coat of arms inscribed with Through Knowledge You Conquer in Latin was displayed proudly above the doors. Women, clad in pink and blue outfits, stood in line waiting to check-in at the registration tables. As they inched their way towards the front, Tania, Natalie, and Rashida chatted and waved at people from other chapters. Sahara smiled to be polite, but she didn't know anyone outside of her chapter so she just stood in line and waited her turn.

After Tania and Rashida received their registration materials, they waited for Natalie and Sahara to get theirs. When the woman sitting behind the table gave Natalie her registration packet, she joined the others, and Sahara took Natalie's place at the front of the table.

"Hi...Sahara Kyle."

The woman flipped to the page with the letters in the middle of the alphabet and looked at her list. Not seeing Sahara's name, she used her finger to go down the rows of last names beginning with "K" one more time. No Sahara Kyle. Then, she turned to the list where the names with "S" were, in case the first and last name had been inverted. Sahara's name wasn't there either.

"Is there any other name that it could be under?" she asked.

"No. Sahara Kyle. That's it," Sahara continued to smile, but she was becoming agitated that it was taking so long. She could hear the women behind her getting annoyed, as well.

"What's the chapter?" asked the Greensboro chapter member looking over her reading glasses.

"Fairchester," replied Sahara. She shrugged her shoulders at Tania whose facial expression asked why she was not finished.

The woman with the reading glasses leaned over and spoke to the woman next to her. "Jackie, do you have the list by chapter? I can't find her on this one."

"Sure," said Jackie reaching in a stack of papers on the table. "Here you go."

The woman with the reading glasses flipped the pages. "Fairchester, Fairchester....Fairchester. Oh, here you are. You're listed as Sahara Allymer-Kyle." She looked at Sahara over the glasses again. "That's you, right?"

Sahara swallowed hard. "Yes, that's me."

"Allymer. Are you related to Cluster Coordinator Fallon?" asked the woman in the pink reading glasses with a smile.

Sahara stood there for a second not knowing what to say. She guessed she should have been prepared for this, but she wasn't. When she found out in May that her Belles & Beaus chapter knew that Congressman Charles Allymer was her father...the same Charles Allymer that was the father of Fallon Allymer-Tate...Sahara thought about resigning her membership. She had carried the secret for so long, and now the whole chapter knew.

But then, nothing happened. No one mentioned it. No one talked about it. It never came up, so, Sahara was lulled into a false sense of security. She almost forgot that her secret was out...until this moment.

"Uh...yes...kind of...," Sahara stammered.

Pink glasses looked at Sahara strangely before handing her a folder and a bag. "Enjoy the conference."

"Thank you." Sahara quickly took the items and hurried over to her friends.

"Goodness! What took so long?" asked Rashida.

"They couldn't find my name." replied Sahara wishing they would change the subject.

"They couldn't find Kyle? It's four letters, for goodness sake," said Rashida.

Sahara lowered her voice. "Well, they didn't have me

under Kyle."

"What did they have you under? I reviewed the paperwork myself before it was sent to the regional director," said Natalie.

Sahara shifted her weight from one foot to the other. Why couldn't they just go inside and sit down? "They had me with the As...," said Sahara.

"The As?" asked Tania still not putting two and two together. However, based on the look that Rashida and Natalie exchanged, Sahara knew they had.

The four of them stood there. Tania in the dark and the rest of them looking uncomfortable. Natalie, finally, put them out of their misery. "You know...A...for Allymer."

"Ohhh...A...." Tania's face took on a reddish hue as she quickly looked at Natalie and Rashida. "Well, let's go inside. It looks like they are about to start."

Thank goodness. Given the number of Belles & Beaus members standing outside the auditorium talking, they probably had a few minutes before the opening session began, but Sahara followed Tania, Natalie, and Rashida into the auditorium. Sahara tried to smile and look relaxed as she made her way down the center aisle and into the row of seats. But, she remembered the look that Tania gave Rashida and Natalie when she understood the mix-up. Like they were guilty of something. Maybe Sahara was fooling herself. Maybe people were talking.

"Good morning, mothers!" said a woman with gray hair, a sharply tailored blue suit, and a large gold Belles & Beaus pin at the podium.

"There's Mrs. Belles & Beaus!" whispered Rashida as Tania and Natalie giggled.

"Mrs. Belles & Beaus?" asked Sahara.

Tania leaned over and said, "That's Gayle Phillips. She's old guard, old school, and any other phrase that begins with old. Her grandmother and mother were in Belles & Beaus. And, she's been in the organization forever. At this point, I'm convinced that she's adopting children so that she can remain a member."

Sahara chuckled. Well, Gayle Phillips was...mature.

Gayle continued, "I have the pleasure of introducing our regional director...the terrific Toni Simpson. Regional Director Simpson hails from the awesome and amazing Alexandria chapter...."

Sahara opened the folder that she received at registration so that she could see what was on the day's agenda. Mrs. Belles & Beaus was reading the regional director's biography that was included in the program. Sahara flipped through the pages to see whom the other speakers were.

Then, her heart stopped. There was a picture of her half sister, Cluster Coordinator Fallon Allymer-Tate. She was speaking today.

Sahara's eyes darted around the room like a scared cat. Was she here? Was Fallon in the room? Sahara hadn't seen Fallon since that time in the hospital...when shit hit the fan. Sahara wanted to know if Fallon was there now, but she was afraid to look behind her. What if they made eye contact?

She could kick herself. Why hadn't she thought about this before she registered? Fallon took a leave of absence so Sahara assumed that meant she would be gone for a year, not just a few months. But, Fallon was the North Carolina cluster coordinator. Of course, she would be at cluster. To make matters worse, Sahara rode with Tania so she couldn't leave. She was trapped.

Suddenly, everyone started clapping so Sahara did the same thing.

"Mothers, we are in a crisis. Can you believe that it is becoming harder for our children to get a decent K-12 education, let alone go on to college? Public schools remain underfunded without the necessary resources to teach our children. Consequently, a disproportionate number of black and brown children are funneled to trade schools and community colleges, instead of four-year institutions. As an organization, we must coordinate, collaborate, and advocate for the next generation. Without an education, they cannot build upon the gains of previous generations," said the woman at the podium before sitting down.

"Thank you to Belles & Beaus alumni and dean at North Carolina Union...," said the regional director before giving final instructions. After she finished, the noise level in the room grew as people got up and started moving. It was time for the first workshop.

"Sahara, where are you going?" asked Rashida.

Sahara looked in her folder. "New Member Workshop. What about you?"

"Membership," Rashida, Tania, and Natalie answered in unison, and then laughed. Sahara guessed they signed up for the same thing so that they could be together.

As the foursome walked out the auditorium, who was in front of them but Mrs. Belles & Beaus, Gayle Phillips. From the audience, Sahara was unable to see the cherry on top of Mother Gayle's outfit. Her pink and blue rhinestone shoes sparkled with a brilliance that only Dorothy's ruby red slippers could rival.

Tania, Natalie, and Rashida said goodbye and walked up the stairs to the second floor where the membership workshop was being held, and Sahara headed down the hall by herself to the new member workshop. She prayed that she didn't run into Fallon.

"Hey, lady," said a voice from behind her.

Nervous, Sahara turned around slowly. What if it was...? However, standing behind her was Emery Edmonds, her Belles & Beaus line sister. She breathed a sigh of relief.

With caramel skin, high cheekbones, and a blunt cut bob that was always laid, Emery Edmonds was beautiful enough to be a model—except she was five foot two.

Yet, while she was not tall enough to parade clothes as a profession, she did not let that stop her from looking as if she had stepped off a runway. As usual she was dressed to perfection in a gray skirt, black and white polka dot blouse, and blue cardigan.

Sahara smiled. "Hi, Emery!" She had never been so happy to see Emery in her life.

"Looks like it is just you and me from the chapter going to the new member workshop." She looked around. "Unless Zora came...."

"No, she isn't here," replied Sahara. "She's at the point in her pregnancy where she no longer wants to go anywhere in this heat."

Emery laughed. "I remember those days. But, she can't be ready to have the baby yet. Isn't she due in November?"

"Yes...but sometimes, you can't argue with this North Carolina heat." Truth be told, Sahara wasn't sure if that was just an excuse.

Emery nudged Sahara. "And, what was that look about?" she asked as they sat down at one of the round tables in the workshop.

"What look?" Sahara asked innocently.

"C'mon..." Emery nudged her again. "That side-eye you flashed says that there is more to this story."

"Well...," Sahara tried to guard her words. Sure, she and Emery were line sisters now, but there was a time when they were enemies, for sure. "I'm not sure what

Zora's involvement will be in Belles & Beaus. Although Zora grew up in the chapter, she never seems interested in black organizations or social events."

"I noticed that. I didn't know if it was because Cass is white or another reason."

Sahara shrugged her shoulders. "Me either."

Emery looked around like she was about to let Sahara in on a deep, dark secret. "I was surprised that Zora joined Belles & Beaus in the first place," she whispered. Sahara shook her head in agreement because she was, too.

"Excuse me. Is anyone sitting here?" asked a woman with a silver Belles & Beaus pin on her sweater. Emery and Sahara looked up and quickly answered no. "Hi, I'm Racquel from the Fayetteville chapter."

"I'm Sahara...."

"Sahara Kyle?"

Sahara and Emery glanced at each other. "Yes," replied Sahara cautiously. The mother didn't look familiar.

"I'm Rashida's cousin. She told me to keep an eye out for you, and, here you are."

Sahara smiled. Seeing Fallon's name in the program had her on edge. She needed to relax.

"I'm sorry," said a woman that was sitting at the table behind where Sahara and Emery were sitting. "Did you say that your name is Sahara Kyle?"

"Yes."

A big smile spread across the woman's face. "I'm Maris Weaver..." The name sounded familiar but Sahara couldn't make the connection. "You know...Maris Weaver...from the art school in Durham."

The light bulb went off. "Maris! It's so great to meet you! Now that I'm working...."

"You mean since you left us to work in finance." Maris poked out her bottom lip in a fake pout.

Sahara laughed. "Well, that's one way to put it." Maris was a great resource when Sahara volunteered at the Fairchester Economic League and coordinated their annual art auction fundraiser. However, since she accepted a fulltime position in the Economic League's finance department, they hadn't been in touch.

Emery and Sahara met more of the new members before the speaker was introduced. Everyone was so nice and friendly. Sahara sat back and exhaled. She was worried about nothing. Everything was going to be alright.

When the workshop started, the speaker, who was the regional membership chair, reviewed the requirements of being a new member in Belles & Beaus. Attend chapter meetings. Host activities. Support programs for children in the community. Participate in conferences. Pay dues.

Sahara knew all of this already. Joy Perry, the membership chair in the Fairchester chapter, had reviewed all these requirements before they were initiated.

Emery leaned over to Sahara. "We could have skipped this workshop. There's nothing that we don't already know." Sahara shook her head in agreement. However, by the questions that were asked, the thorough review of the requirements that Joy provided was the exception and not the norm. After twenty minutes of questions, the speaker finally released them to lunch. Finally. Sahara was starving.

She and Emery walked with the other new members from the workshop to the side of the building where lunch was being served. When they opened the doors, it sounded more like a high school cafeteria than a conference luncheon. The noise was almost deafening. Clearly, everyone was ready to let out a little steam and catch up with their sisters by the level of chatter in the room.

The seating was by chapter so the new members went their separate ways. However, when Sahara and Emery reached the table with the Fairchester mothers, there were no more seats. In addition, there were two Belles & Beaus members sitting at the table who weren't in their chapter. "Sorry," said Sheree, the chapter vice president, with a shrug. "We thought that the new members were sitting together."

Emery and Sahara looked at each other and rolled their eyes before searching for two empty seats. "There! I see a table with some empty chairs. I'll grab them," Emery said as they circled the room for a second time.

Sahara followed her to the table. These mothers had been in the organization a long time. The conversation was about high school requirements and college tours when Sahara and Emery walked up.

Clarissa and Trevor were so young that those conversations were premature for Sahara. However, one of the women looked familiar.

"Hi, aren't you Flora Washington?" Sahara said as she put her things down on the floor. Meranda introduced her to Flora at the Darlings' luncheon a couple of years ago. Although Sahara remembered their interaction at the luncheon being pleasant, now the woman glared at her with a look of disgust that caught Sahara off guard. Had she done something to her?

Wait. Where were her manners? She forgot to introduce herself. "I'm sorry," she said as she extended her hand. "I'm Sahara Kyle."

However, the reception remained chilly. Flora smiled, but it wasn't a friendly smile. Instead, she looked like a cat that was ready to pounce on a mouse. "Oh, I remember, dear." She gave Sahara a cursory handshake and quickly returned to her conversation with the woman seated to her right.

Alright. Maybe Sahara was wrong about their interaction at the Darlings' luncheon. Maybe it wasn't friendly, because whatever happened, this woman was definitely dismissing her.

"Are you ready to get our food?" asked Emery.

"Sure," said Sahara as her stomach rumbled. She tried to push Flora's cold demeanor out of her mind as she went through the buffet, but it was still bothering her. As she waited for Emery to get some salad, Sahara turned and looked back at their seats. The whole table was looking in their direction until they noticed Sahara observing them.

Then, everyone became busy. Eating. Talking. Looking down at the table. Like magic, everyone was now too engaged with something else to have been caught staring at Sahara and Emery. Weird.

When they returned to the table, Sahara quickly ate her food. For some reason, she felt uncomfortable—although everyone was friendly to Emery. After introductions, they asked about her child and how she liked Belles & Beaus. One woman at the table also attended North Carolina Union, and she and Emery realized that they had some mutual acquaintances.

However, with Sahara, it was different. By no means could she say that the ladies at the table were rude—but the interaction was forced. No doubt about it. No one tried to engage Sahara in conversation. Yet, when she would ask someone a question or try to add to the discussion, the response was short and curt. If Emery wasn't talking to her, Sahara ate her food in silence.

And then, there was the body language. Flora Washington positioned her body so that her back was slightly turned to Sahara. It was crystal clear that she was not interested in getting to know Sahara better—even during a thirty minute lunch break. But, Sahara had no idea why.

With her food only half eaten, Sahara threw it away and excused herself to the bathroom. There was no need in prolonging her silent treatment. She might as well freshen up and get ready for the afternoon workshops. While she was in the bathroom stall, she heard the door open.

"I cannot believe that she has the nerve to come here. Absolutely no class at all!" said someone over the running water from the faucet.

"I know. It must be so awful for Fallon...having to see her father's illegitimate child prance around like she owns the place."

Fallon? Her father's illegitimate child? Sahara gulped. They were talking about her.

"Well, we must do our best to protect Fallon. Clearly this girl has no sense of decency, no sense of protocol. Thankfully, little baby Charles came down with a bug which prevented Fallon from attending today. I just think seeing this woman and all her foolishness would be too much."

"And, did you see her? You can look at her and know she's not really an Allymer."

"Agreed!"

Suddenly, the water stopped running. Were they getting ready to leave? Sahara could only hope. Then, she heard the *clickety clack* of their heels against the tile. She held her breath as they passed her stall and that's when she saw them.

The flashy pink and blue rhinestone shoes. One of the ladies was Mrs. Belles & Beaus, Gayle Phillips.

A few seconds later, Sahara heard the door open and close. After listening to make sure no one else was in the restroom, Sahara slowly emerged from the stall. As she stood shell-shocked, she washed her hands under the faucet and thought about what the woman said.

She's not really an Allymer. A shudder went up her spine. And, what was all that *protect Fallon?* Why would Fallon need protection from her? Sahara was as innocent in this situation as Fallon was.

However, those ladies made it clear that wasn't how they felt. As far as they were concerned, Sahara, the *illegitimate child*, didn't belong.

She looked in the mirror. C'mon, Sahara, pull yourself together. Who cares what they think? You don't know them, and they don't know you.

Not necessarily convinced, Sahara looked at the back of her nametag to see what her next workshop was. Of course. It was protocol. However, she didn't remember signing up for that. Maybe this was someone's idea of a joke.

Sahara looked at herself in the mirror once more. *She's not really an Allymer.*

There was no way she was going to that workshop. And, if this was the reception that she'd get in the spotlight, there was no way that she would ever run for LUA president. The tribe had spoken.

THREE

....

"**F**ore!"

Sahara ducked so that she didn't get hit in the head by the wayward ball. She didn't understand the appeal of golf. The outfits. The terrain. The heat. And, don't forget the personal butler forced to walk the terrain carrying a bag full of golf clubs. It seemed like the rich man's version of ladies that lunch—taken to the next level and with servants.

She wiped the sweat from her forehead as she traipsed across the golf course in her flowing pink sundress and sneakers heading back to the registration table. This had to be the worst Green Light Weekend ever. Normally, Green Light Weekend, her LUA chapter's annual fundraiser, was two days of upscale entertainment and relaxation for the area's movers and shakers. Today's activities included a day at the spa for the ladies and golf for the men, followed by a party tonight. Tomorrow, everyone would enjoy a beautiful jazz brunch.

However, this year was different. First, she volunteered to serve as a hostess at the day spa for the ladies. Hence, she picked out this beautiful sundress so she could look like a heavenly pink goddess as she assisted the ladies of leisure. However, when she showed up this morning she was "volun-told" to help with the golf tournament, so she wasn't even dressed appropriately. Thank goodness she kept an extra pair of sneakers in her car for those impromptu trips to the park with her children, or she would be walking around in three hundred dollar Gucci sandals.

Second, everything with the golf tournament was a disaster. Someone forgot to reserve the nice, well-maintained golf course near Jordan Lake that they used in past years. Consequently, when a phone call was placed to confirm the details two months ago, that's when they found out there was no reservation—and the golf course was booked. The chapter was already advertising the golf tournament, so they had to scramble to find a course for the event.

Enter River Valley Golf Course, the only place available on such short notice. River Valley was on the west side of town in an area that was filled with boarded up buildings that were long past their prime. Years ago, River Valley was the place to be for black golfers. In fact, it was the only place for black golfers.

Back then, the course was decent, the fees were reasonable, and the opportunity to network with other black professionals was there. However, once the other clubs allowed blacks to join, most decided to become members of the nicer, more established white golf courses, and River Valley, along with so much in this neighborhood, withered up like a piece of dry hay. Not dead, but long forgotten—until today.

After the location switch, Sahara wondered why some of the sponsors pulled out and registrations were down. However, now that she was here—she understood. She wasn't a golfer, but she knew that the grass looking dry and brown was not a good sign. She overheard some of the players describe it as "a wasteland" and "like playing on overcooked broccoli." Clearly not a positive. River Valley should be renamed Death Valley.

As she walked back, she swatted at the flying insects whizzing around her head. She forgot to add bugs to the list of things wrong with this place. Awful greens. Bathrooms from hell. And bugs. Lots of them.

Sahara saw her husband getting some food, the only thing she had not received any complaints about today, under the tent. Noah, who was normally impeccably dressed, had on red and yellow plaid golf attire from head to toe. Did she mention the outfits? She swore that golf clothes were hideous on purpose. It was another way for rich men to exert their power—by daring everyone not to laugh.

However, as much as Sahara hated to say it, the men's attire was low on the totem pole of things wrong with the day. She was so embarrassed by the event, that she really wanted to keep walking, right to her car, and back home—but she knew that she couldn't do that. She strolled over to Noah, who was standing with Cass, Zora's husband.

Great. Cass was a member of the most exclusive golf clubs in the area, so Sahara really didn't want to hear what he had to say about the tournament.

"Are you guys ready to take home the trophy?" asked Sahara as she patted Cass on the back to get his attention.

"Not quite." He was looking down at his plate of food.

Sahara saw the look of concern on Cass' face and asked, "What's wrong?"

Cass pulled a long, black hair from his plate. "I got a little extra something with my food."

Despite the heat, Sahara felt her cheeks get warmer. "I'm so sorry. Here let me get you another plate." Sahara reached for Cass' plate.

Cass looked awkward. "Uh...that's okay. I wasn't that hungry anyway." Just then, his stomach rumbled revealing his alternative fact. Cass looked off in the distance sheepishly.

"Well, I'm going to speak to someone about this." Sahara spoke with authority to reassure him and walked towards the registration table. However, she was neither shocked nor surprised that Cass found hair in his food. They should hope that was all that lurking in there.

Look at this place. It was a dump. But, Sahara knew better than to "show out" in front of company—

especially white company.

As she got closer to the registration tent, she thought about what she said to Cass. *You guys ready to take home the trophy?* The trophies. Where were they? Sahara hadn't seen them.

When Sahara reached the registration table, she dumped Cass' plate in the nearest trash. "Someone found a hair in their food," she announced to everyone and no one. A collective "Ewww!" went up from the sorors within earshot.

A white woman with a poodle walked past them without saying a word. "Who is that?" asked Sahara.

"The owner," someone replied. "She's 'checking' on things. Whatever that means."

She needs to check the sprinklers on this dry, brown grass. "Does anyone know where the trophies are?" Sahara asked as she looked underneath the registration table to see if there was a box of them under there.

Soror Elizabeth's face was frazzled as she looked up from the stack of papers on the table. "Trophies? Haven't seen them. Soror Christina was supposed to bring them."

The same Soror Christina that took Sahara's cushy spa assignment while she trudged out here in the heat? Sahara swatted at a wasp that was flying around her head as she pulled out her cell phone.

Zit.

She felt a sharp pain in her arm as she saw the wasp

fly away. Terrific. That little sucker stung her. Her only consolation was that he would pay the ultimate price for his disrespect. Or, was that bees?

Sahara scrolled through the contacts in her cell phone. She didn't see Christina's name. "Soror Elizabeth, do you have Christina's number?"

"Yes, let me get it."

A few seconds later, Sahara dialed the phone number that Soror Elizabeth gave her. Please, please, please pick up.

"Hello?" said the voice at the other end.

"Soror Christina?"

"Yes, this is Soror Christina."

Yes! Something was finally going her way. "Hi, this is Soror Sahara. I'm at the golf tournament, but we can't find the trophies. Where did you drop them off?"

"I didn't. They're in the trunk of my car."

Sahara's optimism decreased like a deflated balloon. Why are they in the trunk of her car that is at the spa? They are the trophies for the golf tournament that is happening. Now.

Soror Christina continued, "But, we're pretty busy over here. I don't think I can bring them over...."

There was silence on the phone. Sahara sighed. There was no question that they needed the trophies. "Okay, I'll drive over and get them. Can you...?"

"I'll wait for you. Bye!" replied Soror Christina, and then, she hung up the phone. Great. She was trying to tell Christina to leave the box with the receptionist, but she hung up before Sahara could say it. Hopefully, she would do that. As Sahara walked to her Lexus, she tried to ignore the urge to scratch her arm where she could feel it throbbing from the wasp's sting.

~~~

Sahara sat in the car outside the spa and called Soror Christina again. She didn't answer. It was at most a twenty-minute drive to Midtown where the spa was located. Why wasn't she picking up? Sahara looked down at her dusty, stained, pink sundress, which revealed the remnants of the golf course. She hated to walk into the spa looking the way she did—but Christina wasn't answering the phone—and she needed those trophies. Hopefully, they were at the front desk.

Walking into *Spa by Giselle* was like walking into heaven after being at that golf course. The cool air and the scent of rose and lavender enveloped Sahara as soon as she stepped into the building. This was where she was supposed to be. Everything was clean, pristine, and so relaxing. She took a deep breath so that she could fully enjoy these few minutes that she had in paradise.

"Hey, Donna. Have you seen Soror Christina? Or, better yet, do you have the golf tournament trophies back there?" asked Sahara as she leaned on the front counter in the lobby.

Donna looked official sitting in the black leather chair behind the front counter. "No trophies, but Christina was here a few minutes ago. Let me call in the back to see if she's there." Instead of picking up her cell phone, Donna used a little black walkie-talkie. "Does anyone know where Christina is? Sahara is here to see her."

How big was this spa? Sahara sized the place up. The building was large, but not so large they couldn't get up and easily walk to speak to someone without over-exerting themselves.

But, you know where those walkie-talkies were needed? At the golf tournament. Golf course rules required that they turn off their cell phones, so everyone had to schlep back and forth even to ask a question. They were working in paradise with walkie talkies? Man, Lady Luck dealt her a bad hand.

After a few seconds, a voice on the other end of the walkie-talkie replied, "Soror Christina is getting a massage."

"She's getting what?" Sahara asked as she flicked a piece of grass off her dress.

"A massage," Donna repeated as if Sahara hadn't heard the first time. "We already gave everyone their assignments when she arrived, so Christina is a floater. There really wasn't much for her to do. If she was standing around, why not get a massage?"

Was she kidding? Sahara stared at Donna in disbelief. Why not? Because she signed up to work at the spa, not Christina. Yet, she was hiking back and forth in that wasteland of a golf course, not getting massages. "Well, I need those trophies so someone has to get her."

Sahara made a step towards the waiting area, but Donna held up her hand. "Sorry, Sahara. No can do. Once a service starts, we can't interrupt." She pointed at the *Spa by Giselle* sign. "Rules of the spa."

"I can't believe...I mean she knew I was on the way. What am I supposed to do now? Wait for her to finish her massage?" said Sahara. Donna sat behind the lobby desk trying not to laugh. However, she was failing miserably. "It's not funny," Sahara replied.

Donna contained her laughter and pointed at one of the chairs in the lobby. "You probably only have fifteen minutes max to wait. Pull up a chair so you can sit and talk to me."

Sahara did as she was instructed. To appease herself, when she sat down, she gave into that burning desire to scratch the wasp bite on her arm. Ohhhh. That felt so good. Then, she swiped more grass off her dress.

Donna wrapped her arm around Sahara. "See...we'll talk. You'll relax. You'll get your trophies...and, stop scaring the guests." Donna chuckled as she plucked some grass out of Sahara's hair.

"Again, not funny." Sahara pouted. "You don't even know what we have to deal with over there." Sahara looked around. "You are living it up in the land of luxury with your aromatherapy and detox beverages. We're dealing with ratchetness at a whole other level down there."

"At the golf course?" Donna added smugly, with a nudge. She sat back in the chair. "And, don't be fooled by the calm you see now. It's recent—and probably temporary."

Sahara started, "Well, we don't have enough volunteers so everything is in chaos. The players are complaining about the grounds, which are dry and brown, I might add. Cass found hair in his food before I left. And, let's not forget. We don't have any trophies." Sahara glanced over her shoulder as if doing so would make Christina magically appear.

"It hasn't been all rainbows and unicorns over here either. First, we discovered this morning that the reservation app had a glitch. It recorded names and that's it. We didn't know what service anyone was scheduled for or what time unknown service was supposed to happen. It didn't record any contact information. We had to reach out to sorors to obtain the phone numbers of their guests. It was an absolute nightmare. The spa called in extra staff members to make sure everyone was covered."

Sahara shook her head. "Which I'm sure is going to cost the chapter extra money."

"Exactly. I would be surprised if we make half the money on this that we've made in previous years," said

Donna.

"Same with the golf tournament," added Sahara.

"Alright. Let's call this one a draw," said Donna. "But seriously, we need to figure out what we are going to do."

"Do about what?" asked Sahara, once again trying to ignore the urge to scratch her wasp bite.

"This chapter. I'm serious...." Donna looked around to make sure that no one was listening. "We need to make sure that we, the younger members, get most—if not all—of the positions on the executive board. We need to turn this chapter around—and fast."

"What are ya'll talking about up here?"

Donna sat up at attention like a child who'd been caught with her hand in the cookie jar. However, when she saw whom it was, she relaxed. "What else? How awful this event is."

Soror Gwen rolled her eyes. "Don't get me started, because we will be here all day. We just need someone to run for president. Donna are you going to do it?"

Donna shook her head. "No, I'm running for vice president. We need to convince Sahara to run for president."

Soror Candice turned. "Sahara, you would be the bomb dot com as president."

Soror Gwen joined in, "You would be great, Soror Sahara! You have to do it."

This must be how a fly caught in a spider's web feels.

"I don't know. But, I do hate to see the chapter that Meranda started going downhill. I know that she loves this chapter." Soror Gwen and Soror Candice exchanged looks but didn't say anything. She wasn't sure what that was about.

"Hello, Sorors. I'm glad that things have calmed down to the point that everyone can relax," said Soror Benetta, a good friend of Meranda, as she walked up to the front desk. "And, I see that you've managed to convince Sahara to come over from the golf course to join the fun."

"Oh, we were just leaving," said Gwen and Candice as they returned to the back.

"And, I'm here because I have to get the golf tournament trophies from Soror Christina," said Sahara.

"And, where is Soror Christina?" Soror Benetta looked behind her.

"Um...she's getting a massage," Donna said sheepishly.

"Really?!" said Soror Benetta. She shook her head as she walked away. "Oh you, young sorors...."

The beautiful door chimes sang out melodiously announcing someone's arrival at the spa. Sahara and Donna automatically turned their heads toward the door. It was Emery.

She breezed in, looking her usual effortlessly stylish self. Sahara felt Donna stiffen in the chair next to her.

"Hi, Emery!" said Sahara as she stood to give Emery

a hug over the front counter.

Emery pushed her sunglasses up and embraced Sahara. "Hi, Sahara, my line sister!" Her smile faded a little as she saw the look on Donna's face. "Hi, Donna."

"Hi, Emery. You are here for...?" asked Donna.

For a massage and facial. Sahara saw the services written next to Emery's name on the paper that was in front of Donna.

"A facial and a massage...," said Emery.

"Of course," said Donna giving her a tight-lipped smile. "You can have a seat in the waiting room, and your masseuse will get you shortly."

Emery was no fool and must have sensed the frosty reception from Donna. "Great. Thanks." A smile returned to Emery's face. "See you later, Sahara. We're still on for lunch next week, right?"

Sahara wished that she hadn't brought that up in front of Donna so she quickly added, "Yes. See you then!" Sahara didn't have to look at Donna to know that she was rolling her eyes.

When Emery was in the waiting area and safely out of earshot, Sahara turned to Donna. "Awkward. So, what is the deal with you and Emery? I always thought you were cool. Not best friends, but cool. You act like you can't stand the woman now."

Donna shrugged her shoulders and sat back in the leather chair. "We were cool. I don't know. Since I've been dating Alton...and now that we're engaged...."

"C'mon, Donna. You knew that they knew each other when you started dating Alton. Heck, you told me. And, it doesn't even seem like they are close friends anymore."

"I know. They're not. They talk occasionally, as far as I know, and it always seems forced. Yet, I can't put my finger on it—but something about their friendship irks me."

Jealous much? "Well, you need to get over it. You don't want Alton to think that you are trying to control whom his friends are."

Before Donna could answer, Christina appeared. "That massage was just what I needed." She rolled her neck around and arched her back like she was made of jelly. "Sahara, they said that you were looking for me."

Maybe her brain was now jelly, too. "Remember, I need the trophies." Sahara glared at her hoping that the light bulb went off.

"Right. The trophies. I'll give you my keys, and you can get them out of my car."

Bless her heart. That massage had completely liquefied her brain. "Why don't we go together to get the trophies." The nerve of Christina after she had to wait for her to finish her service.

"Okay." As they walked to the car, Christina said, "Soror, look at your arm. What bit you?" She stepped back like it was contagious.

Sahara looked at her arm. The wasp sting was red

46

and huge. And, now that Christina brought it up, it was itching—again. Christina handed the box of trophies to Sahara and headed back towards the spa. She walked a few steps, put her hand up, and yelled, "Have fun at the golf tournament!" without even bothering to turn her head.

Yea, fun. Sahara wasn't sure that was waiting for her when she returned.

~~~

On the way back to the golf tournament, Sahara thought about their discussion at the spa. Could the young sorors really take over the chapter? Should she run for president? Who else was running? One thing was certain; the chapter was in a rut. Someone needed to shake things up.

After parking, she hoisted the box of trophies out of the car and headed towards to the scoring tent. As she walked through the golf club parking lot, she saw the owner, still carrying her poodle, circling the lot and looking agitated. Sahara didn't know what the lady's problem was, but she strode by her without saying a word.

When Sahara arrived at the scoring tent, she dropped the box on the table. Golfers were finishing up and turning in their scoring sheets. The older soror collecting the sheets looked up when she heard the thud from the box hitting the table.

"Soror Sahara, I was about to send out a search party for you. You were gone so long that I didn't know if you went home or was getting a massage at the spa," said Soror Gertrude.

No, she wasn't the one getting a massage. But, she didn't say anything about Christina. "It took longer to get there...you know...traffic."

"As long as you got them...," she said as she put her hand in the box, and Sahara walked away. "What? We can't use these."

Sahara stopped in her tracks. "What did you say?" she asked, as she returned to the table.

"I said that we can't use these. Look...." She thrust one of the green and gold trophies in Sahara's face. Sahara took a small step back so that she could read the thing.

Lambda Upsilon Alpha Sorority, Inc.

Green Light Weekend 2016

Calf Tournament

Wait. *Calf Tournament?* Ugh. "I'm so sorry. I didn't even look in the box. I just took it from Soror...."

"Whatever the excuse. We can't use them." She turned away in disgust and shook her head. "These young sorors are always in a rush...."

Sahara knew that she was right. Not only should Soror Christina have checked the trophies when she picked them up, but Sahara should have double checked them when she got the box from Christina.

For some reason, Sahara's mind flashbacked to the Belles & Beaus cluster. Again, she felt like a scolded child...correction...a scolded *illegitimate child*. Sahara skulked away and avoided the older sorors for the rest of the afternoon. She knew that her name was mud after this mistake.

When the golf tournament was finally over, Sahara stayed and helped clean everything up. As she walked back to the club to get the last box, she realized that she was the only LUA still there.

Sahara grabbed the discarded box and walked into the club's dining room. The staff was standing underneath the wall mounted television with their eyes fixed on the screen. Sahara wanted to let them know that she was leaving, but something caught her eye.

"Breaking news," said the blonde anchor at the news desk. "It is being reported that Congressman Charles Allymer has an adult child that is not with his wife. Up until this point, the Allymers—Congressman Charles Allymer, his wife Winnie, and his daughter, Fallon—were considered the ideal family. Allymer's career began..."

Sahara's head was spinning. What? Who? How did they know? She looked at the staff still staring at the television oblivious to the fact that her world was collapsing.

She had to get out of there. Noah would know what

to do. She had to call Noah.

Shoot! Her cell phone was in the car. But, that's where she was going. She could call him in the car. Walk, Sahara, walk. Her mind wasn't functioning. But, she could see her car. She was almost there.

Then, she felt her foot land in something squishy. Next came the smell, that awful smell. She looked down at the brown mess smeared all over her sneaker. Dog poop.

She looked around like she expected the culprit to still be there. Aarghh! If she wasn't so close to crying, she would have laughed.

There was no way around it, from the breaking news to the parking lot, it was clear that she was in deep....

FOUR

....

When Sahara walked into the house, she was shaking. "Noah! Noah!" Why was she yelling? She knew he wasn't home. His car wasn't in the garage. Where was he?

She picked up her cell phone to call him again. Everyone at the golf tournament already left. Why wasn't he here? Had he heard? As Sahara dialed his number, she vaguely remembered something about him going with Cass somewhere. No answer.

Calm down, Sahara. The world was not ending. The sky will be blue. The birds will sing. And, everyone will know your big secret—Congressman Charles Allymer is your father.

Water. She should get some water. Make that wine. If there was ever a moment to drink, this was it.

She put her car keys down on the kitchen table and opened a bottle of chardonnay. Think. Maybe she hadn't heard correctly. So, maybe it wasn't breaking news that Charles Allymer had an illegitimate child? Who was she kidding? Even if she didn't hear correctly, it scrolled at the bottom of the television screen.

Sahara picked up her cell phone to dial Noah's cell phone again. It immediately started vibrating. What was going on? Oh, she had a call. This news had her completely unnerved.

Sahara looked at the cell phone again. It was Soror Christina. What did she want?

Sahara started to let it go to voicemail. But, maybe it was important. "Hello?" she said when she tapped the little green button to accept the call.

"Hi, Soror Sahara. It's Christina. I got a phone call from Soror Gertrude, and she said there was a problem with the trophies. I really didn't understand what she was talking about so I figured I would give you a call."

Ugh. She should have let it go to voice mail. She didn't have time to deal with this right now. "What did she say?" asked Sahara. "All I know is that the trophies had a misspelling on them."

Normally, Soror Christina had a laid back, California-type of vibe. Today, she went from zero to about five, real quick. "Get out of here! Something was misspelled? That's not good."

No shit, Sherlock. "Well, did you look at the trophies when you picked them up?" She didn't know why she asked that. She already knew the answer.

"No, when I got them from Soror Benetta, I just put them in my car. I guess that I should have double checked them, but I assumed she did that at the shop."

What? "You didn't pick the trophies up from the

shop?" asked Sahara.

"No, I got them from Soror Benetta. She ordered them and picked them up from the shop."

"Ohhhh." The lightbulb went off. "Everyone thought that you picked up the trophies."

"That must be why Soror Gertrude went on that rant about the young sorors don't do this and the young sorors don't do that."

Sahara shook her head. "You should have stated that her close friend was the one that accepted the trophies." Soror Benetta and Soror Gertrude were also charter members of the chapter, along with Meranda.

"And ordered them," added Soror Christina.

"And ordered them."

Soror Christina continued, "I don't know about you Soror Sahara, but the chapter just doesn't feel the same to me. Green Light Weekend seems so tired now. I wish we would do something else."

"Yes, it has seen better days."

"Well, I overheard Gwen and Candice talking about how the young sorors should take over the leadership of the chapter. It sounds like a good idea, but I don't know if it will work."

"Why do you say that?" Sahara didn't really feel like getting into the disaster of Green Light Weekend, but she was a little intrigued to hear Christina's thoughts. And, a distraction from her real problems was certainly welcome.

"Listen, my mother is a soror, and my father is a member of Rho Nu Alpha. All they talk about is how things are changing, how they don't like the changes, blah, blah, blah. And, I think that a lot of the older sorors feel the same way. The last thing that these older sorors want is for these "young people" to take over their beloved sorority."

Sahara countered, "Well, they say that they want new ideas and new workers...so I think it's a win-win for everyone if we take on some of the responsibility of the chapter."

"They do want those things. However, they don't want to relinquish the power or the control, so where does that leave us?" said Christina.

If Christina was right, where did that leave them? She certainly had an interesting perspective.

"Are you planning to run for anything?" Christina asked interrupting Sahara's thoughts.

"No. What about you?"

"Yes, I was thinking about running for president," replied Christina.

"President? Really?" That was an idea that Sahara couldn't quite wrap her brain around. Christina was a carefree spirit. Sahara couldn't imagine her being organized or structured enough to lead the chapter.

"You sound surprised."

"Well, I am a little." She hoped that she hadn't hurt Christina's feelings. Christina was nice, but she wasn't the hardest worker in the chapter. Donna said she showed up late for her assignment, and she was getting a massage when she knew that Sahara was coming to get the trophies. Sahara also worked with her on other committees in the chapter; she wasn't engaged on those either.

"I'm not sure. Just thinking about it."

"Well, I think nominations close today...so you don't have much longer to figure it out," said Sahara.

"Would you support me if I run?" asked Christina.

Buzz. Buzz.

Sahara looked at her cell phone. It wasn't her.

"Oh, that's my daughter. I'll have to call you back," said Christina.

"Alright, soror. I'll talk to you later," Sahara added quickly. Thank you, Christina's daughter for calling. Would she support Christina's run president? Sahara wasn't interested in touching that question with a ten-foot pole.

Ping.

This time, it had to be her. Sahara looked at the text on her cell phone.

Donna: Sahara, we need you to run for president? Will you?

Sahara sighed. Was she the only person in the chapter that saw this breaking news? Well, maybe that wasn't a bad thing. But, seriously. This LUA election was the last thing on her mind right now.

Sahara: No. Talked to Christina. She's thinking about run-

ning.

    Donna: For what?

    Oh, you know what.

    Sahara: Prez

    Donna: You're kidding.

    Sahara: Nope. Just spoke to her.

    Donna: Well, that can't happen. We need a strong prez. Not sure if that is Christina.

Sahara didn't know if she fit the bill either, especially with this scandal about to break. She remembered the treatment she received at the lunch table at the Belles & Beaus cluster. Thinking back, it was clear that the older members knew whom she was, or more importantly, whom her father was—and, they were not having it.

Mrs. Belles & Beaus, Gayle Phillips said it best. *We have to protect Fallon from the illegitimate child.* Like Sahara being born was an act of war against Fallon. *Clearly this girl has no sense of protocol.*

Sahara's mother always taught to her to shield her father's identity at all cost. Regardless of the toll it took on her. Sahara lived a lie her whole life in order to protect her father's career and reputation.

Yet, these older women had the nerve to say that she didn't know anything about protocol? Please. She followed the rules of protocol when it came to her father and his reputation to a point that it was nauseating.

Nevertheless, she knew that they would never accept her. That was made perfectly clear at cluster. They had drawn a line, and they and Fallon were on one side. The illegitimate child was on the other.

Sahara sighed. With the scandal about her father about to spread beyond this Black social circle into the world, there was no way that she could run for president of the chapter. No way.

~~~

Since the news broke that Charles Allymer had an illegitimate child, he spent the weekend ducking cameras and dodging reporters' questions. And, although her name had not been leaked, Sahara knew that it was only a matter of time.

Consequently, she was on pins and needles and decided to skip the rest of Green Light Weekend. There was no need in torturing herself by going to the party or the brunch. She would be forced to make small talk when she knew that she had this soon-to-be revealed bomb shell hanging over her head. Plus, she would spend the whole weekend wondering who knew, or even—who told.

But, when Monday morning came, she couldn't avoid reality any further. She had to go to work. Oh, how she wished for the days when she was a stay-at-home mom. However, duty called, and she dropped Clarissa off at school, took Trevor to preschool, and headed to the Fairchester Economic League. After spending the weekend fretting over when the shoe would drop regarding her father, work could be a needed distraction. She might as well put a positive spin on it.

Sahara walked into the building and proceeded to her office, where she closed the door. Her desk looked exactly as she left it. Computer off. Papers stacked neatly in front of her chair. Pictures of her family in pretty, little, gold frames.

Yes, everything was just as she left it. It was just her world that had been turned upside down.

"Knock, knock," said Mia Johnson as she opened the door.

Sahara first met Mia, when they both were seeking membership in Belles & Beaus. Sahara got in. Mia didn't. But, things were still friendly between them, and Mia started volunteering at the Fairchester Economic League earlier this year. Consequently, when Sahara moved over to the role of program specialist, Mia took her old job and became the financial analyst working with Mr. Johnson, the finance director. A certified public accountant, Mia was perfect for the role. And, hopefully, having the same last name as Mr. Johnson would be a plus for their working relationship, even though they weren't related.

"Hey, you. You're in here early," Sahara said.

"Lots of work to do." Mia walked into the office and sat down in the guest chair. "I'm glad that you are here." She pulled some papers from behind her back. "I was going to leave these on your desk to sign, but I can just get your John Hancock now."

Sahara quickly flipped through the large stack of papers. "Ugh. It's going to take me forever to read all this."

Mia laughed. "Great! We are on the same page, because I don't have time for you to read it all. It's just the agreement for the scholarship renewal. You know these universities. Twenty pages to say something simple." Mia looked at her vibrating cell phone. "Did you hear about Congressman Allymer? I can't believe that he has a secret love child. The Allymers were like the Huxtables of Raleigh...although we know how that ended, as well. Scandalous! Well, it looks like he's going to hold a press conference."

Sahara's body stiffened. Did she say...? "What was that?" asked Sahara.

Mia held her phone out for Sahara to see. *Congressman Charles Allymer schedules press conference to address rumors.*

Sahara's eyes couldn't focus. The room felt like it was spinning. He...he...was holding a press conference? Everything was going to come out. There would be no more speculation because it would come from the horse's mouth. She was going to be sick.

"Are you okay? You don't look too good," said Mia.

"Yes...I'm alright. I just forgot about something that I need to do." Sahara stood up from behind the desk.

"Wait. Don't forget to sign these." Mia put the papers

on the desk.

"Huh? What? Oh...." Sahara picked up a pen from her desk and quickly added her signature.

"Thank you!" said Mia.

Sahara didn't say anything to anyone as she hurried down the hall, out of the building, and to the parking lot. She opened the door to her Lexus and climbed inside. Breathe. Breathe. Breathe. Her head was pounding, and her heart was racing like she ran a marathon.

A press conference? What was he planning to say? The scene from the television series Scandal when Olivia Pope, dressed in her white track suit, ready for her morning jog, completely unaware of the media circus waiting for her when she opened her front door came to Sahara's mind. Thankfully, Charles Allymer was no Papa Pope, a monster pulling strings behind the scenes. On second thought, at least Papa Pope was involved in his daughter's life.

Sahara thought back to last Thanksgiving when she came face-to-face with her father, and he acted like he didn't even know her. Her own flesh and blood dismissed her like she was a stranger on the street. Sahara had been heartbroken. All those feelings of abandonment, being unlovable, and not accepted that she felt but kept buried all those years came bubbling up. Actually, more like exploded.

But, this? Publicity. Exposure. Humiliation. She wasn't sure that she was ready for this. Sure, the members in Belles & Beaus knew, but she also knew that this information would be kept within *their* circle. Sahara had come to terms with the fact that her secret would probably morph into the worst kept secret in the black elite community. But, it was still *their* secret. *Their* dirty laundry. The whole world was never meant to know.

Aarrgghh! How did this happen? She banged her fist on the steering wheel. Noah would know what to do. She felt around in her purse. No cell phone. Where was it? She looked all over the car. Then, she remembered. It was sitting on her desk. She wished...maybe something was on the radio.

Sahara turned the knob. Music. Music. Music. She needed to find some talk radio or something.

"And Congressman Charles Allymer...." Bingo. She had a winner. "...has scheduled a press conference for two o'clock this afternoon to address the rumors that he has a child...."

Knock. Knock.

Startled, Sahara turned to see Glynda Clayton, the executive director at the Fairchester Economic League, tapping on her car window. "Everything okay?" asked Glynda through the glass.

Sahara put on her best smile and nodded her head. "Yes, I'm okay. Left something in my car." Sahara looked around like she lost something.

Glynda smiled. "Okay. Just wanted to check. I heard you listening to the news that Congressman Allymer scheduled a press conference. Mrs. Allymer must be so embarrassed. You know she's given to the Fairchester Economic League in the past."

"Yes, I remember." Sahara hadn't thought about how Winnie—or Fallon, for that matter—were handling the news since the story broke.

Glynda waved. "I'll see you inside." What would Glynda think when she found out that Sahara was the love child? This was a nightmare.

Two o'clock. That was the time of the press conference. Well, as much as she wanted to, she couldn't sit in the car forever.

As she walked back to the building, Sahara remembered what Mia said. *The Allymers were like the Huxtables of Raleigh.* Well, one thing was for sure. Press conference or not, Sahara was sure that Winnie was not inviting her over for Sunday dinner anytime soon.

~~~

The two o'clock press conference became the four o'clock press conference, which became the six o'clock press conference. The six o'clock press conference then morphed into the eight o'clock press conference. The prime time disclosure guaranteed that this revelation would make the eleven o'clock news. Terrific.

With each delay, Sahara went through a roller coaster of emotions. Relief that for now the secret was safe from the world. That was followed by anxiety from more waiting and the knowledge that eventually everything would be exposed.

She puttered around the house while Noah was upstairs getting the children ready for bed. She couldn't keep her hands still. The waiting was like torture.

In a desperate attempt to stay busy, she cleaned the family room. She even dusted the picture frames on the fireplace mantle. Clarissa and Trevor at the Black Santa Brunch. She and Noah at the Sphinx Masquerade Ball. All of them at her Belles & Beaus initiation. She wondered how her husband and children would be affected when this information became public.

Noah rolled his sleeves down as he walked into the family room. "Look, no matter what happens, we will get through this." He pulled Sahara towards him, and she shrank in his arms.

"Noah, I just don't know. Do you think this will hurt Clarissa and Trevor in some way?" She had to protect her children.

He rubbed her back while he held her close. "They'll be okay. We'll be okay." He lifted her chin up and pressed his lips on hers.

The trumpet sound on the television caught both of their attention. This was it. They moved slowly to the couch in the family room to watch the spectacle.

Any other time, Sahara would secretly ogle the tall, dark, and handsome Fred Hall, the news anchor at the same station as Rowena McGee. However, her favorite Man Crush Monday would be the bearer of bad news so her infatuation was on the back burner today.

Fred straightened his papers, "After three delays, it seems that the press conference that Congressman Charles Allymer scheduled will finally take place. Our reporters are assembled in Washington, D.C. waiting for the press conference to begin. Just to recap, it was reported on a blog on Saturday that Congressman Charles Allymer, representing District 11 in Raleigh in the U.S. House of Representatives has a secret child. Congressman Allymer has refused to answer questions until today." Fred paused. "Okay, it looks like the press conference is beginning."

As they sat on the couch, Sahara twirled her wedding ring as she tried to brace herself emotionally for what her father was about to say. The camera was focused on the brown podium in front of the backdrop with the United States Capitol. The irony of her father confessing in front of a symbol of equality and fairness was not lost on her. When her father walked on the platform and stood behind the podium, Noah took Sahara's hand. A young woman followed him, but there was no sign of Winnie or Fallon.

He looked nice. Everything about Congressman Charles Allymer was formidable. Tall, fair, with wavy hair and a straight nose, Charles Allymer was born with features that naturally made him good and reputable in the eyes of most whites and many blacks. And the title, congressman, elevated his status even higher. The tailored—not too sharp to be considered "trendy" or too loose to be called "ill-fitting"—blue suit that he wore was proper. The red tie with tiny white polka dots signaled he was good and patriotic. The gold cuff links, an adornment used by the common man only in formal occasions, were a nice touch and identified him as respectable and highly regarded.

Yes, her father had thought of everything if he was going to hold on to his powerful position and image. The only thing missing was the "stand by your man" wife. Sahara guessed that Winnie was not willing to play that role publicly today. And, who was the woman on the platform with him? A member of his staff?

"Good evening, everyone," her father said. His voice was steady and calm. Not a hint of anxiety. "I have called this press conference to read my statement. I will not take any questions after I have read it." Noah squeezed Sahara's hand again. "It has been reported by the media that I have a child outside of my marriage. I stand here before you to acknowledge and confirm that I did have a daughter with a woman during an undisclosed separation from my wife. Although my wife and I did eventually reconcile, I am not ashamed of the daughter that I had during that time." He smiled and the woman on the platform stepped forward. "This is my daughter, Sabrina Allymer...."

Sahara didn't hear another word. For a minute, she thought she had blacked out. But, she could still see Charles Allymer's lips moving. Then, Noah was saying something, but she couldn't understand or hear him either. What was going on?

She felt like she was going deeper, deeper, deeper in water. She looked around. But, she wasn't in a pool or anything. Why did everything seem so off? What was going on?

Sabrina Allymer. That was Congressman Charles Allymer's daughter. Sabrina Allymer.

She was cute. A little younger than Sahara. A lot thinner. There was some resemblance with Fallon. Same hair, same complexion—they both got it from their father. Their father. There was another child.

For a second, Sahara felt relief. Her life would be the same. She didn't have to worry about her family's life being disrupted. That was a good thing, right?

Now, it made sense. Why she hadn't heard from him. Why he hadn't reached out. If you were going to tell the world about your illegitimate daughter, your daughter with someone other than your wife, you would call her. Warn her. But, that's why there wasn't a phone call, a text, or an email.

"Sahara, are you okay?" asked Noah.

She forgot he was there. His face was inquisitive, curious...wondering what she was thinking. About the fact that her father had another daughter. Well, another daughter other than the one she already knew about. Sahara threw her head back and laughed.

"Are you, okay?" asked Noah again as he inched closer to her on the couch. Same question. Same face.

Yes, she was alright. Say it. Or, he'll think you've lost your mind. "Yes, I'm okay."

"You don't look okay," he said. Still with the inquisitive, curious face.

She stood up. "I'm okay."

I'm okay. I'm okay. I'm okay. The more she said it, the more likely it was true. However, she couldn't stop the heaviness. He did it to her again. Denied her. He had proclaimed before the world that...what's her name? Sabrina. That was it. He proclaimed before the world that Sabrina Allymer was HIS daughter.

Yet, she still remained a secret. Finally, the water that she was submerged in came flooding out, and Sahara burst into tears.

As she sat in bed the next morning, not ready to start the day, her tears had dried and only the salt remained. She tossed and turned all night. She couldn't get her mind to rest because once again, her father had denied her. Once again, he showed that he didn't care about her. That she wasn't worthy of his attention, of his love...of his legitimacy.

But, Fallon was. And, so was this...Sabrina. Sahara wondered if Mrs. Belles & Beaus would think precious

Fallon needed to be protected from Sabrina, too.

And, how many more children were out there? Maybe this was just the beginning. Maybe there were five...ten...fifteen illegitimate children out there. Who needed the *Real Housewives* when you had *Charles Allymer and All His Children.*

Yet, it seemed that one thing was certain. Congressman Charles Allymer would probably claim them all, before he announced to the world that *she* was his daughter.

As Sahara prepared for work, she couldn't shake her feelings of disappointment and betrayal. AAARRGGHHH!!!! She refused to cry again or anymore. Too many tears had been wasted on a man who proved time and time again that he didn't care about her. That he didn't love her. But, she couldn't stop the pressure that was building in her chest, working its way up, until she felt like she was going to explode.

She wished she didn't have to go to work. Unfortunately, she didn't get anything done yesterday since she was worrying about this big revelation. Well, her prayers were answered. The secret was still that. She couldn't justify taking a day off because there was no revelation.

Buzz. Buzz.

Who was calling her this early in the morning? She picked up her cell phone as she walked downstairs. It was Soror Gertrude. She probably wanted to say something about Sahara skipping out on the rest of Green Light Weekend. Or, as she liked to say, "you, young sorors."

She'd pass. She wasn't in the mood to talk to anyone anyway, and Soror Gertrude with her respectable, privileged friends was at the top of the list.

Unfortunately, Sahara accidently hit the green, *Accept Call* button, instead of the red, *Decline Call* one. Ugh! Could anything go her way?

She had to answer now, or Soror Gertrude would run and tell all her friends that Sahara hung up her. "Hello?" She tried to take the irritation out of her voice, but she wasn't sure that she was successful.

"Good morning, Soror Sahara. It's Soror Gertrude."

She knew whom it was. We have caller id on phones now. What do you want?

Soror Gertrude continued in her slow Southern drawl. "I won't keep you. However, it's mandatory that we include in our report that we contacted everyone who was nominated. So, this is your official call to say that you've been nominated for president, and I'll put down that you declined. Thank...."

"Wait. Did you say that I was nominated for president?" Who had nominated her? She told Donna that she wasn't going to do it.

"Yes, you were nominated for president. I'll just put down that you declined the nomination," said Soror Gertrude again.

"Yes, you can put down that.... Wait. Why did you assume that I would decline the nomination?" asked Sahara, as she poured herself a cup of coffee.

"Well...because you need to learn the chapter. It isn't your time right now."

It wasn't her time right now? What did that mean? And, who put Soror Gertrude in charge?

That was the problem with all of them. The Soror Gertrudes. The Gayle Phillips. And, her father...she couldn't forget him. They thought they were in charge. They thought they were in control.

And, that's where they were wrong. She had power, too.

Sahara smiled to herself. "You know, Soror Gertrude, I think I will accept the nomination." Take that.

FIVE

....

S ahara thanked the Lord for Bluetooth as she weaved in and out of traffic on the busy parkway while she talked to her best friends on the phone. Now that nominations were closed, Donna thought it made sense to get some of the young sorors together before the next chapter meeting to strategize, so she was headed to Donna's place now—and as usual, running late.

Sahara would be lying if she didn't admit that she had second thoughts about running for president. But, she was incensed that Soror Gertrude assumed that she wouldn't accept the nomination. That was the problem with this circle. Old was not always better. Traditions were great, but sometimes you needed innovative ideas and fresh blood.

"They say to never underestimate the power of a woman who knows what she wants, and I know that you certainly have the skills to take that chapter to another level," said Nissa, an assistant district attorney and one of Sahara's best friends from college.

"There's no question that she has the skills," added

Sahara's other best friend, Grace. "But do you really want this, Sahara?"

"Am I tired of the 'powers to be' thinking that they can do whatever they want, say whatever they want...and the rest of us are just supposed to fall in line like 'good little children' and not question them or hold them accountable? Yes. Do I think we need change? Yes. But, am I the one that should be leading the charge? I don't know," said Sahara.

"You don't know?" said Nissa. "Honey, you've already accepted the nomination. You better get your head in the game. Is there anyone running against you?"

That was a good question. "Hmmm...I don't know. I guess that I will find out at the chapter meeting." She hadn't even thought about it. Was someone else running? Soror Christina mentioned that she may run...but she wasn't serious. Or, was she?

Beep! Beep!

Ugh. Why did people in the South drive so slowly? She was supposed to be at Donna's loft fifteen minutes ago, and it would be at least another ten minutes before she got there. However, she shouldn't complain. Now that Donna had moved into Alton's condo in the transitional West Village, she was a lot closer to Sahara than when she lived in her house on the west side.

Sahara beeped her horn at a car that was drifting into her lane. "At the time, I was so angry about everything. My father. That stupid press conference. Green Light

Weekend. Everything. Then, when the nominating chair called and assumed that I wouldn't accept the nomination, I snapped. I was sick and tired of playing by the rules, doing everything right...that I...I don't know. I guess that I felt like accepting the nomination was a way for the underdog to win. You know...like stick it to the man."

"And, by the man...you mean...your father?" asked Nissa.

This summer, Sahara revealed to Nissa and Grace whom her father was. Grace, whose old guard Atlanta family had interacted with him and Winnie on several occasions, was shocked. Nissa, who became more cynical the longer she was an assistant district attorney in Dallas, said that she wasn't surprised. She maintained that she'd never met an honest politician and that included her boss.

Sahara thought for a second. "Yes...no...I mean...I don't know. The whole lot of them, I guess. The whole group. The older sorors in the chapter that refuse to listen to our ideas and think 'their way is best.' They think they are the chosen ones that know best, do best, are best. The Winnies. The ladies in the lunchroom at Belles & Beaus cluster. Mrs. Belles & Beaus, Gayle Phillips. And, yes...I guess...my father. That was my way to stick it to them all."

"Mmmm....I don't think that's a reason to run, Sahara," Grace said softly.

"Well, it's not the only reason...," Sahara said sheepishly as she pulled out in front of the pack of cars she was with and gunned the engine. "I am qualified. I have some great ideas. And, you know that I love the sorority." Grace was also a member of Lambda Upsilon Alpha and was one of Sahara's big sisters when she was initiated.

"Whatever the reason, get that power, boss lady! They say that if you want power, you have to take it," said Nissa.

"They also say that power attracts the worst and corrupts the best," Grace quickly added.

Sahara saw a woman pulling out of a parking space in front of Alton's building so she put her hazard lights on to wait for the spot. "Well, I'm neither. I'm just me. And, right now, I'm only running to be the president of my LUA chapter, not trying to take over the world—or even Fairchester for that matter."

~~~

When Sahara stepped into the lobby, Soror Faye Duncan was already waiting for the elevator. "Oh good! I'm not the only one who is a little late," said Sahara as she embraced her chapter sister.

"Well, I would have been upstairs a little sooner, if I hadn't spent ten minutes looking for place that looked safe enough to park my car. What made Soror Donna pick this place? Her house in Queensbridge Manor was in a nice neighborhood."

Sahara stepped on the elevator and pushed the button to Donna's floor. "I think they wanted to save money for the wedding, and Alton preferred his loft to her house so she moved in with him."

"She should have fought to stay in her house," Soror Faye said flatly. "This neighborhood is too sketchy."

However, she was singing a different tune when they walked into the loft. With its soaring wood-beamed ceilings, exposed brick walls, and amazing view of the city's skyline, it wasn't too difficult to understand why Alton didn't want to give up all this.

Although the meeting hadn't officially started, there were already several sorors seated around the table and a few were standing in the chef's kitchen. Taking the description to heart, Donna stood over the stove stirring the contents of a large black pot.

"Something smells delicious, Soror Donna," said Faye as she walked over to take a peek in the pot to see what was brewing.

"Just a little gumbo," replied Donna.

"Gumbo? What you know about gumbo?" Faye asked with her best Cajun accent.

Donna laughed. "Hopefully, just enough. Alton and I went to the Essence Festival this summer, and he loved the gumbo that we had at one of the restaurants. I wasn't sure that this North Carolina girl could reproduce the flavors, but I found a pretty good recipe online."

While Donna and Faye discussed the cuisine of the bayou, Sahara eyed the four bottles of wine in the middle of the table. Merlot. Riesling. Moscato. And Duplin.

People from North Carolina loved that Duplin wine, but she was not a fan. She picked up the bottle of moscato, another state favorite, and poured herself a glass as three more sorors walked in. Everyone made themselves at home and joined a conversation.

The ladies gathered in the large kitchen were all members of the Fairchester Chapter of Lambda Upsilon Alpha Sorority. Some were originally from Fairchester, but most were transplants. Many were initiated into the sorority as undergraduates, but a few became members in a graduate chapter. Some single. Others married. Most had children. A few did not. Although they were different in many ways, they were all sorors—sisters. And, no one seated in Donna's kitchen was over the age of forty-five.

"I am going to be the bomb dot com at homecoming. Now, I just need to find an outfit to Emery's birthday party that fits in my budget."

"You know that she was let go from her last job. My hairdresser said that there was something funny with the money. I wonder where she ended up?"

"I heard that she was at the ...."

"Sahara, you know Moo...I mean...Rozlyn, right?"

asked Soror Gwen.

"Yes, I know her." But, by no means were they friends. That ship had sailed. "Why?"

"I have a friend that's in Epsilon Iota Zeta. She said that Rozlyn's trying to get in."

Sahara rolled her eyes. "Well, that would be a mistake." And, a switch. She thought Rozlyn had been angling to be in Xi Tau Delta. Some people just wanted to be Greek. The letters didn't matter.

Donna walked over to the table and took the bottle of merlot.

"Hey, hey, hey, young lady! Where are you going with that?" asked Soror Gwen.

"I need it for my dish," said Donna walking over to the oven. She opened the oven door, slid out the roasting pan, and poured the contents from the bottle in it.

Gumbo and a roast? "I'm not trying to be funny, Donna, but when did you become B. Smith? I thought you didn't like to cook," asked Candice as she brought a chair from the living room into the kitchen.

Donna took off the pink apron and sat down at the table with the other ladies. "Trust me. I'm still the take out queen. But, I've been trying to cook more, since I'm going to be a married woman." She flashed her engagement ring around the table to punctuate her point.

"Forget about cooking. When are you going to add a woman's touch to this place? Don't get me wrong the bones are here, and you have a beautiful view—but it could be a little more stylish." said Soror Faye. They all nodded their heads up and down.

"I know," said Donna. Alton's condo looked like the ultimate man cave. Leather sofa, extra large television, stocked bar, and no personality. "I just moved in a few months ago. I don't want to overwhelm him with all my pink and green. Anyway, we are waiting on a few more..." Suddenly, the fire under the black pot on the stove flared up, and the lid started dancing around as water spilled out of the pot.

"Oh no!" Donna said as she jumped up and tried to curtail the damage.

Gwen got up from the table and took the pot from the flame. "Here, let me help you." She took the pot over to the sink. "You have way too much water in here."

"Well, the recipe said to fill the pot with water."

Candice got up and turned off the unattended flame that Donna left burning. "Next time, get a black recipe." She looked at the salt and pepper sitting on the counter and pulled two more bottles out of the cabinet. "And, some more spices for seasoning."

Donna sat back in the chair while Gwen and Candice finished preparing the gumbo and returned the pot to the stove. "Ugh. This is so hard."

"Especially, when you can't cook," said Gwen. Everyone shot her a dirty look so she didn't say anything else.

"What's burning?" asked Soror Trish as she walked into the kitchen.

"Burning?" asked Donna. "Shoot! I forgot about the roast!" She ran to the oven and pulled out a charred piece of meat.

Some of the ladies started laughing and shaking their heads. Sahara stood up. Hopefully, she could distract them from Donna's cooking crisis. "Since most of us are here, why don't we get started." Everyone turned and looked at her. "Thank you to Soror Donna for allowing us to meet in her home...."

A chorus of "Thank you, Soror Donna" and "Thanks, soror," filled the room.

Sahara continued, "Well, all of us have been a little unsatisfied with how things in the chapter have been going lately...."

"Green Light Weekend was a mess!"

"My husband's golf buddies said they have never been to such a poorly run tournament."

"My friend scheduled a massage, but when she got to the spa they told her that she had to get a facial or nothing."

"That party was the worst. The drinks were watered down, and the deejay was whack. I'm a member of the chapter, and I may not go again."

Sahara cleared her throat. "Sorors. Sorors. Yes, there are plenty of examples where Green Light Weekend could have been better, but there are other issues in the chapter...."

"The older sorors don't listen to us."

"The chapter programs are tired. I'm on the program committee, and whenever I suggest something new or different, all I hear is 'we've always done it this way.'"

"Things could be more transparent. Sometimes, I feel like decisions have already been made before they are brought to the chapter."

"Let's be honest. The older sorors don't want our ideas. They just want us to carry out theirs."

Sahara laughed. "You have quickly outlined some of the issues. But, I don't think we want to use this time only talking about what is wrong with the chapter...."

"Because that would take all night and maybe some of tomorrow...," someone said.

With all these disruptions, no wonder the president had a gavel at the meetings. Sahara cleared her throat again and tapped a fork on her wine glass to get every-one's attention. "But, we need to come up with a plan...a strategy...to improve things. Now, who's running for an office?"

"I'm running for Treasurer," said Gwen.

"I'm running for VP," said Donna as she walked over to the table. After people yelled out what positions they were running for there was only one—president—that wasn't spoken for.

"I didn't want to tip my hand too early, so I'm plan-ning to run for president from the floor," said Trish.

Sahara looked at her. "I'm running for president," she said firmly. Out the corner of her eye, she saw Candice elbow Gwen.

"Well, if we both want to do it, we can figure out who should run," said Trish looking around trying to get some support.

Okay, she was going to have to break this down for Trish. "No, I don't want to run. I am running," said Sahara. Trish still looked confused so Sahara continued, "From the nominating committee's standpoint, I'm in the race right now. I'm not running from the floor. I was nominated. And, I accepted."

The light bulb went off, and Trish looked surprised. "You were nominated?"

Why did Trish look like that? Like she couldn't be nominated. But, Sahara remained calm. "Yes, I was nominated, and I accepted the nomination," she repeated.

Trish slumped in her seat. "Oh." Hopefully, that put an end to that.

Donna stepped up and said, "I think Sahara would make a great president. She has a reputation for being hard working and able to get things done. And, I think we have a strong slate of people that are running. But, the question is...can we get the votes?"

Tania added, "Well, of course, everyone here will vote for this slate. And about...." She looked up at the ceiling as if she was calculating something. "Yes, about forty percent of the chapter consists of 'young' sorors.'"

"But that doesn't mean that all young sorors will vote for us," someone added.

Another person chimed in. "Especially the legacies. They may vote the way their mothers vote."

"However, even if we assumed that all the young sorors voted for us, that still isn't enough. We need to get some older sorors to vote for this slate of candidates, if we want to win," said Donna.

"In all honesty, I think some of the older sorors will vote for us. Some of them are just as frustrated as we are are."

"Yes, they're frustrated. But, are they frustrated enough to not vote for their friends?" asked Soror Faye.

"Well, I think that Meranda will vote for me. If I talk to her, I'm sure that I can convince her to vote for our slate," added Sahara. More glances back and forth, but no one said anything.

After a few seconds, Donna said, "Why don't we go through the chapter roster and tally how many votes we think we can get? Alton has a large dry erase board in his office that we can use."

When Donna returned, the meeting morphed into a full-blown strategy session. Who would the competition be? Who could they target for votes? What was their platform? Where would they strike first? When would they start campaigning? Why were they running?

At times, it was hard to hear anything. Everyone was talking over one another trying to get their points across to make sure that their voices were heard. Sahara took a sip of her wine and tried to drown out the commotion for a second. The person that needed to be here was Teri. Organizing, strategizing, promoting...this was right up her alley.

Sahara laughed to herself. When they were trying to get into Belles & Beaus, Teri had profile books, calendars, biographies, and anything else that you could think of documented on the chapter and its members. Sahara had teased that if Teri wasn't careful, someone was going to bring her up on charges of stalking because she had compiled so much information on the chapter members.

However, that was then, and this was now. All this strategizing made Sahara feel that she was out of her league, and unfortunately, Teri wasn't here to help her now. She and Jayla now lived in Mississippi, so Sahara was going to have to maneuver this campaign process without her.

She looked at the white board at the front of the room. It was filled with names and arrows and strike throughs. The question "WHY ARE WE RUNNING?" was in all caps in the middle of the board. Sahara was reminded of her conversation with Nissa and Grace earlier that evening, and Grace's warning that she didn't think Sahara's motivation was a good reason to run.

Just because the decision was made in the heat of the moment didn't mean that it wasn't the right one. She was qualified. She had great ideas. And, she cared about the chapter and its future.

Sahara looked where Donna wrote *Our Slate* at the top right corner of the board. *President – Sahara Kyle* was at the top.

She looked over at Trish who was still pouting about not being able to run for president from the floor. Sahara could withdraw her name, and let Trish run. But, running from the floor was a bigger gamble than being slated, and the flip flopping of candidates was sure to turn some sorors off.

And, to be honest, she was a better candidate with more experience than Trish. If anyone was going to run, it should be her. It *would* be her.

Sahara took another sip of her wine. Now, her only question...was anyone running against her?

SIX

....

SAHARA – 1   *OPPONENT(?)* – 0

D ivision. Cliques. Programs. Votes. It had been two
days since the strategy meeting at Donna's loft,
but Sahara still had the campaign and election on
the brain as she went in to work on Monday. Sure, she
knew that there was no guarantee that she would be
president. However, when she decided to accept the
nomination for president, she hadn't really thought
about the process between nomination and voting. Now,
she was forced to think about platforms, slogans, and
speeches.

Sahara had only been in the chapter long enough to
see one election, but based upon what she heard at the
strategy meeting, the others were the same. The older
sorors ran unopposed so there wasn't much campaigning, and, the biggest controversy at the last election was
that the incumbent president did not receive unanimous
support.

Although Sahara didn't know if she had an opponent...hopefully not...it sounded like things could get
intense with this election. The older sorors would surely
take the nominations as a challenge to their authority

and become defensive. So, the young sorors needed to make sure that their offense was first rate.

"Oof!" said Sahara as someone slammed into her shoulder as she turned the corner in the hallway.

"I'm sorry," said Senator Tyrone Barrett, Meranda's husband. "Oh, Sahara. It's you." The ready smile that always came to his face was slow to emerge today for some reason.

"Hello, Senator Barrett. I didn't expect to run into you—literally." What was he doing here? Then, she remembered. He was on the board of directors for the Fairchester Economic League, but Sahara didn't think they had a meeting today. She always helped compile the information Glynda needed for her presentation when the board met.

"My fault. I have a lot on my mind this morning." He looked over his shoulder as if he wanted to make sure that there was no behind him. "Just got out of a meeting with Glynda Clayton."

"That's where I'm headed. Oh, how is your daughter, Dara, doing? I've been meaning to ask Meranda, but we've both been so busy that we haven't been able to connect." Please don't let any lightning strike her. She had wondered how Dara was doing but purposely never brought her up to Meranda. She knew her neighbor well enough to know that she liked her world perfect—and Dara and her "issues" did not quite measure up.

Senator Barrett's face lit up at the thought of his

daughter. "She is doing well. You know she moved to Atlanta a couple of months ago, and now she's dating someone, a musician, I think."

"I'm glad to hear things are going well for her. She's a sweet girl."

Senator Barrett smiled. "Thank you for asking."

"I don't want to keep you, but please tell Meranda that I said hello. Although, I guess I'll see her at the LUA meeting next Saturday."

"I will, although, I'm not sure if she'll be there. These days, her calendar is busier than mine. She and some friends were holding some late night planning session the other day. Sometimes, I wonder how many galas one town can hold," said Senator Barrett.

In addition to serving on countless boards and being an LUA, Meranda was a member of the Darlings, The Sphinx, and a laundry list of community and civic organizations. She had to balance her own schedule and commitments, along with her husband's busy calendar. Since her husband was a North Carolina state senator, Meranda was always somewhere fabulous schmoozing with local, state, and national politicians.

Sahara laughed. "Sometimes, it isn't about holding a gala, but more so about hosting the BEST gala."

"Well, as long as the cause doesn't get lost during the climb to the top...," said Senator Barrett as he and Sahara parted ways.

Sahara continued down the hallway to Glynda's office and was surprised to find it so quiet. In addition to being the office's social butterfly, Glynda spent a lot of her day making phone calls, and you could always hear her husky voice down the hallway. However, when Sahara reached the office, Glynda's door was closed and the blinds on the small window shut tight.

She had to be in there because Sahara would have passed her in the hallway if she left. For whatever reason, after meeting with Senator Barrett, she was now sequestered in her office like a hermit crab.

Sahara shrugged her shoulders and walked back to her office. She wanted to talk to Glynda to see if she had any specific ideas for the Fairchester Economic League scholarship flyer. It had to be completed by Friday so that she could disseminate it early next week. Well, it seems like it would have to wait.

Back at her desk, Sahara looked through the collection of stock photos that she had. She needed a picture with black people that looked like they could be in college. This photo was a good one...for a campaign brochure.

The children in it were smiling as they played instruments in front of a group of elderly people. The chapter was partners with both an elementary school and a senior citizen community. Maybe they should try to do a joint activity with the two.

She remembered seeing a video on social media that showed when seniors and children interacted in a nursing home, there was a positive effect on both popula-tions. She should write that down. *Greater impact in the community with measurable results.* That would be great to include in her platform.

Focus. Fairchester Economic League. Scholarship. Find pictures for the flyer. That's what she was doing now.

Sahara buckled down and spent the rest of the morn-ing trying to concentrate on the task at hand. However, she was failing miserably. Her mind kept drifting to the upcoming LUA elections. She looked at the green and blue flyer for the scholarship that was on her screen. The font was too simple, and the students weren't quite right. For the past three hours, her only good ideas were related to the upcoming election.

And, Glynda wasn't answering her phone so she couldn't get any motivation from her. Great.

Maybe some coffee would get her on the right track. She looked at the clock on her computer. It was almost lunchtime anyway. Maybe she would grab a sandwich, too. As she walked down the hallway, she noticed that Glynda's office was still closed. Strange. Sahara stuck her head inside Mia's office to see if she wanted to go downstairs with her, but Mia's office was empty. Oh well. It looked like she was on her own today.

Sahara walked outside the old two-story brick build-ing and saw the line for the Chinese restaurant next door was out the building. Unfortunately, she didn't want to wait.

Although the area where the Fairchester Economic League was located was on the outskirts of downtown and not that far from Donna and Alton's loft, it also bordered the fringes of the west side. When the realtors gave the transitional neighborhood the cute and trendy name of West Village, condos and lofts popped up overnight. A few businesses soon followed, but retail and restaurants had not materialized.

Despite the hope, complete gentrification was slow to arrive so graffiti and boarded up buildings were still abundant in the area. Consequently, the food options in the immediate vicinity of the Fairchester Economic League were severely limited. The Chinese restaurant with its bulletproof glass and security bars was the only place to sit down and eat within a six block radius. She'd pass.

However, if Sahara was willing to walk seven blocks toward downtown, she could get some coffee and a sandwich from a local coffee shop. She had to leave early to pick up Clarissa and Trevor today so she didn't want to be gone too long. But, she wasn't in the mood for Chinese food—let alone waiting for it—so she kicked her walking into high gear.

Ten minutes later, she ordered a mocha latte and turkey and bacon wrap from the busy and cute little neighborhood coffee shop. She really needed to get back, but she loved the ambiance with its colorful furniture and light jazz playing in the background. And, the food...Sahara took a quick bite of her wrap to take the edge off. Delicious.

Maybe she could quickly eat her lunch there. All the tables were full, but a woman, at the high-top counter facing the window, looked like she was finished. Sahara stalked her for a few seconds and grabbed her stool when she got up to leave. Victory.

As she looked out the window enjoying her lunch, she realized how much this neighborhood had changed since they moved to Fairchester a few years ago. Like the West Village, this neighborhood was filled with new condominiums and lofts. However, it also had art galleries, craft breweries, and several nice ethnic restaurants. It was probably what Midtown was like five years ago, except smaller and more bohemian. The newspaper dubbed the area as Five Points.

The various shops, boutiques, and restaurants that lined the busy street were patronized by office workers in the daytime, and packed with the residents of the gentrified neighborhood at night. One thing was for certain...what a difference seven blocks made.

Sahara looked at the huge yellow crane, heavy equipment, and workers in hard hats across the street. From the looks of it, the large, decaying building in the middle of the block was about to be demolished. She didn't know what would take its place, but whatever it was, B. A. Montgomery Construction, the company owned by Zora's father-in-law and her husband was now the president of, was building it. And when completed, the building was sure to be leased by B. A. Montgomery Real Estate Services. And once all the yuppies and buppies that moved in started having children, then B.A. Montgomery Construction would build one of the fancy private schools that Cass' family owned. Zora wasn't involved in the black elite circles, but she certainly had snagged a prince in the white one.

Sahara checked her watch to see how she was doing with time. Uh oh. She better get out of there. As Sahara stood up to leave, she saw Mia walking outside. And then, her jaw dropped. Mia wasn't alone. She was with Rozlyn Wormley.

That girl was like a bad itch. Sahara just couldn't seem to shake her.

None of Sahara's friends were close to Rozlyn. And, she wasn't sure what happened between Emery and Rozlyn, but she knew they weren't friends anymore. With Rozlyn and Emery no longer friends, Sahara thought that all ties to Rozlyn were severed, and she wouldn't have to deal with Mrs. Wormley again.

And now, she pops up with Mia. And, she couldn't forget hearing at Donna's house that Rozlyn was trying to become a member of Epsilon Iota Zeta. Incredible. Like a cat, this woman's social life had nine lives.

Sahara watched Rozlyn and Mia through the window as they walked up the street. They were laughing and talking like they were the best of friends. Interesting. Rozlyn used her friendship with Sahara to make inroads with Emery. Her time with Emery was spent studying and copying Emery's style. What was Rozlyn hoping to get from Mia? Only time would tell.

"Are you finished eating, Ma'am?" said a man interrupting Sahara's thoughts.

"Huh? Oh yes...sure." Sahara glanced at the clock on the wall as she gathered her trash. She was in the coffee shop much longer than she planned to be. She needed to get back so that she could finish the marketing flyer for the scholarship.

On the return trip, the seven blocks back to the Fairchester Economic League seemed to take twice as long to cover as it did to get to the coffee shop. Sahara pushed her speed walking into power mode hoping to get to the building quicker...and to get another glimpse of Rozlyn and Mia. But, she didn't see them again.

When Sahara went inside the building, everyone was missing. What was going on? She called downstairs to the receptionist. "Hi, Jonecia. It's Sahara. I got back from lunch, and it's a ghost town up here. Where is everybody?"

"Remember, Glynda called an emergency staff meeting for one o'clock."

"Emergency staff meeting? I didn't know anything about it." Sahara thought about how Glynda's door was closed all morning.

"Well, I sent everyone an email about it around ten." Jonecia paused. "Oh wait. I forgot to include you on it. Oops."

Terrific. "Thank you." Sahara wanted to add "for nothing" but she didn't. She looked at the clock on the computer. She was ten minutes late. Hopefully, she hadn't missed anything important.

When she arrived, the conference room was packed. Sahara squeezed inside and stood against the wall. Mia saw her and waved so Sahara did the same. Everyone that worked for the Fairchester Economic League, except for Jonecia, was there. Marketing. Programs. Community Engagement. Employment & Career Services. Family Support. Finance. Yes, everyone was there.

Glynda Clayton, the executive director of the Fairchester Economic League, stood at the front of the room. Always lively and energetic, Glynda's somber expression and restrained movements were out of the norm. "So, we aren't sure why the membership projections were off, but they are. We've looked at them every which way we can but in the end, we have a lot less money in the bank than we expected.

"Unfortunately, because of the huge shortfall and building expenditures that we made because we thought the money would be there...we're not sure that there will be enough money to cover the scholarships and some of our programs," said Glynda.

People in the room started murmuring and whispering to their neighbors. Did she say that there wasn't enough money to fund the scholarships? A shortfall due to the membership projections? Sahara was a financial analyst when the budget was prepared. She had worked on those numbers.

"In light of these and other issues...."

Other issues? What other issues?

"The board of directors...."

Sahara remembered bumping into Senator Barrett this morning. Is that why....

"...thought it would be best if I stepped down as executive director and served as the deputy director."

There was a collective gasp in the room. Glynda wasn't going to be the executive director? No one knew this place or cared about executing its mission like she did. She had been there longer than most of the employees in the room.

"So...Mr. Johnson will serve as the interim executive director."

Mr. Johnson? Mr. Johnson, the finance director? Sahara could see the glances and the side eyes around the room. Mr. Johnson was one of the most prickly people to work with at the Fairchester Economic League. He and Glynda were always bumping heads. In fact, Mr. Johnson bumped heads with everyone.

Sahara looked around the room, and wide eyes and dropped jaws conveyed the disbelief that everyone felt. With Mr. Johnson was at the helm, the Fairchester Economic League would go from an enjoyable place to work that did great things in the community to a hostile environment. Working full-time was already getting old, this announcement completely killed the notion.

Glynda continued, "Since Mr. Johnson will now serve in the capacity of interim executive director, Mia Johnson will now be the interim finance director."

Another collective gasp went through the room. Mia was the interim finance director? Had that been Glynda's decision or Mr. Johnson's?

Mia was the volunteer coordinator after Sahara became part of the staff at the Fairchester Economic League. When Sahara moved from financial analyst over to the program coordinator position, Mia took her old job. Less than a year after coming to the agency, Mia went from volunteer coordinator to finance director, while there were people working in the office that were in their same positions for more than ten years.

"Are there any questions?" asked Glynda.

There had to be a million questions, yet everyone sat there shell shocked. Then, Angie in accounts payable raised her hand. "When are these changes effective?"

Instead of giving Glynda the opportunity to answer, Mr. Johnson blurted out, "Immediately." People began to mumble.

"Are there any other questions?" asked Mr. Johnson. No one said anything. "Well, if there are no more questions, you are free to leave."

People bolted out of the room like they were leaving the blocks at a track meet. Probably to get on the phone and help spread the news. With this game changer, Sahara was sure that no additional Fairchester Economic League work would be done this afternoon. A couple of people congratulated Mr. Johnson, while a few walked with Glynda out of the conference room.

Sahara decided to follow Glynda. However, Mia intercepted her before she reached Glynda, and Sahara didn't want to seem rude. "Hi, Mia. Wow. Congratulations!"

Mia was beaming. "Thank you! It was quite a surprise."

Sure it was. Sahara continued, "I'm surprised that the projections were off that much. I remember working on them when I worked with Mr. Johnson." Sahara paused. "Actually we...." She now remembered that Mia had helped, too. Since she was a certified public accountant, Mia offered her assistance at the time.

"Me? Oh no...Those projections were done before I got here."

"No, you were here. Remember you were the volunteer coordinator? You actually helped me put them together."

"I absolutely did not compile or help compile any budget numbers," said Mia emphatically.

Sahara clearly remembered that she did but whatever. She wasn't going to argue with her. "Well, I just wanted to congratulate you."

"Thank you," Mia said with less enthusiasm than the first time. "Well, I'm going to get some lunch. They had me in meetings all morning about this."

"Huh? I thought that I saw you out when I was at lunch."

"Nope, wasn't me. We had a meeting right before this all staff meeting. That's where I found out about the promotion."

Sahara was completely confused. She was sure that she saw Mia walking with Rozlyn. Just like she was positive that Mia helped with the budget projections. But, why would she lie?

As Sahara walked by Glynda's office, someone walked out so Sahara poked her head inside. "Glynda, I just want to say that I'm here if you want to talk."

Glynda's eyes were red and puffy. "Come in, Sahara," she said as she smiled weakly. Sahara did as she was instructed and sat down in the chair. Glynda dabbed at her eyes with a tissue. "I don't know what happened."

Sahara hated to see Glynda so upset. Glynda had always been so kind to her and flexible. When Noah was in danger of losing his job, Glynda found the funds so that Sahara could become a part-time financial analyst. And, she was always flexible when it came to Sahara's schedule and picking up her children. "Me either. I worked on those membership numbers…." She started to say "with Mia" but decided to leave that part out. "I don't know how the projections can be so off."

"No, don't worry about that. The projections are only down a little," said Glynda.

Sahara was confused. "Really? You said...."

Glynda looked down. "That's the story that the board of directors let me say...you know...to save face." Tears welled up in her eyes. "For some reason, a number of members have questioned my leadership and the programming at the Fairchester Economic League and requested their money back. That's why I've been demoted."

"Wait...so they paid their membership dues, then requested their money back? That doesn't sound right." Seriously, who does that?

"Well, that's what has been happening. That is why our funds are low—because we've had to issue all these refunds. It's unprecedented." Tears slid down Glynda's cheeks.

Questioning her leadership? And the programs? That was Sahara's department, and she knew that they were doing more things now in the community than the organization had ever done—so that didn't make sense. But, she didn't want to continue to ask questions and upset Glynda. "Let me know if there is anything that I can do. I mean it."

Glynda used the tissue to wipe her tears away. "Thank you, Sahara. I appreciate that, and all the work you've done here."

She sounded like she thought her days at the Fairchester Economic League were numbered, even with the demotion. Sahara walked out of Glynda's office and closed the door behind her. This was awful.

As Sahara headed back to her office, she couldn't help but notice Mr. Johnson and Mia huddled together outside the conference room whispering. And, with Mia over the Finance Department, Sahara couldn't shake the feeling that this shake-up put the fox in charge of the hen house. The only question in her mind...was Mr. Johnson another hen or a fox? Maybe they had more than their last names in common.

Sahara thought about the many disagreements that she witnessed between Mr. Johnson and Glynda. From the looks of his conversation with Mia, it appeared that Glynda had severely underestimated the stakes and her opponent.

SEVEN

....

SAHARA – 1   *OPPONENT(?) – 0*

Everything at the Fairchester Economic League was in turmoil. Mr. Johnson either didn't think his role was an interim one or he didn't know what the word meant. He was changing policies and enacting procedures without consulting department heads. No one liked the new course of the organization, and rumors abounded about Mr. Johnson's ascendancy to the top, as well as the future of the agency. Most people were convinced that Mr. Johnson and Mia had something to do with Glynda's demotion and that they were plotting the dismantling of the Fairchester Economic League. With programs being cut left and right, Sahara found herself with less work to do and more time to entertain the gossip.

On the other hand, paychecks were still needed—so hours had to be logged and work needed to be done. Consequently, things eventually quieted down and everyone became used to, if not comfortable with, Mr. Johnson as the executive director and Mia as the finance director as they navigated the new rules under the interim leadership.

And, with the scholarship and other programs on hold, Sahara moved on to smaller projects. However, she tried to stay clear of Mr. Johnson and Mia. There was something about their alliance that didn't seem right.

The days slipped by quickly and before Sahara knew it, it was the end of the month and time for the LUA meeting. She had been so caught in the drama at work that she put her nomination on the back burner. And, she'd been so busy with Noah and the children when she finally made it home from work that she hadn't talked to Donna or any of the other sorors in their coalition.

Sahara and Meranda normally rode to the meetings together. But, with everything going on, she forgot to call Meranda. But, that could be a good thing. The young sorors agreed to keep their alliance and the offices they sought a secret until the nominations were announced. And, Sahara did not want to slip and say something to Meranda during the ride over to the sorority house.

The morning of the meeting, Sahara turned the key in the ignition and backed out the driveway. Yes, going alone was probably a good thing. She wouldn't accidentally say something that she wasn't supposed to and the solitude would give her time to gather her thoughts. With all the changes at work, the meeting and the nomination announcement crept up on her. Her mind was too preoccupied lately.

However, she couldn't help but wonder why Meranda hadn't contacted her about riding to the meeting together. What was she thinking? Meranda was probably busy, too. Senator Barrett mentioned that she was working late nights on something, and he didn't even know if she was going to attend the meeting.

On the drive over to the Ivy and Pearls Community Foundation Center, Sahara tried to mentally prepare for the next few hours. The nominating committee's report would be towards the end of the agenda. And, Sahara still didn't know if someone was running against her. Since the chapter's president already served two terms, she couldn't run again. However, she wouldn't be surprised if someone else was running for president. In fact, everyone figured that the current vice president would run.

Soror Ada transferred into the chapter shortly after its chartering. She was nice, but she had a reputation for taking on more than she could handle. As a financial executive, she traveled a lot and had a difficult time coordinating the programs. Sahara couldn't imagine her serving as president. And neither could any of the other young sorors. Sahara was sure that she was great with numbers, but she lacked leadership skills in this capacity.

In their meeting at Donna's house, they tried to figure out which of the older sorors would run for what positions. They presumed the current vice president would run for president, and the current financial secretary would run for treasurer. The recording secretary normally moved up to vice president. The secretary positions—both recording and financial—generally were entry points onto the executive board. They weren't sure whom the older sorors had recruited for those positions, but it was rumored that Soror Bonnie and Soror Miriam were running for it.

Regardless, the young sorors strategically put candidates in place that brought more to the table than the usual suspects. It was definitely time that they took a more active leadership role in the chapter. Sahara smiled. The older sorors were used to being in power and running the chapter. They weren't going to know what hit them.

When Sahara pulled into the parking lot of the sorority house, she saw that it was packed. And, there were still twenty minutes until the meeting started. This was a stark contrast to the meetings the past two months. Attendance at September's meeting was light due to sorors preparing for Green Light Weekend. Homecomings were the cause of most absences from the October meeting. However, by the number of cars already in the parking lot, today's meeting was going to be a full house.

After circling the parking lot a couple of times, Sahara came to the realization that there were no spaces. The parking lot was full, and as usual, had its fair share of Mercedes, BMWs, Range Rovers, and a couple of Bentleys thrown in for good measure. She slowly pulled out onto the street and found a spot there.

When she walked back to the Ivy and Pearls Center, she passed a red sports car with the license plate *AngryPnk*. Donna and Alton loved a custom license plate. They could never try to be clandestine. Their cars would always give them away.

That reminded Sahara that their alliance needed to finalize their platform. She passed Tania's minivan a couple of rows later. And a motto or a slogan. Yes, they needed something catchy. Something sorors would remember.

As she opened the door to the building, she saw Meranda's blue Mercedes parked front and center in front of the door. Good. She was here.

And, regardless of how things worked out, Sahara knew that she could count on Meranda's support. If she got a chance before the meeting, maybe she would let Meranda know that she was running so that she wasn't caught off guard by the report. Sahara knew that they agreed to keep everything quiet, but it was the day of the meeting. What would it hurt to say something to Meranda now?

Sahara walked into the brick building and followed the sorors in front of her into the main meeting room, which was overflowing with rows of white chairs. When

Sahara first joined the chapter, everyone easily fit in the room. But, now that the chapter had grown, it was almost standing room only. That was another issue for the next administration to address—their infrastructure and meeting space issues.

"Good morning, Soror Faye," said Sahara as she passed over the green sign-in sheet for visitors and signed the pink paper designated for chapter members. They didn't want to show their hand so they were supposed to greet and interact with each other normally.

"Good morning, Soror Sahara," said Soror Faye, the chapter's sergeant-at-arms. She winked at Sahara before turning to the soror next in line. "Good morning, Soror Ada."

After signing in, Sahara put her purse down in one of the white chairs. As usual, sorors were milling around before the meeting started. Elizabeth, Trish, Donna, Tania. Everyone was there but dispersed throughout the room. Good. Everyone was playing it cool and not tipping their hand. No one was huddled together or talking more than usual. In fact, it was the opposite. They were going out of their way to mix and mingle with the other sorors in the chapter. It looked like any other chapter meeting.

After talking to a few sorors, Sahara excused herself and wandered to the back of the room to look at the chapter scrapbooks and awards on display. That should be safe. It gave her something to do, and she always loved looking through the chapter's history.

A much younger Meranda and many of the older sorors still in the chapter filled the pages of the early scrapbooks. Distributing school supplies. Tutoring elementary school children. Playing bingo with senior citizens. Handing out scholarship checks.

The chapter was so small then, but they did some great things in the community. Sahara was still amazed that Meranda had not only helped charter the chapter but was the first president. Yes, if for no other reason, Sahara had to win this presidency. Meranda was her friend, and she wanted the chapter to return to the level of excellence that it had when Meranda was president.

Sahara opened last year's scrapbook. The chapter was still doing some of its original programs but had added new ones, like Teen Pearls and a county-wide women's health event. There were pictures from their collaboration between the LUAs and the Xis, where they held a self-esteem workshop and pampered the residents at a local battered women's shelter. Emery always served as the co-chair for the Xi's for the project. The president asked Sahara to serve as the LUA co-chair this year.

The chapter was still working hard in the community, but it seemed to have lost some of its luster. Hopefully, they could change that.

Sahara continued to thumb through the scrapbook. There was a picture of her mentoring the Teen Pearls. And, another photo of her at a sisterly relations activity at a ropes course. There she was again in the plenary session at the regional conference. Sahara smiled. She hadn't been in the chapter long, but she certainly had made an impact. No one could argue otherwise.

As she walked back to her seat, she felt better. Less nervous. Sure, their alliance had a lot of work to do, but they were dedicated to the chapter and leaders in the community. Maybe they were overthinking everything, and the election would be simpler than they thought. Sorors had to know that they all loved the chapter, and now, it was simply time for the younger sorors to stand up and help steady the ship.

Sahara relaxed as the president, vice president, and parliamentarian took their seats at the head table in the front of the room. A second later, the president picked up the small pink and green bell and signaled that the meeting was about to begin. Suddenly, Meranda and some other sorors walked in and took their seats on the front row.

The soror in front of Sahara turned and looked at her, and Sahara simply shrugged her shoulders. It was a tradition in the chapter that the first two rows of chairs were reserved for charter members, but where did they come from? Meranda's car was parked out front when Sahara arrived, so clearly she had been somewhere in the building. But, where?

The arrival of Meranda and the rest of the charter members was met with whispers by more than just a few members, and suddenly, the energy in the room shifted. It was definitely more tense. Uneasy. Something wasn't right. However, Sahara pushed her apprehension out of her mind. Maybe she was just nervous about the nominating committee report.

The president called the meeting to order, which was followed by the chaplain's inspiration. Soror DeBerry, normally lighthearted and upbeat, read a meditation that focused on respecting our customs and honoring our ancestors. Some sorors glanced at each other with raised eyebrows—but most sat stiff as boards staring straight ahead. Yes, something was definitely off.

As the meeting progressed, Sahara kept her eyes focused on the president, Soror Hazel, and what she did. She tried to envision herself sitting at the front of the room...holding the gavel...running the meeting. Soror Hazel dressed in her tailored pink suit and pearls always led with a firm hand. One of the charter members, she was big on tradition and even bigger on protocol. When Sahara first joined the chapter, President Hazel took the time to meet with her. Sahara could see herself doing that. Greeting new members and helping them get acclimated to the chapter.

The recording secretary read the minutes from the last meeting and asked for the chapter's approval. The chapter officers gave their reports, providing information about the many meetings, conference calls, and events they attended. When the vice president of programs gave her report on Green Light Weekend, she talked about how well attended and wonderful all the events were. There was no mention of the missteps, mishaps, or mistakes. According to the report, Green Light Weekend was perfect.

Sahara saw more than a few sorors rolling their eyes, and she almost shook her head in disbelief. Clearly, they had reached a new low in that the chapter didn't have any standards. If Soror Ada wasn't willing to acknowledge the mistakes, then how could they learn from them and make the event better? There was no way that Soror Ada could be president.

The committee reports followed presenting post-mortems on finished projects and programs, while updating the chapter on upcoming service activities and events. The nominating committee report was near the end of the agenda, right before unfinished business. You could almost cut the tension in the room with a knife.

Finance. Social. Bylaws. Membership. One by one, the committee chairs sped through their reports. No one asked any questions. Everyone waited with baited breath for the nominating committee report.

Finally, Soror Gertrude stood up and walked to the front of the room. It was show time. "Good morning, Sorors," she said coolly.

"Good morning," they all replied in unison.

With everyone staring intently at her, Soror Ger-

trude seemed uncomfortable for a second. She looked
over at President Hazel, who nodded her head with re-
assurance. That seemed to be what Soror Gertrude
needed. She cleared her throat and continued, "The
nominating committee is comprised of three chapter
members—Soror Benetta, Soror Flora, and myself—who
were elected by the chapter."

Some people started shuffling in their seats. Yes, yes.
They knew all that. Just get on with the report.

Soror Gertrude continued. "Nominations opened on
September 21st and closed on October 15th." She looked
over her reading glasses to make sure that she had everyone's attention, which she did. "For the office of Financial Secretary, there is one candidate—Soror
Candice."

Did she say one candidate? That was interesting. Sahara was surprised that the older sorors didn't recruit
someone for the position. She turned to Candice and
gave her a "You got it, girl" smile. Unless someone ran
from the floor, the position was hers.

"For the position of recording secretary, we have two
candidates—Soror Wanda and Soror Elizabeth."

Okay. So, the current financial secretary was planning to run for recording secretary. That was a miscal-
culation. At the meeting at Donna's house, they guessed
that Soror Wanda would either stay in her current position of financial secretary or run for treasurer. It looked
like she chose a whole new position.

Suddenly, Soror Wanda stood up. "Madam Chair, I would like to withdraw my name from consideration."

The nominating chair looked over at the president for approval. The president nodded her head. "That's fine. I will correct the report." She paused and wrote something on the paper in front of her. "We have one candidate for recording secretary—Soror Elizabeth."

Sahara knew that she wasn't supposed to, but she looked around the room at some of the young sorors. Was it really going to be this easy? Maybe they were worried for nothing. Maybe the older sorors were ready to relinquish control of the chapter.

Then, Sahara saw a sly grin creep on the nominating committee chair's face and a mischievous twinkle in her eye before she looked back down at the paper. The older soror sitting in front of Sahara nudged her friend that was sitting next to her.

"For the office of Treasurer...." Soror Wanda was the best candidate that the older sorors had for treasurer, because it was easy to transition from financial secretary to treasurer. But, it looked like Soror Wanda wasn't running for any position—unless she now was going to run from the floor for Treasurer.

The nominating chair continued, "We have two candidates—Soror Ada and Soror Gwen."

Wait. What? That wasn't right. The vice president was running for treasurer? The two older sorors in front of Sahara looked at each other and smirked. What was going on?

They didn't figured on Soror Ada running for treasurer. Soror Gwen, whom they nominated, was a strong candidate against Soror Wanda, the current financial secretary. But against Soror Ada, who was a financial executive? Sahara wasn't sure. They would have to run an aggressive campaign in order for Gwen to win. Shoot. And, if the vice president was running for treasurer, who was running for president?

"For the office of vice president, we have one candidate—Soror Donna."

Huh? Now, she was thoroughly confused. What was going on? Sahara looked at Donna who shrugged her shoulders. She looked as puzzled as Sahara.

The older sorors were running candidates in some positions, and not others. It was astonishing that they didn't want an older soror to serve as vice president. And, they weren't following their usual succession plan of officers. What in the world was going on?

Sahara couldn't help but look around the room. All the members of their alliance looked shell shocked. None of them had a clue as to what game was being played. However, as baffled as the young sorors looked, the older ones looked confident and certain.

"For the office of president...," The nominating chair paused for dramatic effect as everyone hung unto every word. "For the office of president, we have two candidates—Sahara Kyle and Charter President Meranda Barrett."

Did she hear her right? Did she say Meranda Barrett?

The other sorors in the room must have been just as stunned as Sahara by the match-up. People started murmuring and shifting in the chairs. The president banged the gavel on the table to regain order. "Sorors! Sorors!" Everyone quieted down.

The president looked at the sorors in the room. "Having heard the slate, now is the time to open the floor for nominations. Let's start with financial secretary. The floor for nominations for the office of financial secretary is now open. The floor for nominations for the office of financial secretary is now open. The floor for nominations for the office of financial secretary is now open." The president looked around the room, but no one said anything. "The floor for nominations for the office of financial secretary is now closed."

As the president opened then closed the floor for nominations for each office, Sahara sat in her chair starting straight ahead. Her mind was going crazy. Meranda was running for president? Why didn't she tell her? Sahara would have never accepted the nomination if she had known that. Never.

"Thank you, Madam President," said the nominating committee chair. "The final slate for officers is...for the office of financial secretary is Soror Candice. For the office of recording secretary is Soror Elizabeth. For the office of treasurer are Soror Ada and Soror Gwen. For the office of vice president is Soror Donna. And finally, for the office of president Charter President Meranda Barrett and Soror Sahara Kyle."

They're strategy was all wrong. There were only two positions being contested—president and treasurer. And now, she was supposed to run against her friend, Meranda. Just thinking about it, gave Sahara a headache.

"Since there were no candidates from the floor, all candidates have been certified and can begin campaigning. That's the end of my report," said Soror Gertrude.

Campaigning? There would be no campaigning. Sahara wanted no parts of that or this election.

"Are there any further questions about the nominating committee report?" asked President Hazel.

Everyone was as quiet as a church mouse. A few sorors said, "No," or shook their heads. There were no questions but sure to be plenty of discussion.

"Okay. Thank you, Chair Gertrude."

The nominating committee chair sauntered over to her seat on the front row and sat down. And with the nominating committee report finished, the president moved on with the agenda to unfinished business and then to new business.

However, no one was paying attention. Secret eye signals were being sent amongst friends across the room and whispers and nudges to those seated next to each other. There was nothing else on the agenda that was more important than the news that just was announced.

"Are there any announcements?" asked the president.

Meranda stood up. "Good morning, sorors! I am excited to run for the office of president. As all of you know, I am the charter president of Xi Epsilon Omega. This chapter has done great things with me at the helm, and I believe that we can continue that tradition. One Great Term Deserves Another. Let's Win Together!" She pointed at a pink and green pin on her suit that said the same thing.

After Meranda finished, Sahara saw a few sorors look at her and then whisper. She just stared straight ahead without saying a word. This was a disaster of epic proportions.

EIGHT

....

SAHARA – 0   MERANDA – 1

AAAAAAAAAAAAAAAAAAGGGGGHHHHHHH!
To the outside world, when the LUA meeting was over, Sahara gathered her things and prepared to leave. She got up and even managed to say, "Thank you," to the two sorors beside her that wished her luck.

However, on the inside, she was screaming. What just happened? How did this happen? What was she going to do?

"Hey, let's go outside," whispered Tania. Sahara didn't see her walk up. She felt like a robot. Her body and her mind seemed completely unattached and unaware of what the other was doing.

Go outside. Yes. Let's do that.

Sahara and Tania stood in line with the other chapter members filing out the building. Everyone was eager to digest the slate of candidates and spew their opinions and analysis on the campaign and prospects of each candidate.

As Sahara walked out of the Ivy and Pearls Center, the bright light caught her by surprise so she shielded her eyes. The parking space in the front row where Meranda parked her blue Mercedes was now empty. However, her car was one of the few that were gone. Although many chapter members, except for the officers and some of the committee chairs, left before Sahara and Tania, the parking lot was still packed. The chapter meeting was over, but now it was time for the meetings after the meeting.

There were groups of sorors positioned in various places throughout the parking lot. Some groups had older sorors. Others had young ones. There was a group of North Carolina Union sorors standing by a gray minivan. The 2009 initiates were by the white Honda. And, most of the charter members were standing by a black Range Rover.

The best news anchors and political pundits had nothing on the analysis of the nomination committee report that was taking place right now. Sahara and Tania joined the group of sorors that met at Donna's house by Gwen's green BMW in the parking lot.

"What the hell happened?" said Trish as Sahara and Tania walked up.

"I know! It took everything in me to not sit there with my mouth open. I was shocked."

"And for them to run candidates in some positions and not others. I don't understand that."

"And then Soror Wanda to accept the nomination initially then to withdraw her name today. What was that all about?"

Trish said, "Even if they won both positions...." She looked over at Sahara and Gwen, the only two of their alliance whose races were being contested, to see if they reacted. "...they still wouldn't have the majority of the offices. So, I really don't understand their strategy."

"Well, let me explain it," said Tania. "It's about them keeping the power—while making us do the work."

"Huh? What do you mean?"

"Look at the positions that are not contested—vice president, financial secretary, and recording secretary. Everybody always hates being recording secretary because they have to pay attention, take the minutes, and edit the minutes. Then, they get the pleasure of doing all that for the executive board meetings, too. Fun—said no one ever. One of the most important roles, especially from an archival and chapter history standpoint, but I'm sorry. No one wants to do it."

"Well, I think being treasurer is a lot more work than being financial secretary. You only have to record the money you receive."

Tania replied, "Sure. But, you also have to drive all over town meeting this one and that one, when money is due. It may not require a lot of effort, but it certainly takes up a lot of time—and gas."

Donna chimed in, "And, of course, as the chair and coordinator of all the chapter programs, the vice president is probably the hardest working person in the chapter. Let's not forget about standing in for the president in her absence and the additional responsibilities associated with being second-in-command."

"She's right about that," whispered Soror Elizabeth.

"Well, both president and treasurer are a lot of work—and the older sorors still don't have the majority," said Donna smugly.

"They are a lot of work...but they also have a lot of power. The treasurer controls the finances. Sure, there is a finance committee—but she chairs it. Besides the president, she is the main architect in how the chapter spends its money. And, I don't even have to get into the role the president plays in so many things. Just remember that the president appoints the parliamentarian and the chaplain, which are two other positions on the executive board. President, treasurer, chaplain, and parliamentarian, there is your voting block—and your majority."

Sahara spoke up, "But, what are we going to do now? Meranda and I are friends. I can't run against her, and I'm sure that she doesn't want to run against me."

Tania's analysis was great, but it was theory. What was certain was that she and Meranda were friends, and she did not want to run against her friend.

A couple of sorors rolled their eyes, and Tania said, "Sahara, I love you. But girl, you need to wake up. You don't think Meranda knew that you were running? She and Soror Gertrude are friends. You don't think she told

Meranda who was nominated?"

Sahara thought about what Tania said. Meranda and Soror Gertrude were friends. They both were charter members so there was even a greater sense of loyalty there. However, there was no way that Meranda would knowingly run against her. Would she?

Donna touched her hand. "Look, Sahara. I know this isn't ideal or the way we planned it, but the goals that we discussed are still real—and needed. You have to run. Like Tania said—the president appoints the other two positions on the executive board. Since nominations from the floor are closed, it isn't like someone else can run."

Soror Trish stared at them with this *"I told y'all I should be the one to run"* look on her face.

"We still need you to do this," said Donna.

"That's easy for you to say," said Soror Gwen. "No one is running against you for vice president. I have to run against Soror Ada, whom everyone knows is a certified public accountant and an executive at her firm. I, on the other hand, have been the treasurer of the PTA at my daughter's school, which pales in comparison. There is no way that I'm going to beat her."

"And, there is no way that I'm going to lose a friendship over this election," said Sahara. No way. Meranda had been a good friend to Sahara since they moved here. She got Sahara involved in the chapter, as well as the black social scene in Fairchester. Sure, they attended luncheons and galas together, but more importantly, they supported—not opposed—one another.

"C'mon, everyone. I think everyone is still in a state of shock about the nominations. Let's go home, give this time to digest, and reconvene later." Donna smiled. "Everything is going to be okay."

But, as the group broke up and everyone walked back to their cars, there was an uneasiness in the air. Finally, the light came on. This was not a game, but they just got played.

Score one for the older sorors.

~~~

The entire ride home, Sahara thought about what happened in the meeting and Tania's evaluation in the parking lot. The older sorors didn't want to give up power. They just wanted the younger sorors to do the work. All the planning and strategizing they did at Donna's was out the window. And what about the presidency?

Everyone seemed to think that Meranda knew that she was running. However, Sahara didn't believe that. She was so distracted that she almost ran a red light. Thankfully, she slammed on her brakes before she drove into the intersection. Sahara walked into the house completely out of sorts. She put her keys on the counter and walked upstairs to change her clothes.

"So, how was the meeting, Mrs. Soon-to-be President-Elect?" asked Noah as she finished putting on her jeans.

Sahara pulled the Wellesley sweatshirt over her head. "Not so fast with the title...."

"Why? Is someone running against you?" asked Noah as he sat down on the bed.

"Not just someone...Meranda."

"Ohhhh," said Noah.

"Exactly." Sahara said as she re-fluffed her twist-out in the mirror.

"Well, it certainly isn't ideal, but I'm sure it won't affect your friendship. It's just business. Whether you win or she wins, it'll be fine."

Sahara turned and looked at her husband. "It'll be fine? THAT is the last thing that it will be." Men just didn't understand how women worked.

Sahara only knew of a few examples, but it seemed that people who crossed Meranda were put on a list that they never made their way off. Landy. Tamara. Gretchen. Once Meranda declared you an enemy, you were an enemy for life.

And, Meranda was a powerful woman in these circles. Without a shadow of a doubt, that was one list Sahara did not want her name anywhere near.

But, there was something nagging her. Something that Tania brought up. *You don't think Meranda knew that you were running? She and Soror Gertrude are friends. You don't think she told her?*

"What? What are you thinking about?" asked Noah pulling her out of her head.

"Well...," She almost felt funny saying it aloud, like she was breaching some friendship code. "Some of the sorors think that Meranda knew that I planned to run. Like she wasn't surprised."

Noah looked at her. "I don't believe that. If she was aware, I think that she would call you...not necessarily to ask permission...but to give you a heads up or something."

"Okay...yes. That's what I thought, too." Sahara agreed with Noah, but she couldn't shake the feeling that something wasn't right. She just couldn't put her finger on it.

Sahara went downstairs and grabbed her purse off the kitchen counter. She promised her mother she would call today. But, before she could dial the number, a text message came through.

Meranda: Had another meeting that I had to run to after chap mtg. Get together for coffee on Monday morning at my house?

Sahara breathed a sigh of relief. Meranda wanted to have coffee. She pushed all the worries that Tania and the other sorors stirred up out of her mind. Meranda probably was as shocked and concerned as she was that they were running against each other for president.

Sahara: That sounds great. See you at 9 a.m.

Everything was going to be alright. Noah was right. This would not affect their friendship. She and Meranda would figure something out. Sahara smiled as she dialed her mother's number.

~~~

The sky was dark and filled with clouds as Sahara made her way across the street to the Barretts' house on Monday. November was tricky weather in North Carolina. It wasn't consistent like Baltimore, where you knew that you needed a jacket after September and a coat in November. However, in North Carolina, one day it could be seventy degrees, and everyone would be wearing t-shirts and jeans. The next day, it could be forty degrees, and everyone would be bundled up like it was a blizzard outside. Yet, today was neither hot nor cold—simply gray and dreary—like a storm was approaching.

The Barretts' traditional three-story red brick house was protected from its next door neighbors by a matching four foot brick wall. The black shutters on each of the front windows contrasted with the white, squared portico that shielded the large, black, double front doors. Sahara had always envied how stately the house looked compared to her own French country style home. However, regardless of the style of home, their subdivision—Sugarberry Grove—was still a sought after area, with its historic background, proximity to the lake, and a neighborhood where some of the area's most prominent black families lived. Sahara didn't realize it when they bought it, but moving to Sugarberry Grove and living across the street from Meranda was one of the best decisions they made.

As she walked up the driveway, she noticed the mounds of mulch on top of Meranda's hydrangeas, which were always a warm welcome to the Barretts' grand Neo-Georgian colonial. The landscaper had buried the delicate plants under the earth in hopes that they would survive the winter's cold and snow. With the beauty of the plants missing, Sahara noticed the brick path seemed barren and worn.

Ding, ding, ding, dong.

Sahara could hear the melodious chimes of the front door bell ringing inside. She listened expecting to hear footsteps approaching the door. Nothing. She looked at her watch. It was nine o'clock on the dot. But, it didn't sound like anyone was coming to the door. She checked the text that she sent Meranda.

Yes, she said nine o'clock. However, Meranda never responded. Did she not get the text? Sahara pressed the doorbell again.

Ding, ding, ding, dong.

After a few seconds, there were footsteps. Good. Someone was there.

"Good morning!" Meranda exclaimed as she opened the front door dressed in a gray pants suit and pearls.

Although Meranda was fifty-eight, she had the smoothest, honey-brown complexion, and her long hair was always secured in her signature bun. Not a single hair was ever out of place. Regardless of the location or the time of day, Meranda always looked like a winner.

"Good morning, Meranda," Sahara said as Meranda stepped back to allow her to come inside. Sahara held her arms open to embrace Meranda, who hesitated. That was strange. They always greeted each other with a hug. Why would today be different?

"Dear, I'm afraid that I feel myself coming down with a cold. And, I don't want to get you or the children sick," said Meranda.

That made sense. And, that was probably why Meranda left so soon after the meeting. She wasn't feeling well.

Meranda smiled. "I see the weather made a turn for the worse. Let's go into the sitting room for some tea. That will take the chill off."

Sahara smiled. "Yes, that would be great. Thank you."

Meranda led Sahara through the spacious foyer by the Marge Carson credenza and past the wrought iron staircase with the paintings by Jonathan Green, Paul Goodnight, and Annie Lee along the wall. Sahara had been in the Barretts' home many times. Committee Meetings. Holiday parties. And, that one time with Dara. However, she never tired of seeing the ornately decorated house.

They walked through the European-inspired, two-story family room with its brown and gold damask ceiling-to-floor open draperies and similarly patterned sofa and chairs and past the kitchen with the white cabinets and large, beige and black granite island. Meranda had an eye for design, and it showed in her clothes and in her home. Similarly, she also had a knack for adding the perfect special touches to events she chaired for the sorority and other organizations she was in.

Finally, they arrived in the keeping room. "Please have a seat, dear," Meranda said. "I will be back in a moment with our tea."

Sahara could hear Meranda moving around in the kitchen. She smoothed her skirt. Why was she anxious? Meranda wanted to discuss everything. They would figure something out. So, why did she have butterflies in her stomach?

After a few minutes, Meranda returned with a tray that she set on the small, round coffee table. Meranda sat down in the yellow upholstered club chair to the right of Sahara. "Here we are, dear. Let me pour some water in your cup," said Meranda.

Sahara followed Meranda's lead and took a tea bag from the wooden box filled with exotic teas. "Thank you, Meranda." Sahara took a sip of her tea and noticed her hand was shaking. She wasn't sure why she was nervous—but she was. "Are you and Senator Barrett going to Shaw's anniversary gala?"

"Yes, we'll be there. I'm looking forward to it," said Meranda.

Sahara tried to relax. "Noah and I were thinking about going. I heard about it from one of the Belles & Beaus members."

"Well, if you have the opportunity to go, you should definitely take advantage of it." Meranda took a sip of her tea.

That's an interesting choice of words. Very interesting. Again, something wasn't right. She could feel it.

"Well, dear, I'm sure that you are wondering why I invited you over...," continued Meranda.

Sahara sat up. "No, trust me. I was as shocked as you were when Soror Gertrude announced that we were both running for president. What do you think we should do? Should I drop out or do you want to...."

Meranda started, "Actually, dear, I was thinking...."

Then, it came to Sahara. The perfect solution. "Oh my goodness, I don't know why I didn't think of it sooner! We can work together. Do the bylaws allow for co-presidents? That would be great! We just need...."

Meranda interrupted her. "I'm sorry, Sahara. There seems to be some sort of misunderstanding...."

"Misunderstanding?" Sahara was confused.

Meranda's eyes narrowed. "I have every intention of running for president. Let me correct that. I have every intention of being president—not co-president—but president."

Sahara was shocked to hear Meranda's frankness. "I...I...I thought you invited me over to figure out how to handle this situation. To figure out what we should do."

Meranda looked like she wanted to laugh. "Dear, I already know what I'm going to do. I'm going to be the next president of the chapter." She smiled. "But, I invited you over to say that it would probably be best for you to drop out of the race."

What? Sahara couldn't have heard her correctly. "You are telling me to drop out of the race?"

"No dear, I would never do that." Meranda took another sip of her tea and put it down on the coffee table. "I'm merely suggesting that it is in your best interest."

"In my best interest?" Sahara almost laughed out loud. "How is that in my best interest?" Sahara's hands were still shaking so she put her tea on the table.

"Well, I have the votes...and you know with your recent issues, you wouldn't want to make any further protocol faux pas."

Protocol faux pas? Sahara had no idea what Meranda meant. "What do you mean by recent issues? And what mistake have I made?"

Meranda pursed her lips in annoyance and then looked over her shoulder like she wanted to check that no one would hear her. She was always so extra. Weren't they the only ones in the house? "You know...with Charles Allymer being your father."

Sahara was taken aback. "I didn't realize that Charles

Allymer being my father meant that I had committed some protocol faux pas."

"Well, you have to admit, dear. Both you and Fallon Allymer being in Belles & Beaus makes things a little awkward. And, Winnie Allymer is a powerful woman— even outside of Raleigh. Now, I understand why she had so many questions about you..."

Sahara remembered the time that she saw Winnie and Meranda eating lunch at Triangle Hills in Raleigh. *She is awfully loyal to you.* That's what Winnie told her once about Meranda.

But now, Sahara wasn't sure that was accurate. And, what did Belles & Beaus have to do with the sorority?

Meranda continued, "And, I'm not sure who in the chapter even knows that Charles Allymer is your father. However, I'm sure that you wouldn't want your family issues to become a distraction for the chapter."

Sahara's back stiffened. Her family issues? A distraction for the chapter? Sahara couldn't believe the nerve of Meranda. "Well, as far as I'm concerned—my family is Noah, Clarissa, and Trevor—and they would never be a distraction for the chapter." Sahara was so upset that her voice was trembling. "And, I am a little surprised to hear you talk like this, Meranda. Of all the people in the chapter, you know me...."

Meranda smiled sweetly but her eyes flashed with anger. "Well, I think it's clear that I didn't know you as well as I thought."

Touché. When they met, Meranda asked if Sahara was related to Charles Allymer. Sahara told her no. But, no one knew. And, if it was up to her, the world would still be in the dark.

Meranda continued. "And, as charter president of the chapter, I have to do what I think is best for the chapter. And, right now, that is taking over the helm and resuming the leadership."

Sure, she and Meranda socialized in the same circles, but to be clear, Meranda was the one to introduce Sahara to this world. However, Sahara thought they were friends. Yes, this was a world of pearls, poise, and protocol, and she knew that proper decorum and appearances were important to Meranda. However, she never dreamed that it meant more to her than their friendship. Sahara admired Meranda and thought of her as a mentor...family. But, to hear her now, it was clear that Sahara was wrong about Meranda and their relationship.

Sahara stood to her feet. "Well, thank you for letting me know where you stand." Meranda stood up, but Sahara put her hand up. "Please, finish your tea. I can see myself out." If Meranda thought that she was going to roll over and hand her the presidency, then she better buckle up because they were in for a bumpy ride.

NINE

....

As the first morning sun slowly crept into the bedroom, Sahara expertly moved her hips back and forth as she straddled Noah. As he lay on his back watching his wife's breasts jiggle to the rhythm of their morning lovemaking, Noah felt his yearning increasing with each stroke. He grabbed Sahara's ass and guided her to move faster. When he felt like he was ready to explode, Sahara arched her back and let out a deep moan. His eyes rolled back into his head, and his toes curled as they climaxed together. A few seconds later, Sahara climbed off him and collapsed on the bed. There was nothing like morning sex to get your day started right.

Sahara's shallow breathing told Noah that she quickly fell back to sleep, so he covered her naked body with the comforter. What was that Chris Brown song? *Back to Sleep.* He smiled as he stood up and walked to the bathroom. He would be forty soon—but he still knew how to put in some work.

The water poured out of the gold showerhead and flowed over Noah's six foot one frame like the Elk River

Falls. He lathered up his washcloth and spread the soap suds on his chestnut brown skin as he spent the silence and the solitude reminiscing about the sweet sensations that he just experienced. He didn't like that Sahara and Meranda couldn't come to an agreement about this presidency situation—but he loved helping Sahara work out her aggression.

Noah grabbed the blue towel from the hook next to the shower stall and wrapped it around his waist. As he brushed his teeth, he looked at himself in the mirror. The gray hairs seemed to have multiplied overnight on the top of his head, and he spotted even more when he was taking his shower. Without a doubt, all that drama with Dwight at work was the cause of most of it.

Thankfully, things at the bank finally quieted down and were good. Not great, but good. One of the senior vice presidents still seemed to take pleasure in questioning his recommendations. However, Tad, the senior vice president of business banking, was always a jerk—even before all the shit with Dwight.

And, since Dwight's position as executive vice president had not been filled, he knew that Tad had his sights on the title. However, Noah did, too. That's what made today so important—and he hoped a good sign.

Noah walked to his closet and put on the clothes that he selected last night. The charcoal pinstripe suit paired with the light blue shirt and dark blue tie looked suave, but still classic. After he put on his Tom Ford glasses, he looked in the mirror one more time. The line from Slick Rick and Doug E. Fresh's *La Di Da Di* popped into his head. *Fresh, dressed like a million bucks....* Yes, that's exactly how he looked and felt.

As he walked out the room, he noticed the crumpled sheets on the now empty bed. A smile came to his lips as he heard the sound of bacon sizzling from downstairs.

When they lived in Baltimore, it was far enough north that turkey bacon and chicken sausage were the norm. He even made the mistake once of asking for "real bacon" when they were at brunch with his mother-in-law in D.C. The waitress looked horrified before saying, "We're a restaurant, not a garbage dump. And, there is nothing 'real' or 'healthy' about eating any part of the filthiest animal on earth—so we don't serve that here." He ended up reluctantly eating the only "meat" they had—a black bean sausage. And, that didn't even come from an animal.

But, that was one of the beautiful things about being back home in North Carolina again. Pork was king, and he could eat all the bacon, barbeque, and sausage that he wanted. Morning sex and bacon? Shoot. There was no way that this day could wrong.

"Looking good, babe," Sahara said when Noah walked into the kitchen. Knew it—-a million bucks. She turned off the stove and put the pancakes and bacon on plate.

"Thank you. Well, you definitely are giving me the

red carpet treatment this morning," replied Noah as she set the plate in front of him.

"Anything for my man...." She sat in the chair across from him with a cup of coffee. "So, whom do you think will be there? Anyone we know?"

Noah took a bite of his bacon. "Cass...and of course, Tyrone...."

"Senator Barrett? State legislators can serve on the Education Council?"

"Yes, they can...I think there is a limit or something."

Sahara looked suspicious. "Hmmm...sounds fishy to me. Just the thought...."

Noah could see where this was going. He put a forkful of pancakes in his mouth, because he wasn't going to need to speak anytime soon.

"I can't believe that she had the nerve....," said Sahara getting up from the table. She busied her hands by cleaning the pans she used for cooking breakfast while her mouth was occupied with her latest rant about Meranda.

He should have known better to mention Tyrone Barrett. Sahara talked for days about her shock and the "audacity" of Meranda to ask her to step out of the race as if she had no chance of winning. She finally stopped obsessing about it the last couple of days, and he had to open his mouth and get her started again. He couldn't win for losing.

Noah shoveled the remaining pancakes and bacon into his mouth as he tried to nod in the right places and throw in a "You're right, you're right" at the correct times to give the appearance that he was paying attention. For the life of him, he couldn't figure out why these women kept up so much drama. All the strategizing, alliance building, and score taking was just too much for him sometimes.

Thank goodness men didn't have all those issues. And, he hoped that whatever was going on with Sahara and Meranda didn't affect his relationship with Tyrone.

"I know she's the charter president and all...but that doesn't mean that she knows everything. It's time for some changes...."

"Thanks for breakfast, honey." Noah slid his empty plate into the sink and kissed her on the cheek.

"Huh? What? You're finished already?" Sahara looked sheepishly. "I guess I've been talking about Meranda the whole time...."

"You have...." Noah grinned and took her into his arms. "But, I still love you anyway." His manhood began to stiffen as he felt her curves under her robe. Unfortunately, he didn't have time for a second round so he loosened his grip on her quickly.

"Tell Cass that I said hello...and Senator Barrett," said Sahara.

Noah ignored her eye roll at the end and grabbed his keys. Sure, Cass and Tyrone would be at the Education Council meeting—but they weren't the ones that he cared about seeing. No, Noah made sure that he was dressed to impress for one person in particular. And, not even another round of morning sex was worth being late today.

~~~

Luck was on his side. Noah's red BMW slid into a parking space a block from the large, white domed Capitol Building on East Edenton Street. And, the parking meter still had time on it. Yes. No need in testing Lady Luck right now, so Noah added a few more coins to the meter and joined the myriad of blue and black suits advancing upon the state's center of power.

Noah tugged on his jacket and stared straight ahead. As the first African American senior vice president at Regional Southern Bank, he was used to being the only black person in high-level meetings. However, there were other African Americans that worked in other areas—IT, HR, and administration. Regardless of position, if he passed another black person he would give the customary "nod" or eye contact as a show of acknowledgment.

However, as the only black person in this sea of white faces, he felt like an outsider...an imposter. Further illuminating the scam, once inside the building, as the others moved with purpose through the halls on their way to offices and meetings, Noah had no idea where he was supposed to go. "Excuse me. Where is the Education Council meeting?" he asked the woman sitting behind the information counter in the lobby.

"Let me look it up on the computer." She began to type what seemed like an encyclopedia on the computer given the length of time the *clickety clack* of the keys could be heard.

"Noah, is that you?" said a large booming voice behind him.

Suddenly, he felt his body relax. He didn't need to turn around to see whom it was. He heard that voice every summer and spring break as a child growing up in Charlotte. And, it belonged to the person that he wouldn't have passed up the opportunity to see.

Noah turned and faced the tall older black man with an oversized belly standing behind him. He was an older version of his Cousin Donald. "Uncle Russell? I didn't expect to see you here."

They embraced quickly—as if they were old classmates that randomly bumped into each other rather than family that had not laid eyes on one another in years. Noah felt Uncle Russell's large stomach press against his own toned body and felt slightly repulsed.

Memories when he was a child of Uncle Russell saying that it was easy for uneducated men to stay in shape because manual labor was hard, back breaking work flooded his mind. Then, Uncle Russell would rub on his belly and say, "This right here. This is the mark of good living." Noah's husky cousin, Donald, would chime in, "Well, then, I'm living well, too." Father and son would laugh as Noah felt ashamed of the tall, lean physique he inherited from his own father, a dishwasher in a restaurant. Noah shook the memory out of his head.

"It's good to see you, nephew. It's been too long." Uncle Russell said as he patted Noah on the shoulders. "I have to let Donald and Aunt Brenda know that I saw you."

Noah smiled. Yes, please do. He wished he could be a fly on the wall when his smug cousin heard that they ran into each other here.

"So...where are you headed?" asked Uncle Russell.

"To the Education Council meeting," said Noah.

Uncle Russell's face changed. "The Education Council meeting?"

What's up with the echo? Noah knew that Uncle Russell was not hard of hearing. "Yes, the Education Council meeting," he repeated assertively.

"Oh, I thought that we were proposing candidates for the empty seat at this meeting. I didn't realize that there was already a vote."

Noah had no idea what Uncle Russell was talking about. "No, I'm not a new member. I'm here for Mr. Walton. I'm his proxy." Noah smiled, pleased that Jeremiah Walton, the president of First Southern Bank had selected him as the proxy. Yes, the year at the bank had been a rocky one, but things looked like they were firmly back on track. Noah oftentimes represented the bank or Mr. Walton at diversity events. But, the Education Council was the governing body of the state's university system. For Mr. Walton to choose him to be his proxy at the meeting elevated Noah to a whole other level.

However, Uncle Russell was not impressed. The scowl on his face grew deeper. "You're Jeremiah Walton's proxy?"

Again with the echo. Yes, your poor nephew has a seat at the table—at least today. Yes, he's living the good life and doesn't need a big gut to prove it.

The lady behind the counter interrupted their conversation. "Hello, sir. The Education Council is meeting in the third floor conference room. Do you need directions on how to get there?"

"I'm going there. I'll show him where it is," said Uncle Russell.

As the elevator doors in the Capitol were closing, someone shouted, "Hold the elevator, please!" Then, a black briefcase swung in between the doors to prevent them from shutting. A woman on the elevator quickly pressed a button, and the elevator doors retreated. A second later, Cass Montgomery, dressed in a blue pinstriped suit, stepped onto the elevator. "Good morning...Noah...Russell..." He nodded in their direction as he said each name.

"Good morning," they both replied in unison.

As they rode the elevator to the top floor in silence, Noah quickly glanced first at his uncle and then Cass. Even though everyone else on the elevator got off on the second floor and they were the only three on it, each man just stared straight ahead without saying a word.

No small talk. No "how's the family." No comments about the Panthers win. Nothing. There was no mention of the weather, but the air certainly was chilly in there.

The elevator came to a stop, and Cass held the door open for them. "After you, gentlemen."

Uncle Russell darted out so fast and down the hall that Noah felt forced to walk with Cass. He knew that Uncle Russell was caught off guard seeing him, but he didn't expect this. What was going on with these guys?

"I think it's great that you will be at today's meeting for Jeremiah. Hopefully, we can make it so that you have your own seat at the table soon," said Cass with a wink.

Noah wasn't sure what that meant, maybe it was the vote that Uncle Russell mentioned, but he appreciated the warm welcome. At least Cass knew that Noah would be there, even if Uncle Russell didn't.

They entered a large board room, where the table and chairs were configured into a large square in the middle of the room. People were milling around and talking, and a buffet was setup in the back of the room with food. So, this was the Education Council meeting.

When the media spoke of the Education Council, it

was with an air of prestige and prominence. The thirty-two member board oversaw the seventeen campus university system of North Carolina. Appointed by the State Legislature, you needed some connections and some clout to become a member.

Alexander Byers, MobileComp's chief executive officer. Joseph Floyd, a major developer in Raleigh. Walter Powers, the owner of a chain of restaurants. These were a few of the faces Noah recognized. All white males—like pretty much everyone else in the room. There were only a handful of women and only three minorities—Uncle Russell, Tyrone Barrett, and Yvette Oliver, a partner at the law firm Sheridan, Ellis & Ashton and a board member of a mentoring program where Noah volunteered.

Although the Council was supposed to be non-partisan, from reading the newspapers, Noah knew that most of its members were Republican and major political donors. So much for impartial and objective education in the state.

For the second time that day, Noah stood near the door not sure what he should do. Put his briefcase down in one of the seats? But, what if there was pre-determined seating arrangement? Should he join one of the groups talking? He certainly didn't want to waste the networking opportunity. He looked over at Uncle Russell, Tyrone, and Yvette huddled in the corner. He wasn't sure what they were talking about but it had to be intense by the looks on their faces.

"Walter, here's someone that I would like you to meet," said Cass as he approached Noah. "Walter, this is Noah Kyle, a senior vice president at First Southern. Noah, this is Walter Powers."

Walter extended his hand. "It is nice meeting you, Noah. I've heard great things about you from Jeremiah. We're glad to have you here today." He paused. "Can you excuse us? I need to have a word with Cass."

"You can put your briefcase down right there." Cass pointed at a chair at the front of the room. "I think we are starting soon."

Noah nodded as the two men walked away. He tried to hide the grin spreading on his face. It sounded like Mr. Walton had been talking about him to some pretty important people. This could bode well for his career. Very well.

As others moved to the table, Noah walked to the seat where Cass pointed. While Cass and Walter Powers stood at the front of the room deep in conversation, Uncle Russell, Tyrone Barrett and Yvette were still huddled in the corner in the back. Whatever was going on, apparently, neither side wanted to include him.

After a few minutes, Cass sat down next to Noah and Walter Powers sat to the left of Cass. Surprisingly, even though they spent the last fifteen minutes talking to each other, Uncle Russell sat on one side of the room, and Yvette sat on the other. And, Tyrone Barrett didn't move to the table at all but instead took a seat in the room's gallery seating. That was strange.

"If everyone can take their seats, we are ready to start the meeting," said Walter Powers.

The few people that were moving around the room sat down.

"I call the meeting to order at 9:02 a.m.," said Walter.

After the invocation by one of the members, the secretary began the roll call. "Andrews. Burris. Byers. Caine. Edgars." As expected, each person made their presence known. Did she skip Barrett?

Noah looked over at Tyrone sitting in the gallery, instead of at the table. Why was he there? Noah knew that Tyrone was on the Education Council. He saw it listed on Tyrone's biography a thousand times.

"Jarrett. Langley. Lawrence. Montgomery. Newman. Oliver...."

No Kyle. But, that made sense. He wasn't officially part of the Council, so his name wasn't part of the official roster. He probably had to speak up when she said Jeremiah Walton's name. Noah sat there waiting for his turn.

"Thompson. Walton...."

But before Noah had a chance to say anything, Tyrone stood up. "Excuse me, Chair Powers, but it seems that Jeremiah Walton is not in attendance today but has sent someone in his stead. I don't believe that is in accordance with the Council's bylaws."

Really? Tyrone was trying to stop him from serving as a proxy? Is that what all that whispering was about in the back of the room before the meeting?

Walter Powers and Cass exchanged glances and a smile came to Walter's lips. "Thank you, non-voting member Barrett. However, there is nothing in our by-laws that states that Mr. Walton cannot send someone to be his proxy."

C'mon, Tyrone. Mr. Walton wouldn't have sent him if it wasn't allowed. This sounded like stirring the pot for no reason.

"But, the standing practice is that a member that is unable to attend is merely marked as absent not...," Tyrone countered.

Walter Powers held up his hand to stop Tyrone. "Practice is not policy. Why don't we simplify things and take a vote?"

"I move that we allow Noah Kyle to act as Jeremiah Walton's proxy," said Cass immediately.

"I second," said another gentleman at the table.

"Are you ready for the question?" There was silence. "All those in favor?" asked Walter Powers.

"Aye," said most of the room in unison.

"All those opposed?"

Uncle Russell and Yvette Oliver raised their hands. Noah was surprised that Tyrone didn't vote with them. That's right. Walter Powers addressed him as a non-voting member. Noah looked at Uncle Russel and Yvette

Oliver. That meant there was one less person stabbing him in the back.

"The ayes have it," said Walter.

"Walton...," repeated the secretary.

"Noah Kyle present and acting in his stead," said Noah, and the secretary nodded in his direction.

"Worthington. Wylie."

"Thank you. Let's continue with the agenda. We'll now have the budget report." said Walter Powers when the secretary finished.

Cass stood up in front of his seat. "The budget committee met and now makes the recommendation that the Center of Poverty, Work, and Opportunity be closed. It does not directly benefit students nor produce scholarly work. Quite simply, it is a drain on the system's finances, and that money can be used elsewhere."

Uncle Russell raised his hand, "Chair Powers, I disagree with this recommendation. Off the top of my head, the Center has hosted a poverty summit, published papers on the Medicaid crisis and the racialized concentration of poverty in North Carolina. If I had more time, I could produce a more extensive list."

"Or, does the fact that the Center presented a paper that was critical of the use of vouchers for use in private schools and criticized businesses, including the budget committee chair's own, refusal to pay their workers a living wage have anything to do with this recommendation," said Tyrone.

"I take offense at the suggestion that the recommendation is personally motivated," added Cass.

"However, you will benefit...," said Tyrone.

Walter Powers lightly banged a small gavel on the table. "Let's keep it friendly, gentlemen." Some people shifted and fidgeted in their seats.

"I, for one, am surprised that this is being brought forward for a vote," said Yvette Oliver.

Did she say that she was surprised? Mr. Walton gave Noah a list of how he wanted him to vote on motions as his proxy. Noah was instructed to abstain from any new motions that were not listed. However, the motion about closing the Poverty Center was on his sheet of paper. Noah was supposed to vote yes.

"We have presented the information, handouts, and the recommendation," said Cass as he waved his hand at a stack of papers on the tables.

"Are you ready for the question?" There was silence. "All those in favor of closing the Poverty Center," said Walter Powers.

Like the first vote, everyone raised their hands, except for Uncle Russell and Yvette Oliver. When Noah's hand went up so did Tyrone's eyebrows. Uncle Russell and Yvette were the only ones that opposed. The motion passed, and the Center would close.

Thankfully, the rest of the meeting was uneventful. Reports were given on public affairs, university governance, military affairs, personnel and tenure without much discussion or disagreement.

"Now for the educational planning, policies, and program report," said Walter Powers.

One of the few women in the room stood up to give the report. It all seemed pretty humdrum until she said, "The Committee feels that the standards have become too low at certain schools and the minimum admission should be raised...."

Tyrone, Uncle Russell, and Yvette looked agitated.

"And the tuition cut..."

The three of them looked at each other.

"...at the following institutions...Elizabeth City State, UNC Pembroke, Winston-Salem State, and Western Carolina."

Whatever was going, Noah could tell that voting member or non-voting member, Tyrone Barrett was not having it. Tyrone stood up. "I am shocked that something of this magnitude would be brought to the table without any warning."

The committee chair gave Walter Powers a *"I'm not even about to deal with him"* look. In response, Walter Powers banged his gavel. "Senator Barrett, as a non-voting member of the Education Council, you are entitled to speak. However, that doesn't give you the right to be disrespectful. If your outbursts persist and you don't adhere to the rules of decorum, I will be forced to silence you according to our rules."

Uncle Russell jumped up. "I want it noted in the record that I protest this verbal bullying by the chair." However, Tyrone did not need anyone to come to his defense. He was not going to let a little resistance stop him from speaking out. He and the committee chair went back and forth like they were playing a tennis match. Occasionally, Uncle Russell and Yvette Oliver would chime in. However, everyone else watched the proceedings as if they were bored and disinterested.

Everyone except Cass. He didn't say anything, but the amusement in his eyes and the curl to his lips indicated that he was entertained by the whole situation.

That is until the resistors wore the committee chair down, and she requested to rescind the recommendation and consult with her committee. Now, it was Walter Powers and Cass's turn to look irritated and perturbed, while Tyrone sat back like a cat that had eaten the canary. After the heated discussion surrounding the SAT scores and tuition cuts, the energy drained from the room as the final committee reports were given with no opposition.

When Walter Powers adjourned the meeting, most people hurried out, ready to go to the office and get some work done. However, a few lingered and discussed the discord in today's meeting. Noah hoped to avoid all the politics and slip out unnoticed. Unfortunately, Tyrone Barrett and Uncle Russell cornered him in the hallway after he left the room.

"Noah, I don't know what their agenda was about today, but you have to convince Jeremiah to vote against raising the SAT scores and cutting tuition at those recommended schools," said Uncle Russell. Oh, so now they wanted to include him in their alliance.

"I understand that raising the SAT scores, especially with its cultural bias, could be detrimental to some students, but how could lowering the cost hurt anyone?" asked Noah. He received financial aid to go to college, and he didn't understand why they weren't in favor of college being more affordable for students.

"Requiring higher test scores, which results in lower enrollment, and tuition cuts translates to schools having less money to operate—so they'll have to make cuts. They want to turn these schools into community colleges and trade schools," said Uncle Russell.

Tyrone shook his head in agreement. "Sure, they threw in a couple of primarily white institutions as a red herring, but make no mistake. This is about defunding HBCUs and stopping the pipeline for minorities and poor people to move up the socioeconomic ladder." Tyrone looked at Noah. "You have to convince Jeremiah to vote no to this. Others will follow his lead."

Now that Tyrone and Uncle Russell clarified the ramifications of the proposals, Noah understood their concern. Although his own alma mater, North Carolina Union, wasn't on the list, he knew the majority of African Americans in North Carolina and the country were educated at historically black colleges and universities.

However, convincing Mr. Walton to vote against the recommendation would be a hard sell. In his mind, Noah pictured the sheet of paper that he received from Mr. Walton. Clearly written at the bottom was: *Motion on raising SAT scores and tuition cuts vote yes.*

Uncle Russell stated that he didn't know what Walter Powers and Cass' agenda was. Noah didn't know either. However, whatever it was, Mr. Walton was definitely a co-conspirator.

TEN

....

SAHARA – 0   MERANDA – 1

As Noah's BMW pulled off the freeway exit for PNC Arena in Raleigh, the night was lit up, not with stars, but with white car headlights. They followed the brake lights of the car in front of them and joined the thousands of cars slowly snaking their way to the Chris Rock concert.

"See, that is exactly what they do." Sahara said as she put her lipstick on using the mirror in the car's sunshade. "They close rank under the guise of this 'establishment' and 'tradition' mess. It's just not right."

"I'm not sure that is exactly what they were doing...," said Noah keeping an eye on the car in front of them in case it hit the brakes suddenly.

Sahara looked at Noah. "Did Uncle Russell tell you what they were doing?"

"Well...no...but...."

"And tradition and establishment are the same hand Meranda is playing with this election. At church on Sunday, I innocently mentioned the LUA election when we were in the fellowship hall to a few church members that are in my chapter. Don't you know that Meranda already contacted them, and they agreed to give her their support? A couple of sorors said that their husbands are in the Rho Nu Alpha chapter with Senator Barrett, and they asked their wives to support Meranda. Can you believe that? I thought he would be focused on his upcoming re-election, not acting as a consultant to Meranda's campaign."

Noah's eyebrow went up. "Wow. I didn't realize that it would get so serious."

Yes, it was. That is exactly why she needed Noah to talk to his Theta brothers and get their wives on her side. She needed to fight fire with fire.

Noah continued, "Well, it does sound a little like what was going on in the Education Council meeting. Everyone had their alliances and their agendas, and I was on the outside absolutely clueless to what was going on and what side I was supposed to be on."

In the beginning, Sahara didn't think there were sides, because everyone just wanted what was best for the chapter. However, clearly there were. "That is exactly how I feel," she said as she smacked her lips and looked at her freshly applied lipstick one more time. And, without a doubt, she knew whose side she was on. Her own.

After they parked in the VIP lot, Noah showed the attendant their tickets, and he and Sahara walked through the metal detectors and into the arena. They took the elevator up to the level with the suites. Noah's line brother, Jason, worked for a pharmaceutical company that had an arena suite and was able to score seats for tonight.

It was nice to have a date night. It had been a while since they'd gone to something outside of the usual galas and fundraisers. Sahara and Noah walked in the suite, and they could see that the party had already started.

The room was full of people, mostly Thetas. Some were solo. However, many were with wives or girlfriends and what looked like a few "side chicks" for good measure. Hot 97.5 was blaring from the speakers. The food and drinks were overflowing. Wings. Meatballs. Fried shrimp. Wine. Tequila. Rum. The food was hot, and the bar was fully stocked.

"What's up, Noah!" Jason came over and gave Noah some dap. "It's great seeing you, Sahara."

Sahara hugged Jason. "Thank you for inviting us."

"Yea, thank you...," said Noah.

Jason smirked. "I really just invited Sahara...but I guess she had to drag you along." Their other line brother, Isaiah, walked over and Sahara left the three of them laughing and joking with each other.

After making herself a plate of food and getting a Cosmopolitan from the designated bartender, Sahara walked past the flat screens on the wall and sat down in one of the suite's leather chairs. She was enjoying her Buffalo wings when the wife of one of the neophytes sat down in the seat next to her.

"You're Sahara, right?" said the short woman with gray eyes. "I'm Jackie."

"Yes, and you're Donovan's wife." The woman shook her head up and down. "I think we met at the Theta fundraiser last spring," said Sahara.

"That's right. That was right after Donovan was initiated so it was blur of faces and introductions that night."

Sahara laughed. "Yes, if you aren't familiar with it, entering the world of Black Greeks can be overwhelming, especially if you've never been exposed to it."

"It was for sure." Jackie paused. "I mean my mother is an LUA, but she was initiated after I was an adult."

Sahara perked up. "Your mother is an LUA? Is she in a chapter?"

Jackie put a forkful of barbeque in her mouth. "Yes, the one here in Fairchester."

"Really? What's her name? I'm an LUA so I should know her." Maybe Sahara could get Jackie to talk to her mother about voting for her. Anything was worth a shot.

"Marva."

Sahara sank into her chair. She knew Soror Marva. They worked together on the political action committee. She was also a regular guest at Meranda's table for the Darlings luncheon. Sahara was sure that Meranda already had her vote.

Jackie moved over a seat when the show was about to

start so that Noah could sit next to his wife. Sahara took a sip of her Cosmopolitan and pushed the thoughts of Soror Marva and the election out of her mind. There were plenty of votes up for grabs so there was no need in her dwelling on the fact that one person was voting for Meranda. Plus, tonight was about spending time with Noah and enjoying the show. She snuggled up against Noah and prepared to be entertained.

Chris Rock delivered without a doubt. Between his divorce, Trump, and pop culture, he had plenty of material, and Sahara never laughed so hard. And, from the sounds of it, Noah enjoyed himself as well. He laughed harder than she did at most of the jokes.

She smiled. Tonight was a good night. Maybe they should hang out with Noah's Theta brothers more often. It was a nice break from the tuxedo and gown's crowd they were used to.

After the show was over, people mingled in the suite finishing off the food and the liquor, not wanting the night to end. Sahara saw a familiar face, one of her LUA chapter members, and made a beeline for her. "Hi, Cynthia! I didn't know that you were here."

Cynthia took a sip of her drink. "Yep. I came with Andrew." She pointed at a guy that Sahara didn't know. "We got here late so I'm behind on my eating and drinking." She raised her plate to emphasize her point. "Did you like the show?"

"Loved it, loved it." Sahara could see Noah out the

corner of her eye, and he looked like he was ready to go. The way his hand kept sliding up her thigh in the darkness towards the end of Chris Rock's monologue, she knew that he was ready for the show to continue at home and for her to step up to the mic. Consequently, she didn't have much time to make her pitch to Cynthia. "I'm sure that you know that I'm running for president, and I would love to be able to count on you for your support."

The expression on Cynthia's face changed. "Um...I'm sorry, Sahara. I already told Meranda that I would vote for her."

Another vote for Meranda. Sahara felt the wind come out of her sails. Cynthia quickly added, "It's not because I don't think that you would be a great president. However, Meranda got to me first. I wasn't at the chapter meeting so I didn't know that you were running for president when she asked for my support."

"Don't worry. I understand," said Sahara trying to put a positive spin on the situation.

"Well, it was great seeing you."

Sahara smiled. "Yes, see you later."

She and Noah walked out of the suite, and Noah pushed the elevator button. This was going to be a lot harder than Sahara expected. Meranda was definitely leveraging her connections and memberships to get support for the election. Clearly, Meranda wanted to win—but Sahara did, too.

As Sahara and Noah walked out the arena and to their car, they saw Donovan and Jackie. Everyone smiled and waved goodbye. "I'll tell Rozlyn that I saw you," said Jackie.

"Excuse me?" asked Sahara. She couldn't have heard her correctly.

"I'll tell Rozlyn that I saw you," repeated Jackie. "That's how I know you. I'm friends with Rozlyn."

Rozlyn. She just could not get that girl out of her life. Sahara gave Jackie a fake smile and walked away. On second thought, maybe they didn't need to hang out with this crowd anymore.

~~~

Like a mini-science fair on steroids, children were spread throughout the employee cafeteria in MobileComp at stations for coding, computer demonstrations, interactive simulations, and electricity. There was even a parents workshop on internet safety in one of the conference rooms. When the workshop was over, Sahara and Emery escorted the Belles & Beaus mothers to the employee lounge where hot food and cold beverages waited so the parents could network while the children rotated through all technology stations.

"Well, I'm going to say it. I'm impressed Sahara and Emery. This was a great age group activity. No one would believe it was your first one," said one of the mothers.

Sahara and Emery smiled at each other. At cluster back in August, they decided to do a joint age group activity with Clarissa and Riley's age groups. Reynard, Emery's husband, was able to get his company to sponsor the event by providing the supplies for the activities, staff members, and even food and snacks. All Sahara and Emery really had to do was to mail the invitations and buy thank you gifts for the staff.

"Well, everything is pretty much all Reynard and Emery's doing. I just get to take the credit along with them," said Sahara, and they all laughed. Sahara stifled a yawn. She was struggling this morning because of the late night at the Chris Rock concert.

"Emery, what's up with that guy?" asked one of the mothers as she pointed at one of the MobileComp employees.

"Honey, he is *fi-ine*. Kind of reminds me of Remy from *Queen Sugar*," said someone else.

Another mother chimed in, "Remy will always be Robert to me. I just can't see him with anyone but Vanessa Huxtable."

"I hope that he and Charley work out. I like them together."

"Well, anyone is better than Davis. See, that's what always happens—too many women go with the guy with money and think that they will be happy."

"Oh, c'mon! Charley loved him, too. It wasn't just

about the money."

"Let's just be clear. Charley is a boss. Whether she married Davis for love, money, or both—she didn't need to. He thinks he's in charge? Please, she is the one pulling the strings."

"You're right about that!" Two of the moms high-fived each other.

As the conversation drifted on to talk about Issa Rae's *Insecure* and the upcoming movie, *Black Panther*, Tania turned to Sahara. "Let's go over here and talk."

When they were safely out of earshot of the other mothers, Tania asked, "So, have you had a chance to talk to anyone about the LUA race? I talked to Bridget and Emily at the Belles & Beaus executive board meeting, but Meranda got to them first at the Sphinx meeting. However, that doesn't mean that you can't flip them."

"I'm not surprised," said Sahara. "It seems that Meranda's reach is much further than I thought."

"That's an understatement," added Tania. "I had no idea that she wanted to be president again—or this badly. Well, we don't need to give up."

That was easy for her to say. Sahara sighed. "Right. We just need to think of something. Something that will capture the chapter's attention. Let them know that we mean business, and can get the chapter moving forward."

"I agree. Right now, everyone knows that the chapter is in a rut. However, I guess some people would rather stick with the traditional path, which is safe, rather than the new and unknown," said Tania.

"Well, let's try to think of something—a program, event, fundraiser—something that will show that we mean business and can take the chapter far. If they'll give me a chance."

"And still keep trying to get people's votes."

"Yes." Sahara looked at Tania. "I can't lie. I'm starting to get a little nervous."

Tania returned Sahara's worried expression. "I am, too."

It was almost time for the age group to be over. Sahara and Tania walked to the front of the cafeteria, where the children were getting ready to give the parents a wrap-up on what they learned. At the end, everyone clapped and gathered their jackets.

"Thank you!" said the children.

"Great job, moms!" said the parents.

As people filed out of the building, Sahara and Emery began to clean up. "It seems like everyone enjoyed the activity," said Sahara.

"They better had. It was great," replied Emery.

Sahara laughed. "Right!"

Emery got a serious look on her face. "So, I heard that you are running for president of your LUA chapter."

Sahara scowled. "Yes, but I don't think it is going very well." Did everyone know? Emery was a Xi for goodness sake. She was the last person Sahara expected to care about this LUA business.

"You're up against some fierce competition. You know, Meranda is no joke."

"Yes, I know." Sahara remembered her conversation with Meranda after the meeting. She was so mad...and hurt...about Meranda's insistence that she drop out of the race that she double downed and was even more committed to winning. However, now she was having second thoughts. "Maybe I should just drop out."

"She's hard core, but that doesn't mean that you should drop out." Emery touched Sahara's shoulder. "I think you would be a great president."

That was sweet of her to say. "From what I hear, you are one of the few votes that I would get." Sahara smiled. "Oh, that's right. You can't vote."

"Well, there are some LUAs in my Marigold chapter and at my church. I definitely don't mind putting in a good word for you."

Sahara's face lit up. "Would you?" Then, she paused. "Or, do you think that would be weird?"

Emery got a twinkle in her eye. "I know being a Xi, I shouldn't be all in y'all's business...so I'll do it discreetly."

Sahara hugged her. "Thank you."

"No problem. You know I got your back," said Emery.

~~~

Tracy: Talked to Emery. Don't worry. You have my vote.

Sahara got the text from Tracy Moore as she walked out of the Fairchester Economic League on Monday afternoon. Tracy Moore was a principal at a high school in Durham. Sahara didn't know her well, but she was also a Marigold. This made the fifth text that Sahara received since talking to Emery after the age group activity on Saturday, and she felt like doing the Toyota jump. She would need a lot more votes to win—but it was a start. Sahara got into her Lexus and pulled out of the parking lot.

However, instead of driving to the preschool, she headed towards Midtown. The Fairchester Economic League originally planned to hold the scholarship reception at the Marriott in that area. However, with no money for a scholarship, there was no need for a reception. Thankfully, the Marriott agreed to refund the deposit, and Sahara was on her way to pick it up.

TLC's Creep was on the radio, and Sahara turned the volume up. She used to love this song. She still remembered the silk pajamas T-Boz, Left-Eye, and Chili wore in the video and the little dance they did as the wind blew on the trio. She was singing at the top of her lungs, when she was interrupted by the cell phone ringing. It was Donna.

"Hey!" said Sahara after she hit the green button.

"Where are you? Please don't tell me that you are

stuck at work like me," said her friend.

"No, I am headed to the Marriott. Have to pick up something for the Fairchester Economic League. What's up?"

"Tania told me about your conversation at the Belles & Beaus activity so she thought that I should give you a call." Tania had to be more concerned than she was letting on. Donna continued, "You can't worry. I know it seems like Meranda has it on lock, but she doesn't. We got this."

"Well, yes and no...."

"What do you mean by that?"

"Forget it," said Sahara quickly.

"No, say it," said Donna.

"Well," Sahara started. "You keep saying we, when we aren't in the same boat...."

"Go on..." All the extra sweetness that had been dripping from Donna's voice was gone.

"No one is running against you...so yes...you got this, for sure. I, on the other hand, am running against one of the most well-connected women in Fairchester...so our outlooks are a little different. In fact, we are nowhere near being in the same boat," said Sahara probably with a little more attitude than she intended.

"I didn't realize that you felt that way." Donna said curtly. "I consider all of us—you, me, Elizabeth, Candice, Gwen—that we're all running as a slate...."

"But, we're...."

Donna interrupted Sahara before she could finish. "I get it. Different. Not the same boat. Blah, blah, blah."

Now, it was Sahara's turn to be irritated, but Donna was the one that took a deep breath. "Look, I get it." Her voice was calmer. "But, you have to know that all of us are working on this. Remember, it's not just you that has an opponent. Gwen does, too. And, I know that things haven't started as we planned. However, trust and believe that we are trying to ensure that we get the ending that we want. There is no way that I want to be the vice president if Meranda is president. No ma'am."

Sahara had to admit that she felt a little relieved to hear Donna say that. "Well, I do have a little good news of my own." Sahara paused. "I got a text from Tracy Moore and some other sorors saying they were supporting me."

"Tracy Moore? Really?" Donna must have realized how it sounded. "No offense. She just seems like someone that would be firmly in Meranda's camp."

"Well, I guess Emery convinced her to vote for me."

"Emery? What does Emery have to do with this?" asked Donna.

"Well..." For some reason, Sahara felt like she should tread lightly. "Emery said that she would talk to some of the sorors that went to her church and in the Marigolds."

"I don't think it's right to have that Xi all up in LUA business..."

Sahara knew that Donna was right. However, she also knew that Emery said that she would help her, and Emery did just that. And frankly, she needed all the help she could get.

"I just don't think it's right," Donna repeated. "I know that you've flip-flopped about Emery since you've become Belles & Beaus sisters, but I don't like her. And, I don't trust her."

Sahara didn't even feel like arguing with Donna about this. "Well, I'm sorry that you feel that way. But, let's talk about this later. I'm almost at the Marriott." She was about ten minutes away, but there wasn't any point in prolonging the conversation.

"Okay, bye."

"Bye," said Sahara but Donna had already hung up.

Sahara pressed the disconnect button, but her mind was still on the conversation. She was annoyed and a little hurt that Donna called her a flip-flopper. Sure, she and Emery didn't get off to a great start, but most of that was Rozlyn's fault. Was she supposed to hold on to that forever? Emery already knew Sahara's deepest, darkest secret—and Sahara didn't plan to tell her any others anytime soon—but couldn't they at least be friendly towards each other. They were Belles & Beaus sisters now. Couldn't they also be friends? Donna didn't seem to think so.

The parking lot of the Marriott was full. Sahara had to go down several levels in the parking deck before she found an open space. Using her mirrors, she carefully backed into the spot. As she was about to get out of the car, she noticed the license plate of the car on the other side of the parking lot.

NDALWYR?

Wasn't that Alton's car? But, what was going on in the car was what caught her eye. Two people were kissing and groping like there was no tomorrow. Her first thought was get a room. However, since they were in a hotel parking deck, it was clear that they already did that or planned to do it.

Maybe she was wrong. It couldn't be.... But, Sahara was pretty sure that it was Alton. Who else would be driving his car?

After the two lovers unraveled from their embrace, the driver started the car and backed out of the parking space. Guess that answered that question. They were leaving from their rendezvous. Sahara slid down in her seat but kept her eyes fixed on the car.

The Porsche roared up the parking deck ramp towards the exit, but not before Sahara got a good look at the driver. It was Alton. However, due to the angle of the car and the fact that she slouched in the seat, the passenger remained unseen.

But, Sahara was certain of two things. The passenger was a woman—with expensive taste. She didn't see the woman's face, but she couldn't miss the red Hermes bag in her lap. And, she definitely wasn't Donna, who was at work and probably still fuming over her conversation with Sahara.

She put her head back on the car's headrest. Who was the woman? And, what was she going to do? History had shown her that making the wrong decision could have disastrous consequences.

ELEVEN

....

SAHARA – 1   *MERANDA – 2*

S ahara picked up the deposit from the Marriott event coordinator, but the last thing on her mind was the Fairchester Economic League. That night all that she could think about was seeing Alton kissing some woman in his car. There was no mistaking the passion in their embrace. And, the car was in the Marriott's parking deck so that could only mean one thing. They had been there. But, was this a one-time thing or something ongoing? And, should she tell Donna?

Her mind kept flashing back to the past...to that moment when she was in Teri's bedroom and realized that she'd seen it before. She chose to say nothing then...and look what happened.

No, she knew that she had to tell Donna. And, she knew Donna's first question would be who was the other woman. Sahara had no idea. It was too dark in the parking garage to see the woman's face, and when Alton drove away, his body blocked Sahara's view. Yes, Sahara had to tell Donna what she saw, but she owed it to her friend to provide as much information as she could. And, that meant finding out who was the other woman.

The weight of the secret led to a restless night of tossing and turning for Sahara. Every time she managed to fall asleep she had the same dream. There was a *pop, pop, pop*. Then, a door would fling open, and a woman would crawl out and collapse on the snow-filled street.

However, in the dream, the woman was Donna. Sahara didn't have to be a psychiatrist to know what the dream meant. By the time Noah's alarm rang, Sahara was relieved that she had an excuse to be awake.

While Noah was in the shower, Sahara got up from bed to cook breakfast. As she passed the dresser, she saw the check from the Marriott sitting on the dresser. She had been so distracted after seeing Alton that she hadn't even put it in her purse.

Shoot. They accidentally made the check out to her. Maybe she could sign it over to the Economic League. She quickly dropped it in her purse so that she wouldn't forget it when she was leaving for work later this morning.

Since she didn't sleep well, Sahara was moving slower than usual. Before she knew it, she only had a short time to get breakfast on the table, herself ready for work, and the children up and dressed for school. Gone were the days that she and the children could leisurely eat breakfast and lounge around in their pajamas. With Sahara working, their life required much more coordination and included schedules and afterschool care. When they moved to North Carolina, Sahara wanted to return to work. Now that she had to work, she hated it—and days like today were no exception.

Suddenly, Noah came running down the stairs. "Sahara! Turn on the television!"

What in the world? Was there some breaking news? She turned off the stove so the eggs wouldn't burn and walked over to the family room. Noah was standing in front of the television with the remote in his hand.

Rowena McGee with WRTD was sitting at the anchor desk in a red suit, "As reported at the top of the hour, the Carolina Times received an email from an anonymous source highlighting financial improprieties at the Fairchester Economic League and an attempt by leadership to sweep the problems under the rug. Our calls so far have gone unanswered, but we have been able to confirm that there were recent management changes at the organization. Councilman Darren Kirk is calling for a full investigation of the agency."

Sahara and Noah looked at each other. This was not good. She better hurry and get down there to see what was going on. "Noah, can you...,"

"Don't worry. I can take the kids to school today," said Noah.

Sahara shot him a brief look of appreciation before running upstairs. She quickly showered and threw on some clothes. Before she walked out of the bedroom, she grabbed her purse from the dresser. The refund check from the Marriott to the Fairchester Economic

League was lying on top. Could someone at the hotel have tipped the media off to the Economic League's financial troubles? The timing had to be a coincidence. The hotel manager was very reasonable when she contacted them about canceling the event. No, the anonymous sources had to be someone else. But, one thing was for sure. With the spotlight being on the agency's finances, she needed to get this check there right away.

Sahara came downstairs and heard Noah leaving a message for his secretary that he would be late. She quickly kissed Clarissa and Trevor, who were now awake and at the kitchen table. As she backed her car out of the garage, she couldn't help but wish that she was eating breakfast with her babies instead of driving into work to deal with this catastrophe.

~~~

When Sahara walked into the building, she expected it to be in a state of all hell breaking loose. Instead, everything and everyone was strangely calm. Had they not seen the news this morning? The only telltale sign that she had not hallucinated the news segment were the phones. They were ringing off the hook, and the receptionist could not keep up.

Sahara walked into Glynda's office and sat down in the guest chair. When she became the deputy director and Mr. Johnson the executive director, he and Glynda switched offices. It seemed strange to see Glynda's items in the glorified veal fattening pen and on these strange walls.

Glynda looked up and put her finger to her lips for Sahara to keep quiet. "Can you believe this?" she said in a whisper after she closed the door.

Following Glynda's lead, Sahara scooted the chair closer to the desk so that Glynda could hear her. "What is going on? I came in early expecting everybody to be in crisis management mode based on what I was hearing in the news. Instead it looks like any other day at the Fairchester Economic League."

Glynda shook her head. "Yes...makes me wonder about whom the anonymous source is."

Sahara opened her eyes wide. "You don't think...." Could it be Mr. Johnson? He was shady but not that devious. Or was he? And, what would he gain from having the media spotlight on the Fairchester Economic League now? He was in charge.

Glynda got a gleam in her eye. "All I know is that if I was the executive director and this story broke, I would have pulled documents and prepared to meet with the board of directors on how to handle it. Frank is sitting in his office probably playing Sudoku puzzles. And, he instructed everyone, including the receptionist, not to answer the phone."

Had she heard Glynda right? No wonder the phones were constantly ringing. "He did what?" Public relations

101 was that you give them something...*no comment at this time...we'll issue a statement later*...something. Not answering the phones, especially when the story was regarding a financial issue, made it seem like they had something to hide or worse. Kind of like locking the doors in a bank run, people would start to think that someone was fleeing the scene with all that money.

Glynda continued, "You heard me. I had to go behind his back and tell Jonecia at the front desk to at least say that there would be a statement later."

"Thank goodness." Sahara paused.

"That is why I wouldn't be surprised if Frank is the anonymous source." Glynda shook her head up and down.

"But, what would he have to gain? I mean he works here too. Plus, he was the former finance director."

"Well, there are some things that you don't know about Frank."

Sahara and Glynda were not friends. Sure, outside of work, they attended the same luncheons and galas. But, at those events, Sahara would say they were more cordial, than friendly. And, at work, Glynda was the consummate professional. But, it looked like she was about to spill some serious tea.

Glynda continued, "Frank has never been...how shall I say...a fan of the Fairchester Economic League."

Sahara was confused. "What? Then, why does he work here?"

Glynda leaned in closer. "Well, in a nutshell, he's the gatekeeper for the good old boys."

Gatekeeper for the good old boys? Who the hell were the good old boys? Glynda sounded like a conspiracy junkie. However, all Sahara could manage was a mystified, "Huh?" Glynda was not making any sense.

"Frank has been here since the inception of the Fairchester Economic League. As part of the agreement to get funding from the state, the board of directors agreed to let the legislature approve the director of finance. The only one that they would approve is Frank. And, he has been making it hard to get anything really done since then."

Sahara thought back to all the discussions between Glynda and Mr. Johnson that she witnessed. He didn't really like to think out of the box or fund anything beyond basic programs. If Sahara hadn't taken the art auction to another level, they would still be trudging along, not really making an impact. "I can see that."

"And, didn't you find it interesting that if there was an issue with the money that it would be the director of finance that would be the one that would become the new executive director?" asked Glynda.

Sahara did wonder why Mr. Johnson was the one to take over for Glynda if the budget was off, and he oversaw the organization's finances. But, was it been for another reason? Was there been a bigger issue than refunds being issued?

It made Sahara speculate about what really was going on. Maybe the "good old boys" were trying to get control of the Fairchester Economic League. The new governor was fighting the legislature's power grab before the governorship changed hands—so she didn't put it past them. But, what did they want to do with it? The handling of the current crisis was not a good sign—especially if Mr. Johnson was the anonymous source and the creator of it.

As Sahara got up to leave, Glynda said, "I don't know where this is going. Defunding the scholarship was probably the first step. You probably want to start looking for another job."

Sahara returned to her office and thought about what Glynda said. She should start looking for another job. As the phones in the office continued ringing, Sahara had to admit that was probably good advice. But, she didn't want another job. Heck, she didn't really want this job. But, at least it was flexible and allowed her to work around her children's school schedules. Another job may not be so lenient. No, if she had to work, she needed to work here.

Sahara looked in her purse for her cell phone when she saw the check from the Marriott still in there. What did Glynda say? *The defunding of the scholarship was the first step.* Sahara sat back in her chair.

What if they held some sort of gala or luncheon to fund the scholarship? A lot of organizations had scholarship fundraisers. Why shouldn't the Fairchester Economic League? But, with all the press about financial improprieties, the agency probably couldn't get away with trying to hold another fundraiser now. Plus, they didn't have the manpower to spare with the art auction coming up.

But, what about Lambda Upsilon Alpha? There was no question that scholarships fit with their mission. But, there was also the human interest element of it— stepping in to save the day so that these students could continue to get scholarships for school. And, if she and her friends took on the project, this could certainly tip the election scales in their favor.

The more Sahara thought about it, the more she was convinced that it could work. But, first she wanted to talk to Donna about it. Ugh. She still hadn't talked to Donna about Alton. Shoot! With all the drama going on with the Fairchester Economic League, seeing Alton with another woman had slipped her mind.

Well, she already decided that she wanted to figure out whom the other woman was before she approached Donna. And, in the meantime, she could talk to Donna about holding some sort of event to benefit the Fairchester Economic League scholarship recipients.

Before Sahara left for the day to pick Trevor up from preschool, she grabbed the piece of paper off her desk where she scribbled some ideas throughout the day that she wanted to discuss with Donna. With the Fairchester

Economic League's contacts and the purpose of funding college scholarship, Sahara knew that they couldn't go wrong.

As she walked down the hallway, she passed Mia's office. Mia looked up and waved. Sahara smiled and waved back. And, there was no way in hell that they needed to let Mr. Johnson or Mia anywhere near this event—or the money.

~~~

Noah pulled his car up to the black box in front of the large black gate and punched in the guest security code. After a few seconds, the gates separated and the red BMW entered the master planned community. After a series of turns down the wide streets, Noah and Sahara pulled up in front of the brightly lit, three-story home sitting on the large lot. Cars lined both sides of the street as far as the eye could see. Sahara would have second-guessed her decision to wear black Louboutains tonight if it wasn't for the saving grace in the middle of the circular driveway—the valet. Okay, Emery took this party to a whole other level with that.

Noah took a ticket from one young man as another took his car keys. Sahara couldn't help but feel excited as they walked up the stairs to the front door. This was her first time attending Emery's birthday party. In a way, she felt like she had finally arrived.

"Sahara! Noah! Thank you so much for coming," said Emery when they walked inside the house. Dressed in gold two-piece jumpsuit with a beautiful red rhinestone pin with her initial on her chest, Emery looked stunning.

Sahara handed her the wrapped gift she was holding. "Thank you so much for inviting us."

"The food is over there, and the bartender is in the dining room. Please mingle, and have a good time!" Emery said before she was off to greet some other arriving guests.

So, this was Emery's birthday party. Emery and Sahara were never close enough for the Kyles to get a formal invitation. Well, Sahara was close to getting one the first year that they were in North Carolina...but then....well there was no point in dwelling on the past. They were here now. And, so was everyone else.

People from all the fraternities, sororities, and social clubs were mixing and mingling on the ground floor and in the basement. Xis. Gammas. LUAs. Rhos. Belles & Beaus. Marigolds. Darlings.

The Sphinx Masquerade Ball was the premier event for Fairchester's black establishment, and Emery's birthday party was the place to be for the city's young, black, and fabulous. Well young-ish. They were all approaching forty.

After getting a Cosmopolitan and something to nibble on, Sahara spotted Donna standing by the dance floor looking miserable, like she was passing time. "Hey, Donna! I was looking for you."

A smile broke through the scowl on Donna's face. "I am so glad to see you!"

"Really? By the look on your face, you don't even know that you're at a party," said Sahara with a smirk.

Donna laughed. "Well, you know how I feel about *your girl*. I tried to back out of coming tonight, but Alton insisted. He said he would even come without me. So, then we got into a huge fight. Needless to say...I am not a happy camper." Donna gulped down the rest of the drink she was holding.

Sahara was glad that they decided to come. She still hadn't told Donna about seeing Alton with another woman. But, earlier this week, she had figured that Emery's party would be a great place to play detective and see if Alton let on whom the other woman was. She had to be here. Everyone was. And, who could resist parading that beautiful Birkin bag with such a captive audience.

"So...." Donna lowered her voice so Sahara moved closer so that she could hear. "I talked to some of the sorors about the scholarship concert, everyone loves it!" said Donna. "You are absolutely right. It has the sophistication and the wow factor. If we can pull this off, there is no way that we won't sweep all the positions."

"I think so, too," said Sahara.

"We got this!" Donna raised her hand, and she and

Sahara gave each other a high-five.

"We got this!" Sahara repeated with a giggle.

Donna took a sip of her drink. "Changing the subject...Since I am supposed to be a grown woman, I have to say that I'm sorry."

Sahara's eyebrows went up. "For what?"

"For going off about Emery the other day." Sahara looked around to make sure that no one could hear them as Donna continued, "I think that I'm just feeling crazy and hormonal getting ready for this wedding."

"You've had too much to drink if you are getting all mushy on me," said Sahara as she nudged Donna. She knew how stressful planning a wedding was. "It's okay. You know that I love you."

Donna hugged her. "Thank you, and I love you, too."

A little while later, Alton came to get Donna so that they could dance. As Sahara watched them move across the dance floor in Emery's family room, Sahara couldn't help but feel sad for her friend. She had enough single friends to know that Donna was the beacon of hope for every single, professional black woman still looking for love after 35. She'd found her king—but apparently, he had a chick on the side.

Maybe it was a one-time thing. If so, was destroying Donna's happiness worth it for one mistake? But, how could she know that it was only one time? And, what was the saying? Once a cheater—always a cheater.

Back on the case, Sahara watched to see if Alton

looked too long at any one woman or seemed nervous as anyone walked by. No, the whole time that she watched him, he looked like he only had eyes for Donna.

As Sahara walked to the bar to get another drink, she tried to remember anything that would help her identify the woman. She didn't seem tall. Her hair wasn't short. She could see it swaying as she and Alton pulled apart from their embrace. Shoot, she wished that she had gotten a better look at her. The only thing that Sahara saw clearly was that red Birkin handbag in her lap as Alton drove away.

With a second round of liquid courage in hand, Sahara made a point of looking at every woman that was at the party. She eliminated everyone that was at least Alton's height or taller. And everyone with short hair. But, that still left about half of the women in the room. Should she eliminate everyone that was married? No. Just like Alton was cheating on Donna, his side chick could be cheating on someone, too.

"Are you having a good time?"

Sahara turned and saw Emery standing next to her. She was so busy playing detective that she hadn't heard Emery walk up. "Yes, I am. This party is great! And I love your new house." Sahara couldn't help but glance to see if Donna saw her with Emery, but thankfully Donna was still dancing with Alton and only had eyes for him.

"I'd been trying to convince Reynard to sell that

house at Magnolia Estates for years so we finally did it."
Emery smiled. "Do you want a quick tour?"

"Oh, I would love to see it. But, are you sure? I don't
want to take you away from your guests."

"It's no trouble at all."

Sahara felt like a VIP as she and Emery quickly circu-
lated through the basement and the rooms downstairs.
The house looked big from the outside, but the first impression didn't do it justice. It was humongous. After
looking at the upstairs sitting room, Riley's room, and
three additional rooms, Emery showed Sahara the master bedroom. It was like a mini-palace. If she and Noah
ever moved, she had to have a bedroom like this.

"And, this is my absolute favorite place in the house,"
said Emery opening the door to her huge walk-in closet.

For a minute, Sahara thought that the heavens
opened and started singing "Hallelujah, hallelujah, hallelujah!" The custom closet with its dark wood and bright
lights was to die for. She changed her mind. Keep the
bedroom. If she could have a closet like this, she would
be good. She wouldn't need or ask for anything else.

She salivated over the row of clothes, shoes, and ac-
cessories. You couldn't help but be a fashionista with a
closet like this. "Can I live here? Not in your house. In
this closet," asked Sahara.

Emery chuckled and said something that Sahara
didn't hear. For at that moment, Sahara had stopped
lusting over Emery's closet but instead was fixated on an

item on one of the shelves. Sitting as proud as a pea-cock, on display was a red Birkin handbag.

TWELVE

....

SAHARA – 2   MERANDA – 2

When Sahara opened her eyes the next day, she knew that she had at least one too many Cosmopolitans last night at Emery's party. Her head was pounding, and she felt like she'd been banging it against a wall. Her mouth was dry like cotton. And, her brain was in a fog. Unfortunately, she did remember one thing about last night—Emery's red Birkin handbag.

Maybe she was mistaken. Well, the bag in Emery's closet was definitely red. And definitely a Birkin. There was no doubt about that. But, maybe she was wrong about the purse in the woman's lap being a Birkin.

However, deep down, she knew she was right. Her mother had a gold Birkin handbag. With its handmade leather and palladium hardware, Sahara could spot the luxury item anywhere.

She slowly rolled over and looked at the clock on her nightstand. 10:22 a.m. Ugh. She had missed church. She wanted to go to church. Scratch that. She needed to go to church to get some guidance on what to do.

Ping.

She grabbed her cell phone from the night stand and

scrolled through her text messages.

Noah: At church. Didn't want to wake you.

Emery: Talked to Kim and Charnelle at the party. They said that you can count on them.

Donna: Heard through the grapevine that Soror Gretchen and Soror Danika are voting for Meranda. Both are in Raleigh Darlings chapter with Winnie Allymer. Heard that she got to them. Sorry. : (

Emery: Just thought about it. Marigolds are using The Atrium for Swing into Spring. I know the event coordinator. Can see if he is willing to give you deep discount for scholarship concert. Interested?

Sahara rolled back on the bed after sending a response to Noah. She just wanted to close her eyes and make everything go away. This was a complete and utter nightmare. She was prepared to tell Donna that Alton was cheating after doing some detective work to find out the identity of the other woman. But, now that she knew that the other woman was Emery, Sahara wasn't so sure about what to do.

Donna wasn't only her soror, but she was also her friend. She and Tania were one of the first LUAs that she met in Fairchester, and they had welcomed her with open arms. And sure, she and Emery had a rocky start, to say the least, but they were initiated into Belles & Beaus together and were now friends. Heck Emery wasn't even in the sorority, and she was working harder than some of her friends in the chapter to get her elected.

Sahara closed her eyes. She didn't know what she was going to do. She didn't want to hurt her friendship with either woman. However, she also knew how serious the impact of holding on to a secret like this could be.

One thing was certain. Secrets and friendships were not a good combination. She wished that she wasn't anywhere near the Marriott parking deck that day. But, unfortunately for her, she couldn't turn back the hands of time.

Sahara looked at the clock again. 11:04 a.m. She may have missed church, but she told Zora that she would stop by today to see the baby. But first, some aspirin and then some breakfast—because another thing that didn't mix was babies and hangovers.

~~~

After the security guard checked her name off the list, the gates parted and Sahara drove through. Walnut Forest and Sugarberry Grove were both on Jordan Lake and adjacent neighborhoods. Although the houses in Walnut Forest looked like the homes in Sugarberry Grove, they cost twice as much and had a manned guard's station. Sahara pulled up to the Montgomerys' stately home with its two-story marble columns and second floor balcony and got out of the car.

A few seconds after ringing the door bell, the doors swung open. "Sahara, I'm so glad that you could come," said Zora as she and her three-year-old son, Darius stood in the doorway.

Sahara handed the pink diaper cake and small gift bag to Zora as she stepped inside. "Are you supposed to be walking around? And, where is the baby?"

Zora and Sahara embraced. "The baby is in the nursery with the nanny. And, yes, I believe that it is okay for me to move around." Zora stepped over some bubble wrap on the floor. "Excuse the mess. I think the movers are at lunch."

Movers? In the three years that Sahara knew Zora, she was only in Zora's house a couple of times. But, each time she was impressed with how neat and orderly everything was. It was almost like a real family didn't live there, like it was staged for a magazine or television show. However, today, there were boxes and packing peanuts all over the place, and the furniture was wrapped in clear plastic. "Are you moving?" asked Sahara. She didn't see a *For Sale* sign out front.

"I thought that I told you." Zora shrugged her shoulders. "With Cass taking over the family business and the new baby, we thought it was time for us to move into something larger."

Larger? Zora's house had to have at least five bedrooms with a basement and a huge pool and outdoor kitchen in the large backyard. Well, she wasn't mad at them. Cass was the president of a multi-million-dollar enterprise now, it certainly was nothing wrong with wanting the lifestyle to show it.

"So, when are you moving? It looks like soon."

"Not soon enough for Cass' sister. Our house was supposed to be finished and ready for us to move in six weeks ago, but with all the rain that we got last month, everything was delayed."

Sahara wasn't sure what that had to do with Cass' sister so she asked, "Oh, is she helping you decorate the new house?"

Zora laughed. "No, we hired someone to do that. Cass' sister and her family are moving into this house."

"Oh...," said Sahara a little surprised. So, they weren't selling their house. They were giving it to Cass' sister. Now, that was money.

"She's taking Cass' old job...so I guess why not get the old house, too. It's owned by his family's trust anyway. But, let's go upstairs. It's too much of a mess down here."

If Zora's house was part of a family trust, Sahara had significantly underestimated the wealth of the Montgomerys. "So, where's the new house?" Sahara asked as she followed Zora to the second floor.

"Well, our closest neighbors are Cass' parents, but they aren't too close." Cass' parents lived in this magnificent house on a horse farm on the outskirts of town. Sahara had never been inside, but she knew the area. If

Cass and Zora were moving there, without a doubt, they moved up to the big leagues.

Yes, she had underestimated their wealth—significantly. She guessed Cass wasn't as much of a rebel as she thought. It seemed like he was embracing the privilege that having a wealthy father gave him.

The few times that Sahara was at Zora's house, she never went upstairs. But, the second floor looked exactly as she expected—pristine with everything in its place. "Let's go in my room!" said Darius as he took Sahara's hand and pulled her into one of the bedrooms. King-sized oak bed draped with a blue and gold duvet. Beautiful blue walls with whimsical swirls. And, enormous stuffed animals were sitting through the room like they were guards standing watch over the prince. Yes, everything looked like it was part of a magazine.

Except for the nursery. When Sahara walked into the room, she was caught off guard by the simplicity of the room. No colorful walls. No abundance of toys. Just a crib, a dresser, and a rocking chair in the corner that looked like it had seen better days. Maybe since they knew they were going to move, they didn't want to waste the energy of decorating the nursery.

The room looked drab, but one thing that stood out was the beautiful brown baby asleep in the crib. "Look at her! She is absolutely gorgeous!" said Sahara as she walked over to the crib and lifted the tiny person out of the crib and held the baby in her arms. Oh, this was dangerous. She could feel the desire of wanting another child rise as she looked down on the sleeping infant.

As they walked to the upstairs sitting room, Sahara couldn't help but stare at the beautiful baby. Unlike her blue-eyed brother, her ebony skin was as dark and smooth as her mother's. Her dark brown eyes twinkled as she took the world in for the brief minutes that her eyes were opened before returning to their resting state. Sahara closed her eyes and inhaled deeply to take in the sweet aroma that only a new baby could provide. "I want one," said Sahara as she held the baby close to her chest.

"Ha! I forgot about how sleep-deprived you are with a newborn so anytime you want her please come get her," said Zora.

"I may take you up on that."

"Please be a good friend and take her," Zora repeated as she laughed. "So, what's been going on with you? Did you go to Emery's birthday party last night?"

Sahara wished she could forget the whole night. Instead, she said, "Yes, it was as fabulous as I thought it would be." Except for the whole Emery was cheating with Alton revelation. "But, things have been crazy at work...."

Zora started fidgeting. "Yes, Cass told me there were a lot of financial issues at the Economic League. When things like that happen, it is definitely best for it to be brought to light. It's a shame that we can't do better. Frank Johnson will make sure that the right thing is done there."

It's a shame that we can't do better? It is definitely best for it to be brought to light? And, how did she even know whom Frank Johnson was? Sahara had dismissed Glynda's idea that Cass had something to do with the anonymous email that was sent to the media, but now she wasn't so sure. It seemed like Zora was privy to a lot more details than most.

"It's an unfortunate situation. And, the whole thing has left the Fairchester Economic League scholarships up in the air," replied Sahara.

"Well, I heard that you and Donna were planning to hold a scholarship concert," said Zora. Sahara's spidey sense started tingling. Yes, she was certainly in the know for someone that was busy with a newborn. But, maybe that wasn't a bad thing. Zora explained, "Alton mentioned it to Cass."

Of course. Alton and Cass were college roommates at Duke. "Well, while we are on the subject, maybe you and Cass would be willing to be a sponsor. Most of the scholarship recipients attend historically black colleges, including your father's alma mater, North Carolina Union," said Sahara.

"Hmmm...I'm not sure if that would be something that would interest us. I mean if the students were going to Duke, Elon, UNC-Chapel Hill...maybe...."

"Having attended Wellesley, I know it's important to support your own alma mater...." However, Sahara had no idea why she would throw in Elon and Chapel Hill. She didn't think that they had ties to those schools. "And, I get it. I went to a predominantly white institution, too. But, hbcus still educate the majority of African-American students. With the assault on education in this country and this state, it's important that we continue to help black students get an education in hopes of moving them up the socioeconomic level."

"I'm all for education. I just don't think that we should encourage students to attend HBCUs," said Zora.

Sahara tilted her head. What you talkin' about, Willis?

Zora continued, "The standards are lower, many don't finish. College isn't for everyone, and I think some of the students that attend them would be better served by attending community college or learning a trade."

Sahara tried to hold back her anger. "You realize that Noah went to an HBCU." Learning a trade? So, that's what they were pushing their young people to do now? Education was how most people in this country moved up the socioeconomic ladder. If it wasn't, why would so many wealthy people intent on holding on to their power in the world spend so much energy trying to destroy public education?

Zora looked sheepishly, "I'm not saying that every student that goes to an HBCU should go to a community college. But, some people are just more cut out for learning a trade, that's all."

Sahara looked down at the little brown baby in her arms and said a little prayer that the privilege that her father's wealth could give her would be more abundant than the dislike of her complexion she was sure to face outside her home, and maybe, inside it. And, in that moment, Sahara knew why Zora agreed to move near her in-laws' horse farm. She was full of shit, and she hoped that her new surroundings would mask the odor.

~~~

Saturday was a bust. Sunday was a bust. Unfortunately, Sahara knew that Monday was not going to be any better. She had jury duty.

As she drove downtown to the courthouse, she tried to not get irritated. This was her civic duty—one of the most important civic responsibilities behind serving in the military. But, she couldn't help thinking about all that she had to do. They had a ton of things to do for the scholarship concert. And, she still had actual Fairchester Economic League work that she was getting paid to do—at least for now—that she needed to complete. She showed up, but she prayed that she didn't get selected.

Sahara hurried up the courthouse steps. The summons said to be there at eight o'clock in the morning, and she was already five minutes late. She tried to wait patiently in the line to pass through the metal detector but watching the minute hand on her watch move further along the clock made her antsy. Finally, she was near the front of the line.

"Everything out of your pockets!" yelled the burly officer, before Sahara proceeded through the large machine.

BEEP!

She looked around to see if it was someone else that had caused the alarm. Nope. It was her.

"Anything in your pockets, ma'am?"

"No, I don't think so." Sahara patted herself on the sides to reinforce the point.

"Okay, go back through again, please." She walked around the metal detector to start the process again. She tried to not look at the annoyed faces waiting in line.

"Do you have on a watch?"

"Yes." But, so did most of the people that passed successfully through before her.

"Here." He held out a small white bin. "Some of the heavier watches they make now can cause the detector to go off."

Sahara took her watch off and put it in the bin. She held her breath as she walked through the metal detector for a second time. No beep. She exhaled as she took her watch out of the bin and put it back on her arm.

"Thank you for your patience, ma'am."

Sahara gave him a small smile. "No problem." But, now she was fifteen minutes late.

She followed the halls looking for the room that was on the summons. Room 1415. She went down one hall then another. Why didn't they just have a sign? *All Potential Jurors Here.* That would be simple. Finally, she found what she was looking for.

She opened the door not knowing what to expect. Maybe she would be dismissed because she was late. Would they make her come back tomorrow? That would be absolute torture. Maybe she would get in trouble, whatever that meant.

Room 1415 was simply a large waiting room. People were sitting in chairs, reading magazines, staring at their cell phones, and looking bored. Great. Now, she was glad that she was late. Sahara walked over to the raised information desk at the other end of the room and presented her jury summons. The female officer behind the desk looked at the paper and then typed something on the computer in front of her.

"The judge will be in here shortly. You can have a seat."

Sahara looked around the room. There were all types of people sitting in there. Men and women in business suits clearly irritated that they were forced to endure this. Women smacking on gum and talking on cell phones like they didn't have a care in the world. Men with hoodies and sagging pants that made you wonder if they were in the right room.

Sahara slid into one of the empty seats by a young

white man that didn't look too threatening and pulled out her cell phone. Email. Facebook. LinkedIn. Instagram. Twitter. She viewed them all, and they were still sitting in the waiting room. How much longer would they be in here?

An hour later, the judge dressed in his long black robe walked into the room with a bailiff in a brown uniform trailing behind him. A few people stood up like the king had entered.

"Thank you for being here today. Serving on a jury is one of the greatest responsibilities of a citizen of this great country," said the judge after he had everyone's attention. "Is there anyone that does not reside in this county?" Everyone looked around but no one indicated that they were an outsider. "Is there anyone that has served on a jury within the past six months." A woman in a suit and a black guy in saggy jeans raised their hands. "Please proceed to the information desk." Both looked relieved. "Finally, has anyone been convicted of a felony?" Everyone looked around the room to see if a hand went up. After a few seconds, the white guy next to Sahara slowly raised his hand. "Please go to the information desk." Sahara clutched her purse a little tighter as the guy did as he was instructed. "Again, thank you for your service, and now, the bailiff will divide you into groups."

The bailiff quickly divided the remaining jurors into four groups of approximately twenty-five to thirty people each. Sahara was in the third group. "Group One, you will be escorted to courtroom five. Group Two, you will be escorted to courtroom seven. Please keep up with your group."

Sahara's ears perked up as the bailiff continued to stand in the middle. Her group was next. "Group Three and Group Four...you can wait here for now."

Sahara felt like the wind was let out of her sails. She didn't really want to be on a jury—but she had enough of the waiting game. Doing something was better than doing nothing. Sahara sighed. Back to email, Facebook, and Instagram.

Ping.

She had a text so she switched over to her messages.

Donna: U still have jury duty? Downtown for meetings. Free for lunch?

Hmmm. She knew that she needed to talk to Donna. But, was this the best day?

Sahara: Yes, downtown. Don't know about lunch. Will let you know if they free me.

Donna: Okay.

After another forty-five minutes of playing on her phone, Sahara became antsy and a little hungry. She thought about Donna's text. She got up and walked over to the information desk. "Hi, do you know when they are going to call us back?" Sahara stared at the officer who continued to type on her computer like Sahara wasn't standing there talking to her.

After what had to be the longest pause in the world, the officer's hands stopped moving, and she looked at Sahara. "If they don't come get you in...." She looked down at the clock on her computer. "If they don't come get you in fifteen minutes, you'll be released for lunch."

"And then we'll be done for the day?"

"No, you can go to lunch. And, in one hour, you have to return here."

"Oh," said Sahara. How long was this going to drag on? This really was torture. "Thank you," she said to the officer as she turned to leave.

"You're welcome," said the officer as she returned to the computer. Whatever she was working on had to be super important. As Sahara walked back to her seat, she sent Donna a text.

Sahara: Looks like we will be released for lunch in 15 mins. Where do you want to eat?

Donna: Luigi's in Five Points?

Sahara: Sounds good.

Sahara put her cell phone back in her purse. Now, she just needed to figure out what she was going to say to Donna. And, the jury was still out on how she would respond.

~~~

"Hey, girl!" Donna said when the hostess brought Sahara to the table where she was seated almost hidden behind the restaurant's lavishly decorated Christmas tree.

"You got here quickly," said Sahara as she sat down at the table.

"I'm doing an audit at Game Masters Corp, which is in the building next door."

The waiter walked up to the table and asked, "Ma'am, can I get you something to drink?"

"I'll have what she's having," Sahara said as she eyed the glass of white wine in front of Donna.

"Perfect," said the waiter.

"So, how's jury duty?" Donna asked after the waiter left the table.

"Probably not happening. My group is still sitting in the jury waiting area."

"So, you don't have to go back."

"Apparently, I do," Sahara took a sip of the wine that the waiter placed in front of her. "Wonderful. That was to the wine, not the waiting."

After giving the waiter their lunch orders, Sahara said, "So, I got an email. We have The Atrium for the scholarship concert."

"That's what I'm talking about," said Donna.

Sahara continued, "With the four singers and two dance troupes that have agreed to perform, we're in a good place. It would be great if we could get one or two more but if not, we'll be fine. Now, we just need to start marketing."

The waiter put their food on the table, and everything looked delicious. She loved Luigi's.

"Uh huh," said Donna absentmindedly.

"Is everything okay?" asked Sahara as she took a bite of her pasta. Heaven.

"I just have a lot on my mind...with the wedding and stuff..."

Stuff? What stuff? Sahara shifted a little in her chair. "What's going on?"

"Something just feels off with Alton and me. Don't get me wrong. I love him. I love him with all my heart and like I've never loved anyone else. But...I just don't...How did you know that Noah was the one? Like the one that you were supposed to marry and be with forever?"

Sahara circled the rim of her glass. "I didn't know at first. I didn't know...and still don't...that it will last forever. But, it always felt right. Not perfect. But right."

"I see...." Donna sat back in the chair.

Sahara wasn't sure what Donna was feeling, but this seemed like the sign that she asked God for. "Well, I've been trying to figure out how to tell you something," Sahara said.

Donna's body stiffened as she continued to eat her food. "What it is?"

Now, that Sahara had started there was no way that she could stop—but she wanted to do just that. She loved Donna. She was there at the start of Donna and

Alton's love affair and witnessed it grow and blossom. She hated to be the messenger that could kill it. "I don't know how to say this." Sahara paused.

Donna was staring at her. "Just say it."

Sahara took a deep breath. "I saw Alton with another woman."

Without skipping a beat, Donna snapped, "I don't believe that."

Huh? Sahara had prepared herself for anger, tears...even laughter. Disbelief had never crossed her mind.

"Who did you see him with? Where?" asked Donna like she was trying to catch Sahara in a lie.

Feeling a little defensive, Sahara replied, "Well, I was at the Marriott trying to get the deposit back for the Fairchester Economic...."

"Get to the point, Sahara," Donna said curtly as she crossed her arms. "Where did you see Alton? What was he doing and with whom?"

Sahara sat up in the chair. She didn't know if Donna was on offense or defense, but she clearly was on the attack. "I saw him kissing a woman in the parking deck of the Marriott."

"They were just standing there making out?"

"Well, no. They were in his car."

"And, you happened to park next to him?"

"No," Sahara said slowly. "I happened to park across from him."

"And, you were facing each other?"

"Well, no...but...I could see their shadows."

"You could see their shadows?"

"Yes, I could see their shadows. It was dark and the car was facing the wall so it was hard to see...."

"Well, how do you know they were kissing if it was dark?"

Alton may be the lawyer, but Donna knew how to cross-examine a witness. "I...uh...well...their faces looked like they were close together."

"But, I thought they weren't facing you."

"Well, they weren't. I could mainly see the back of the seats but their faces came close together."

"Well, could they've just been talking? The car is really small."

Sahara thought back to the day. It had been dark. She guess they could have been talking—but that seemed like a stretch. But, maybe it was possible? Score one for the defense. "I guess...."

Donna cut her off before she could even finish. "Okay, let me get this straight. You thought it made sense to tell me that you may or may not have seen my fiancé kissing...talking...you're not sure...another woman. But, you're not sure what you saw because you only saw their shadows. Is that right?"

Sahara whispered, "Yes."

"I can't believe you, Sahara." Donna picked up her purse and stood up. "Thanks for lunch."

Winner Takes All

As Sahara watched Donna stomp out the restaurant, she took a sip of her wine. Well, that went well.

THIRTEEN

....

SAHARA – 1   *MERANDA – 2*

The thirty-story granite and glass building commanded a prominent place in Raleigh's downtown skyline. As the driver helped Meranda out of the black town car, she noticed the building's sleek lines and recent facelift. Apparently, even buildings weren't allowed to age—or hold on to tradition for that matter. Meranda and Tyrone walked into the building under the yellow and red Wells Fargo sign. However, it would always be the Wachovia Building to her.

As men and women hurried past them into and out of the building on the cold January morning, Meranda and Tyrone strolled past the security guard and to the appropriate elevator bank. If they had been to the Cardinal Club, downtown Raleigh's premier dining club, once, they had been a million times. Providing the right ambience and exclusivity, it was a great place for Raleigh's business leaders and politicians to network and meet over a meal.

As they waited for the elevator, Meranda fixed Tyrone's tie and brushed the lint off the lapel of his suit jacket. She wanted to make sure that he looked his best.

When you look good, you feel good. And, she wanted to ensure that no matter what, Tyrone felt good today.

The elevator door opened, and they stepped on. They were the only two occupants for the express ride to the top of the building, but they stood silent, each deep in thought, until they reached the penthouse. As the elevator doors opened, Tyrone took Meranda's hand into his own, and they exited. Team Barrett was here.

"Good morning, Senator Barrett. Mrs. Barrett, good morning. I know that we spoke on the phone but I didn't realize that you would be joining us today," said Bobby, Tyrone's campaign manager who was waiting when they reached the lobby.

Meranda gave Tyrone's hand a small squeeze, and a smile came to her lips as he did the same. A second later, Tyrone extended his hand. "Good morning, Bobby. I want Meranda to be here. She's really the brains behind the operations."

Bobby smiled. "Well, you won't get any argument from me." Whether he agreed with it or not, she was here to stay. Tyrone needed her.

As they walked into the private room in the back of the club, Carl Hopkins, Michael Phillips, and Horace DeBerry were seated around the table. Everyone in Tyrone's inner circle, all good friends and members of The Shield and The Coalition of Sentinels, during the last campaign was there. Well, except one.

"Where's Noah?" asked Tyrone. Most of the room

looked down at the table, but Bobby stared at Meranda.

"Well, with everything going on...I thought it best to have this meeting without him," said Meranda as she sat down. She didn't bother explaining the "everything," and she didn't think Tyrone would question it. At least not then.

Tyrone took his seat at the head of the table and didn't say anything. "Why does everyone look like we're at a funeral?" His remark was met with nervous laughter that seemed to highlight, instead of alleviate, the tension in the room. "C'mon. It can't be that bad," said Tyrone. No one said anything.

Carl Hopkins and Michael Phillips fidgeted with the papers in front of them. Horace DeBerry finally got the courage to say something. "Well, let's lay out the facts, and go from there."

Ready to take any positive sign that he could get...even if it was miniscule...Tyrone said, "I'm ready. Give it to me."

Horace took a deep breath. "Well, the positives are that your approval rating among your black constituents is at one of the highest levels it's been since you became senator." Trump's assault on democracy forced most black politicians to have an increased media presence, if for no other reason than to speak out against his foolishness.

"Well, that's good news. Anything else?" said Tyrone.

"Your legislative concerns that have received media

attention...mental health and education...help win over some independents," added Bobby.

"That's great news!" Tyrone exclaimed. Meranda could tell by Bobby's tone that there was another shoe to drop.

"But not enough....," added Horace. "I'm going to put it to you straight, Senator Barrett. We have two big problems. One is directly related to you. The other has nothing to do with you."

"I'm not following." Tyrone started squirming in his chair. Meranda patted his hand that was on the table and looked at him. *Everything will be okay. We will get through this.*

Horace started again. "I think everyone agrees that your last re-election campaign was close...a nail biter." Trailing in the vote count most of the night, it wasn't until the final surge of votes from the west side, which was predominantly black, that Tyrone edged out his opponent, a newcomer but a Tea Party favorite.

"Well, this is the South, and we still won," Tyrone said optimistically.

"Yes," said Bobby. "But this time you have two things working against you."

What was this good cop, bad cop? Maybe forbidding them from inviting Noah was a mistake. Just spit it out, for goodness sake. Tyrone was a grown man, not some child, that they needed to coddle.

Bobby continued. "We know the Republican base has

been energized and will come out to the polls. And, from the last presidential election, we know that they will support the ticket regardless of whom it is and what baggage they bring to the table."

Carl stopped fiddling with his papers and chimed in, "That's definitely true. We saw in your last race that the Republican base was willing to vote for someone with no government experience. Then, we saw the same dynamic in the presidential and state elections. Too many citizens will vote for anyone white and male, even if it isn't in their best interest."

All this back and forth was getting on Meranda's nerves.

"And unfortunately, we can't depend on donations from Jeremiah Walton and Cass Montgomery—which means that we can't depend on the donations from their friends either. And, we believe the amount of cash you had to spend is what tipped the scales in your favor last time."

Tyrone drummed his fingers on the table. "Damn, white boys. They'll screw you every time. Sometimes wearing a red tie. Other times with a blue one."

"What if we compensate the loss of the funds from Jeremiah and Montgomery with other donors?" asked Meranda. She already knew the answer, but she wanted to make sure that Tyrone knew that no stone went unturned in trying to find a solution.

Horace said, "I guess it is possible. But, we don't

know whom that person is. We contacted the party to see how much assistance they would be willing to provide, but their polling has the seat flipping as well."

Meranda repeated the words in her mind. Their polling has the seat flipping as well. The words stung like a slap across the face. Seat flipping.

Everyone remained quiet as Tyrone drummed the table staring at everyone and no one. Then, he leaned forward and said, "So, what you are telling me is that I don't stand a chance in hell of winning this thing—of being re-elected."

Everyone looked like they were afraid to speak. Finally, Bobby said, "We're not saying that you can't win. We're saying that your chances—"

Tyrone cut him off. "Why isn't Noah here? All this double talk. He would give it to me straight."

Everyone looked at Meranda. Well, Noah wasn't here so she guessed the task fell to her. She took a deep breath and exhaled slowly.

"No, Tyrone. You're not going to win." Not this time, baby. They had played many cards and negotiated many deals to keep Tyrone's political career on track. However, now they needed to play the hand that they were dealt. It was time to cash in the chips.

Tyrone didn't say a word. He sat back in the black leather chair, put his hands behind his head, and stared intently at the back wall. Meranda knew that he was trying to take in everything. Trying to register everything he heard.

The longer he stared at the wall, the more Meranda became concerned. She could feel him falling, falling, falling into that dark hole.

Tyrone had a brilliant mind, and he needed to be busy, to be useful, to feel like he was contributing. When he didn't...she'd first seen his fear of not being needed or important overtake him when they were in college and a science professor told him that being a physician wasn't his calling. He eventually pulled himself out of it and became an engineer. As one of the few black engineers at IBM in those days, he had advanced quickly—but then he got passed over for a major promotion, and it was back.

Hopelessness. Despair. He couldn't work. Couldn't sleep. Couldn't eat.

But, once again, he found a glimmer of hope, a reason to move from the darkness into the light....a seat on the school board suddenly was open, and he had been very involved and engaged with the issues because of their children. Winning that seat on the school board, led to the North Carolina House, and then the Senate.

And now, that door was closing. But, Meranda refused to let the darkness take her husband again. "Well, let's get in front of this thing so that Tyrone is in control."

"That's a good idea," said Bobby. "What are you thinking?"

"We need to get to work on securing his next position...something high profile that seems like a natural extension of the causes that he's championed. Except mental health." That was too close to home. If anyone started digging, then that could be the end of his public career for good.

"Okay...no mental health."

"And, he needs to play a part in picking his successor...," added Meranda.

"Whom the Republicans will run?" asked Michael.

"No...his successor in OUR community. Who will take up the torch and make sure that our community's needs are addressed? We need to make sure that the leadership gap is filled with someone that will maintain Tyrone's legacy."

"Agreed," the men sitting across from her said in unison.

"And, what about the Education Council?" asked Bobby.

Being on the Education Council had always been a positive for Tyrone. But, Meranda heard through the grapevine that Rowena McGee of WRTD was investigating as she put it "the attack on education." His association with the Education Council could be a negative and drag him down. Or, he could be seen as trying to fight the system within it, if framed correctly. Either way, the affiliation could work to his advantage for positioning him for what was next. "Let's just sit where we are for now. He's part of the Education Council, but he's a non-voting member. Hopefully, that will protect him from any negative press that could be coming down the pike."

"Yes, but his continued criticism could show that he's still making the people's wishes known...," said Horace.

"Or, ensure that he is not brought forward again when his term is up," added Carl.

"Yes, let's just hold our current position on that for now," Meranda reiterated.

"Sounds good," said the men.

They spent the next hour strategizing and covering other details. And, then just like that, they had planned the final details of Tyrone's career as a politician. She just had to make sure that the end of this chapter of Tyrone's life did not mean an end to her position in the community, as well. More than ever, she needed to win this presidency.

~~~

Meranda sat in the back of the limousine and stared out the window as the car sped down the freeway behind the police escort. She tried to tune out Tyrone who was on the phone as she watched the occupants of the passing cars wonder what very important person garnered the special treatment. She and Tyrone spent so much time traveling from one event to another that ordinarily, she would take advantage of the opportunity to catch up on some work or return some phone calls.

However, she suspected that with Tyrone not running for re-election, time would be plentiful as requests for event appearances became infrequent. Often feeling that she was pulled in so many directions between accompanying Tyrone to his civic and social obligations and juggling her own community work and commitments, Meranda always wished for more hours in the day to get everything completed. Surprisingly, now that the wish was on the horizon, the thought absolutely terrified her. What was she without all this?

The limousine came to a stop in front of the executive mansion, where the governor lived, and the driver helped Meranda out the limousine. As she and Tyrone walked on the red carpet to the front door, Meranda saw Senator Angela Bryant and Representative Rosa Gill entering the mansion. After four years of Republicans controlling the state's house, senate, and governorship, it was great to have a Democrat back as the state's top executive.

"Thank you," said Meranda as she and Tyrone handed their coats to the housekeeper when they entered the airy entrance with its elongated hallway and lofty ceiling.

Given the length of Tyrone's tenure in state government, Meranda had been to the executive mansion many times. However, the frequency of her visits did not stop her from being in awe of the magnificence and tradition of the home of the state's first family every time she entered. With the beautiful red and gold carpet with the names and terms of the state's first twenty-five governors and state symbols woven into its fabric at her feet and the grand staircase with its pine railing and hand-carved decorations in front of her, it was easy to imagine all the balls and galas with their pomp and circumstance that were held in a building of this splendor over the years. And, Meranda felt fortunate to say that she had been to more than her fair share.

Tyrone and Meranda quickly made their way past the morning room and to the other side of the long corridor, where they could hear talking and laughter. As they entered the gentlemen's parlor, they were greeted by the roomful of people that were not only Tyrone's colleagues, but many he and Meranda considered friends. It was a tradition for the governor to host a small breakfast for the Black Legislative Caucus on Martin Luther King Jr's Day of Service to thank them for their public service and efforts in keeping MLK's dream alive before everyone scattered to service projects and commemorative events in their own districts.

While Tyrone hurried towards the governor, Meranda made the rounds like a seasoned political spouse. She spoke to Representative Brockman about the chances that House Bill 2 would get repealed fully. The economic impact of the loss of NBA All Star Weekend to

Charlotte was the topic of her discussion with Representative Cunningham. And, she and Senator Foushee strategized about the upcoming Women's March and how they could get women of color involved in the local march in Raleigh.

Sure, many of the spouses were not as engaged as she was in the political issues facing the state and the country. When Tyrone first became a state representative, one well meaning wife actually told Meranda that she never cared about any of that "stuff" and left politics to her husband. When you are privileged and went from your father's house to your husband's home and was used to a man taking care for you, Meranda guessed that you could think like that.

However, she felt it was her duty to leverage the opportunities that Tyrone's position afforded her to advance the causes—like education, the working poor, and health care—in which she was interested. And, over the years, she was able to leverage her access and her connections to benefit the organizations in which she was a member, especially LUA.

However, when Tyrone left office, there was no way around it, his power and influence would wane—even with a political appointment. Yes, he would still have clout and influence. But, real power...that remained to be seen.

Meranda smiled as she saw Tyrone mingling with everyone. He was determined to continue his career in public service, just in another role. And for that to happen, he needed to use his network to find the right position.

But, people liked Tyrone. They always had. With his easy going smile and mellow nature, people always fell for his good, old country boy charm.

That was what attracted her to him many moons ago when they were students at Howard. And, that charm would help him land his next role. She was positive of that.

"Are you ready to go, Meranda? The driver is outside," said Tyrone startling her.

Meranda quickly regained her composure. "Yes? Oh sure. I'm ready."

As they walked away from the staircase, she glanced at the ladies' parlor across the hall. Long ago, when the men retreated to the gentlemen's parlor to discuss politics and business, the women would escape to the proper and genteel ladies' parlor. Frankly, Meranda never cared for the room.

The driver held the door open for Tyrone and Meranda as they hurried inside the limousine to flee the cold. Before the car pulled off, Meranda took one long look at the grand executive mansion. State senator or not, Tyrone would be invited to other events at the executive mansion. Whether his spouse would be invited was another question.

During Tyrone's time in public office, they saw many

people come and go in state and local politics. However, Meranda didn't foresee their time with this level of access would end so...abruptly and with such finality. She needed time to prepare and get her ducks in a row.

The limousine maneuvered the streets of downtown Raleigh then sped along Interstate 40 to West Fairchester High School so that Tyrone could make an appearance at the MLK Day of Service Unity Project held by all the sororities, fraternities, and other black organizations. After breakfast with the governor, Tyrone would stop by a few events commemorating the day. However, regardless of the number of invitations that he received, Meranda insisted that he give remarks at the Unity Service Project every year. All their friends and many of his black constituents were at this event so attending, even if it was only for a few minutes, gave him a lot of bang for his buck.

Tyrone resumed his phone calls and responded to emails, while Meranda checked herself in the mirror. Ordinarily, she would have worn something patriotic to fit in with the various events of the day. When it came to political events or holidays, you could never go wrong with red, white, and blue. However, today she opted for a kelly green suit with a pink scarf. They would only be there for a minute, but she didn't want to miss out on the opportunity to look presidential for sorors in attendance since she and Tyrone would be center stage.

...ecked her watch as the driver pulled up ...e front of the gym and came to stop. They couldn't be there long. Tyrone was expected at the nursing home on the other side of the city, and those old ladies became cranky if he kept them waiting.

Even though it was cold and windy, there was a small group assembled outside. As Meranda exited the car, she pulled her fur coat around her tightly. When you look good, you feel good.

One of the ladies said, "Good morning, Mrs. Barrett. I'm your handler for the day." The day? If they were here for more than thirty minutes, that would be a surprise. However, Meranda handed the young lady her purse so that her hands could be free. As they entered the gym, Meranda could see that the stations spread out in the room had been abandoned and everyone was gathered near the stage—until they walked in.

As people rushed her and Tyrone to say hello and to shake their hands, Meranda knew that this was what rock stars felt like. And, it felt good. As the majority of the crowd engulfed her husband, Meranda's handler maneuvered her to the reserved seat they had for her near the stage.

"Can I get anything for you? Water? Coffee?" asked the young lady as she put Meranda's purse in the chair beside her.

Meranda settled in her chair and crossed her legs. "How about some tea?"

The handler suddenly got a confused look on her face. "Tea? I don't know...," Meranda raised her eyebrow, and the handler continued. "Tea...sure...I'll see if I can find some." Then, she scurried off.

As Tyrone and his entourage made the rounds, Meranda watched as people ran to shake his hand, thank him for his work in the community, and to take pictures. He really was a local celebrity, and the people loved him. No, she didn't have to worry about Tyrone. He would land on his feet. But, lacking Tyrone's charm and easy going style, the question was would she.

FOURTEEN

....

SAHARA – 1   *MERANDA* – 1

The purple lighting that illuminated the building made it stand out like a beacon against the night sky. With only a few months of planning, the Stars for Education charity concert was finally here. The line of cars creeping along Brier Creek Parkway waiting to deposit their passengers at the entrance of The Atrium was a testament to Sahara's marketing skills and connections in the community. From what Meranda heard, the young sorors had the event plastered all over social media, and the concert even had its own hashtag. One of the sorors in her Sphinx chapter was a marketing director, and she said that having the hashtag was a big thing.

Meranda could only pray that tradition and establishment still meant something in this new world that placed more emphasis on likes and follows than decorum and structure. She preferred more *Downton Abbey* and less *Real Housewives*, please.

The black limousine pulled in front of The Atrium, and the driver in his suit and cap got out and opened the back door. Tyrone dressed in his black classic Armani tuxedo exited the vehicle and waited for the driver to help Meranda out of the car. She finished the glass of champagne she was enjoying before exiting. It was going to be a long night.

She smoothed her floor-length, gold gown. She thought about wearing something black, but why not make a splash, even if it wasn't her event. The Barretts proceeded up the stairs that were covered with tealights with a red spotlight in the middle that glowed as if it was a red carpet. Cute.

Meranda knew exactly what Sahara and her team were trying to do with this concert. Sure, the loss of the Fairchester Economic League scholarship would be devastating to some of the students. And, partnering with the sorority to fund them was a great way to make sure that the educational needs of these students were still met.

However, Meranda wasn't stupid. Sahara was also leveraging the concert to win votes. She wanted to show that not only could she lead an event that had a powerful impact on the community but that it could be high profile and bring a lot of publicity to the chapter. To be frank, it was a page Meranda from her and Naomi's playbook back in the day when they were trying to get into this circle.

Touché, Sahara. She definitely taught her well.

However, regardless of the fact that she and Sahara were running against each other, Meranda knew that she had to show her support of the event. To not would be seen as unsisterly and indicate that she was not willing to put the chapter's interest above her own feelings. Sure, she could be petty, but that wasn't anyone's business—so here they were.

Meranda and Tyrone walked into the lobby of The Atrium, and a small smile came to Meranda's lips. The idea was from their playbook, the execution clearly wasn't. Sure, the venue looked great. Black columns with metallic gold stars on top looked like soldiers at attention. Long velvet ropes were on both sides of the red carpet marking the passage from the building's entrance to inside the main ballroom. And, photographers were positioned in front of step-and-repeat banners taking pictures of the event's patrons. Yes, the special touches were there to make it an upscale event.

And, the lobby was filled with people. However, with all the posting and sharing on social media, someone forgot to state what the appropriate attire was at this type of event. Like Meranda and Tyrone, some were dressed for the Oscars with formal gowns and tuxedos. However, others were dressed for some video award show, with ladies in short, tight dresses and men in skinny jeans. Meranda's eyebrows went up when she saw one couple gyrating and making out in the corner. Oh my.

Soror Gertrude, dressed in a black, floor-length gown, waved at Meranda as she and her husband walked by. Soror Gertrude's eyes became wide as saucers as a young man with a gray sweater and pants walked by with his arms around a young lady in a pink leather dress that looked like it had been molded onto her body. Meranda was pretty sure that she could see the young lady's butt cheeks. Okay. She wasn't the only one that was taken aback by some of the outfits here.

When the event was proposed to the chapter, Sahara said that they would try to cast a broader net and market to a greater audience. From the looks of things, all sorts of types were pulled in with tonight's catch.

"Good evening, Meranda...Tyrone," said Soror Gertrude. Meranda turned and gave her soror a hug as Tyrone and Judge Hawkins shook hands. "So, what do you think?"

"The venue is nice," said Meranda.

"Yes, it is. I'm surprised that they were able to get The Atrium with ticket prices so low."

"Well, I heard that Emery Edmonds was able to get them a discount."

"Isn't she a member of Xi Tau Delta? Why would she help them with an LUA event?" asked Soror Gertrude.

"She and my competition were initiated into Belles & Beaus together."

"Oooohhhhh," said Soror Gertrude. "Well, if Emery was able...and even willing, for that matter...to get The Atrium for a discount, they must be close."

Meranda pursed her lips and gave a sideways glance.

"I guess so." But, even she knew that must be a new friendship. It was not long ago that Sahara thought Emery blackballed her from getting an invitation to the Sphinx Masquerade Ball. Not that long, at all. It was amusing how quickly things could change, and yesterday's enemy could be tomorrow's best friend.

"Thank goodness it is almost time for the concert to start. I can't watch anymore of these butts shaking in these too short dresses," said Soror Gertrude.

Meranda laughed. "Well, for that reason and the fact that I'm starving. I wonder what they will serve for dinner."

"Dinner?" Soror Gertrude laughed. "Dear, there's no dinner." She pointed across the lobby. "There were some hors d'oeuvres over there. You better hope there are some left."

She had to be kidding. However, Meranda could see there were buffet tables set up on the other side of the lobby. Meranda looked over at Tyrone who was deep in conversation with Judge Hawkins. It sounded like they were discussing the upcoming state's elections. She begged Tyrone to not let anyone know he wasn't running for re-election just yet. It would be better to announce his departure and future plans at the same time to leave the impression that he was leaving one for the other. And, on top of that, she needed to sew up this election before anyone got wind of the change.

However, maybe Judge Hawkins had some contacts

that could be beneficial to Tyrone—so she didn't want to interrupt their conversation. "I need to powder my nose so I'll walk over and see what's available."

"Good luck," said Gertrude as Meranda made her way across the lobby to the food stations. As she suspected, the dress code had not been an abnormality in her corner. All the older sorors and guests were dressed to the nines. However, most of the young people attending, including chapter sorors, were more casual. Meranda chuckled. The old folks thought that it was Fairchester's version of the Kennedy Center Honors. Apparently, the young people thought it was more Showtime at the Apollo. Well, she guessed they would see once the concert began who was right.

Her stomach rumbled. And, no dinner? No wonder the tickets were so inexpensive. She would have gladly paid more to have a more appropriate crowd and something to eat. Gladly.

Meranda eyed the bar but decided to make the food stations her first stop. However, Soror Gertrude was right. Everything was picked over. Well, from the remnants, it seemed like a decent assortment of heavy hors d'oeuvres that went above and beyond the normal cheese trays and meatballs. Baby crab cakes. Grilled apricots with brie and prosciutto. Buffalo chicken balls.

She quickly made a small plate and ordered a glass of wine. The tomato, spinach, and bell pepper stuffed mushrooms were absolutely delicious. She hated to look greedy but the food was so good—and she was hungry. She missed lunch working on a project for her Sphinx chapter. Meranda looked over her shoulder to make sure that no one saw her take a couple more mushrooms and another crab cake.

As she stood there eating, she saw Sahara talking to Emery on the wall opposite her. Neither looked like they were going to Oscars—but they weren't casual either. Sahara had on a long-sleeved, green sequined cocktail dress. Emery wore a cocktail dress also. However, hers was red with a patterned mesh at the top and on the sleeve. They both looked nice, not formal, but nice. However, not as nice as Meranda, because that would never happen.

Meranda observed them as they stood there talking. Emery said something to Sahara, which made her throw back her head and laugh. A second later, Emery was laughing, too. There was nothing phony or fabricated about the interaction between the two. They were comfortable with each other...friends.

She took a sip of her wine. My how things have changed. The two enemies were now friends. Or, were they...what did the young people call it...frenemies?

Meranda noticed that she wasn't the only person watching the interaction between Sahara and Emery with interest. Two other women to her right were staring intently. She knew the signs anywhere. The crossed arms. The pursed lips. The rolling eyes. Clearly, they weren't fans.

Wait a minute. Meranda recognized one...no both...of the women. The taller one with the blonde hair, she was easier to place. She was the new finance director at the Fairchester Economic League. Mia Johnson. That was her name. Meranda met her at the art auction last year and a networking event that the Fairchester Economic League hosted that Tyrone forced her to attend this summer. Yes, that was definitely Mia. She would remember that blonde hair anywhere.

Now, the other woman...Meranda couldn't quite put her finger on how she knew her. Short, thick—as they liked to say—and wearing a black dress that it would take some heavy machinery to pry off her body. She certainly wasn't anyone in Meranda's circle. But, she did look familiar.

Meranda looked back at Emery and Sahara. It would come to her. Then, she looked back at the woman. Sahara. That's how she knew her. The woman was one of Sahara's friends. Rhoda? Ronnie? Rozlyn. That was her name. Sahara introduced Meranda to her a couple of years ago...maybe at Green Light Weekend. However, she hadn't seen her recently. And, if the death stare that she was giving Sahara and Emery was any indication, Meranda wasn't surprised she hadn't been around lately.

"Here you are, dear. I've been looking for you," said Tyrone as he kissed her on the cheek. "Are you ready to find our seats? The concert is about to start."

The real action looked like it was here, not on any stage, and Meranda didn't want to miss any fireworks. However, she turned and smiled at Tyrone. "Of course, dear. Just let me finish my drink." Meranda drank the last of her wine and put the empty glass on the tray carried by a passing attendant. "I'm ready."

Tyrone and Meranda walked into the building's main hall and were blown away. The room was transformed into a purple paradise under the stars. White tulle cascaded down from the ceiling as white stars glowed on it and the walls. Rows and rows of gold chairs faced the stage giving everyone what felt like a front row experience of heaven.

Meranda was impressed and a little annoyed. For every negative that she found with the event, there were two positives. She couldn't afford for this to be a win for Sahara.

Thankfully, even though she and Sahara were running against each other, Meranda and Tyrone were still seated up front, and the other charter members and executive officers were placed appropriately, as well. They weren't ones for tradition, but at least, the young sorors knew better than to play with protocol. She was, after all, still the charter president. Win or lose, they couldn't take that away from her.

The concert was an assortment of singers and talent. Some good. Some could have been better. But, Meranda could see what they were trying to do. Big Band. Blues.

Jazz. Rhythm and Blues. Hip Hop. They wanted to have a little something for everyone.

Unfortunately, that left everyone with nothing. It would have been better to book fewer artists that could perform more than one genre. That would have resulted in less down time between acts and given a more consistent show. But, she had to admit that it was a great first effort, especially for something completely new that had to be planned in a short amount of time. It just needed a little tweaking.

Meranda discretely turned to see how people were reacting to the concert. Some were moving to the music. She could hear others tapping their feet. Whenever one of the singers asked for crowd participation, the audience was all in. The event had its rough edges, but people were definitely enjoying themselves.

Consequently, Meranda was worried. She had to win this presidency. There were no ifs, ands, or buts about it. With Tyrone leaving office and out of the spotlight, she needed something to...what did the young people say...keep her relevant. She needed something to keep her relevant.

Being the wife of a state senator had opened many doors for her. But, without that, where would she be? It would be easy to dismiss her along with the end of Tyrone's political career. No, she needed something to keep her at the forefront—if only for a little while—and to help with the transition.

And, who knows? Maybe she could follow in Benetta's footsteps and run for regional director after this and then a national position. However, in order to do that, she needed to be relevant, which meant that she needed to be president of the LUA chapter.

After a few more songs, the lights came up and the emcee came out on stage, "I hope that everyone is enjoying the concert so far." There was some mild clapping. "C'mon, you can do better than that! How is everyone enjoying the concert." This time he got an exuberant level of applause and foot stomps. "That's more like it! Well, we are going to take a fifteen minute break so go to the bathroom, get another martini, and we'll see you in fifteen minutes.

Meranda's stomach started growling as she and Tyrone made their way to the lobby. The crab cakes and stuffed mushrooms had worn off. Donna, her fiancé, Sahara and Noah were in front of them. Meranda didn't expect them to be overtly gloating over the success of the event, but they didn't look like they were speaking. You could cut the tension with a knife. Well, that wasn't good for their alliance.

Donna was running uncontested, yet she knew all the young sorors were running as a "ticket" so to speak. But, it certainly looked like number one and number two were off to a rocky start.

"Would you like another glass of wine?" asked Tyrone when they reached the lobby.

No, she really wanted another crab cake, but she could see from here that the hors d'oeuvres were long gone. She guessed that wine would have to suffice. "Yes, thank you."

As Meranda waited for Tyrone to bring her wine, Soror Gertrude walked up to her. "So, what did you think?"

"I have to admit. Well done."

"There are some negatives...the food, some of the singers are pretty bad, and the crowd...." Meranda could hear Gertrude talking but something else had caught her attention. Donna and Alton were speaking to Emery and her husband, Reynard. Alton and Reynard were both in the same fraternity. But, something was off. The men seemed normal, cordial. But, the women...again you could see the friction. They were talking to each other but even from here, Meranda could tell that the interaction was forced.

And then, there was Mia and Rozlyn hovering around again like vultures. What was the deal with these two? Or was it one? Mia looked upon the couples like she was amused. But, Rozlyn. She was agitated...and angry. Arms crossed. Tapping her foot. She certainly didn't like something that was going on. Interesting.

"Meranda, are you listening to me?"

"Huh? What?" Meranda was so busy people watching that she forgot that Gertrude was talking. "Yes, yes...of course...." Meranda turned towards Gertrude so that she could focus on what she was saying, but then there was movement out the corner of her eye. She strained her neck so that she could hear what was being said, but she didn't need to bother. Rozlyn was speaking loud enough for everyone to hear. Terrific. Let the fireworks begin.

"Hi Emery. Hi, Reynard," said Rozlyn. "I guess since you moved, you both think you are too good for me, huh?" She moved around them like a snake circling its prey. "Emery, you have been a naughty friend and haven't returned my calls..." Rozlyn wagged her finger back and forth at Emery. By the look on Emery's face, she was trying her best to maintain her composure.

Rozlyn continued, "And, Reynard...you, too...have not returned my phone calls, or been all in my DMs like usual. However, given our conversations, I guess us not talking would make you a faithful husband now." Emery's husband, Reynard, stood there. He didn't seem embarrassed, more so curious, as if he wondered where Rozlyn's musings were headed.

However, if Rozlyn failed to evoke a reaction from Emery based upon their own communication breakdown, Rozlyn's revelations about her husband had her visibly boiling mad. However, Rozlyn wasn't finished. "C'mon Emery. Don't play the 'hurt wife' game for us. You know and I know that you've known a long time what type of man your husband is. A dog. And that has nothing to do with his fraternity." Rozlyn laughed. "The real question is does he know that you are one, too. I mean what else would you call a wife that sleeps with her husband's fraternity brother, right Alton?"

The look of anger on Emery's face changed to horror, as Reynard went from amused to bewildered. "What is she talking about?" asked Reynard. "What? You two?" He looked back and forth between his wife and fraternity brother. Then, he grabbed Alton. "Are you sleeping with my wife? Are you sleeping with my wife?"

The look of guilt on Alton's face said it all. Before anyone could stop him, Reynard pulled back and punched Alton in the face. A loud "Ohhhhh!" erupted from the crowd that thought they paid good money for a charity concert. Getting to see a boxing match was a bonus and made it money well spent.

Melee ensued as the crowd rushed forward to get a closer look so that they could capture the brawl on video and post it on social media for all the world to see. In the meantime, Emery and Donna were screaming and trying to tear the two fraternity brothers apart. As the ladies, finally separated the two men and sent them to their respective corners, Sahara ran up, "What is going on?" she cried.

However, with the fight over, the amateur videographers and freelance reporters clammed up and became busy uploading the footage to social media.

#CharityBoxingMatch
#LambdaUpsilonAlpha
#BoxingandBougie

#HeGotKnockedTheEffOut

As Emery and Reynard skulked off without saying a word, Sahara turned to Donna. "What happened?"

Donna, who was helping Alton with his ripped tuxedo and nurse his bruised face and fat lip that was growing larger by the second, turned to Sahara. "Did you know?" she yelled.

Taken aback because she probably thought that she was the one asking the questions, Sahara asked, "Did I know what?"

"DID YOU KNOW THAT EMERY WAS SLEEPING WITH MY FIANCÉ?!" screamed Donna.

If it was possible for a black person to turn white, Sahara did. And, that was all the admission that Donna needed. A second later, her hand slapped Sahara's face so hard that all the color came back to her skin as her cheek glowed red. Once again, the crowd reacted with a loud "Ohhhhh!".

Having missed the ruckus, Tyrone appeared beside Meranda's side completely unaware and thus unfazed by the uncouth behavior of the night's coordinators. "Here's your glass of wine, dear." he said.

Meranda smiled and waved it off. "Make it champagne." It was time to celebrate.

FIFTEEN

....

SAHARA – 1   *MERANDA* – 2

Although it was only a little after six, the darkness hugged the sky like a warm blanket on a cold winter night. Not used to a lot of traffic, the narrow road criss-crossed through the countryside like a race track daring Noah's BMW to open its engine and devour the asphalt. The rolling hills were hidden by the nighttime sky—only illuminated by the distant flickering of the occasional lights from a distant house set far back from the road.

However, Noah refused to be tempted. Even nestled in his seventy-thousand-dollar car, he hated to be on dark roads at night. You never knew when a hairpin curve or even more dangerous, a waiting police car, would appear. While Noah was not that far from home in Sugarberry Grove geographically, this was horse country, where some of the most powerful men in the area lived. Financially, Noah was on another planet.

Was that...? Noah realized that he missed his turn and stopped the car. He maneuvered it in the right direction and tried again. Noah made a right turn down the gravel road onto the private road that led to Cass and Zora's house.

Gone were the iron gate and guard that were at the entrance to the Montgomerys' old neighborhood, Walnut Forest. Maybe you didn't need home security when your house was in Timbuktu. No one just happened to be this far out. If someone was on your property, either you invited them or they were up to no good and you introduced them to your shotgun. In the South, guns equaled power. The bigger, the better.

Noah parked his car at the end of the row of vehicles wrapped around the property. As he got out of his BMW, he saw Meranda getting out of the blue Mercedes in front of him. "Mrs. Barrett? Is that you?" asked Noah. "Let me escort you up to the house."

So Meranda and Tyrone were here. He didn't expect to see them. Cass and Zora weren't part of their typical crowd. Noah knew that Meranda blocked him from the meeting where Tyrone decided not to run for re-election. At first, he was angry that she froze him out because he worked hard on Tyrone's last campaign and continued to serve as an advisor. He wasn't saying that he would have drawn a different conclusion, but he deserved to be there. However, Tyrone contacted him later and informed him of the decision.

In the darkness, Meranda had difficulty recognizing who was speaking to her. When it registered that it was Noah, she hesitated for a second but still let a smile come to her lips. "Noah, how kind of you, dear." She looked towards the car as if she was waiting for some-one to come out. "Is Sahara not with you?"

"No, I had to wrap up something at work and wasn't sure that I would be able to attend. She should already be here."

When Sahara told him that Meranda was also run-ning for president, he didn't think it would be a big deal. Someone would win and appoint the loser to a high profile position. End of story. But, they were acting like they were Democrats and Republicans. The Hat-fields and the McCoys. Sharply divided, although he knew that each ultimately wanted what was best for the chapter. They just disagreed on what that was.

Meranda exhaled and relaxed a little. "Yes, Tyrone and I came separately, as well."

Aside from Meranda barring him from the meeting, things were different with him and Tyrone. Noah didn't know if it was the fact that his political career was end-ing or this election with Sahara and Meranda. But, things were different...and probably had been so since the Education Council meeting, if Noah thought about it.

Before they could ring the doorbell, the door opened and a woman dressed in a maid's uniform opened the door. "Good evening," she said. "I can take your coats." A maid? Noah knew that Cass and Zora had a nanny, but the maid was new. They were definitely in the big leagues now.

"Thank you," said Noah as he and Mrs. Barrett gave their coats to her.

The outside was rustic and rural, but the inside of the house was polished and sophisticated. The two-story foyer was massive with its white marble floors, crystal chandelier, and double spiral staircase. Meranda said, "Beautiful," when they stepped inside, which was followed with "Where's the bar?" two seconds later.

The room was filled with people. Some black, but mainly white. A few Asians. No Indians or Latino. A lot of movers and shakers. Mayor of Raleigh. President of University of North Carolina-Chapel Hill. Was that Coach K, Duke's basketball coach? Yes, it was. Even Walter Powers and some other members of the Education Council were there.

Noah still wasn't sure what exactly this event was and why he was invited. The invitation that they received included something about a Celebration of Service...whatever that meant.

He scanned the room for Sahara and saw her talking in the middle of the room to someone. Noah quickly made his way through the crowd to her. She smiled and introduced him when walked up, but her reception afterward was a little chilly to say the least. He exhaled slowly through his smile. What did he do now?

After a few minutes, the young man excused himself. Sahara immediately turned to Noah and said, "So, why did you escort Meranda in here?"

He should have known being nice would get him in trouble. "We parked near each other. I was just trying to be a gentleman and walk her inside." He flashed a grin showing off the dimple in his chin, which he knew that she loved, and gave her a little nudge. "That's alright, isn't it?"

She rolled her eyes at him. "I guess. If you must be a gentleman." She took a glass of white wine off the tray of a passing waiter and took a sip. "It's going to be a long night."

"Why do you say that?" asked Noah, as he waved off the waiter that attempted to give him a glass.

"Well, I didn't expect to see all these people...." Her eyes skimmed the crowd. "...that I know."

Sahara was still reeling from the disaster of the charity concert last weekend. After Alton and Reynard's fight, many of the older guests left so the performers in the second half performed to a half empty hall. Sahara spent the rest of the night crying.

He tried to tell her to focus on the positive—that they raised more than enough to cover the Fairchester Economic League scholarships for the year. However, she had been on the phone all day the next day. It seemed all anyone was talking about was the fight. She was convinced that her chances of winning the presidency were doomed. Noah was surprised that she was willing to come tonight.

"The only one that you need to have eyes for is me,"

said Noah trying to reassure her.

"Alton..."

"Huh? Alton?" Noah was confused.

"Alton just came in," said Sahara as she rolled her eyes in disgust.

Great. Now, she was going to spend the rest of the night agonizing about the charity concert. Thanks, Alton. And, of course, he made a beeline for Noah and Sahara when he saw them.

"I don't want to talk to him," said Sahara under her breath.

"C'mon. At least be cordial." said Noah.

"Trust me. Alton has said and done enough. I don't want to hear anything coming out of his mouth." She took a quick sip of her wine. "Look, there's someone that I know." She sauntered off before Alton reached them.

"What's up, man," said Alton a few seconds later.

Noah gave him some dap, "It's good to see you. I think."

Alton looked over his shoulder. "I was hoping to talk to you and Sahara, but I see she dashed out of here when she saw me coming."

"Do you blame her?" asked Noah.

"You're right, man. I know that I really messed up," said Alton as he looked down on the floor.

That's putting it mildly. Noah shook his head. "I'm not going to lie to you, Alton, you have." He paused.

"So, what's up with you and Donna?" Sahara and Donna were friends now, but Donna was his girl from college. He was the one that introduced Donna to Sahara, and Donna was good people. She and Tania helped him when he was pledging Theta, and he never forgot that.

Alton rubbed his neck. "Right now, she's at Tania's house. She won't see me. Won't take my calls. Nothing."

"And, when she does talk to you, what are you going to say? I mean is everything over with you and Emery?"

Alton looked like a man in love. The question was with whom. "If not, then you need to leave Donna alone." Noah believed in the guy code just like the next dude. However, Alton wasn't frat, and his loyalty was to Donna.

"Man...It's like Emery has a hold on me that I can't shake. It's like she's a drug, and I'm an addict. But, you know what I mean...," Alton trailed off.

Yes, Noah knew the hold that she had on men—all too well. Even back in college, there was just something about her that was intoxicating. But, it wasn't just the sex. It was her confidence, the way she owned a room...just knowing that she picked you and every man in the room wanted her...it made you feel...like a king.

"Yea, I do." Feeling guilty about reminiscing about Emery, Noah glanced over at Sahara. Thankfully, she was busy talking. She was completely unaware of his brief stroll down memory lane.

"But, I never meant to hurt Donna. I love her. I really

do. It's just that Emery has my mind all messed up...."

"Well, you know that you have to make this right, Alton. You have to clean up this mess."

Alton shook his head. "You're right. I know." Something caught his eye. "There's Cass. I have to talk to him about something. Catch up with you later?"

"Alright, I'll talk to you later."

Alton took a step but stopped. "Please tell Sahara that I'm sorry. I never meant for my dirt to ruin their event...or her friendship with Donna."

"I'll let her know," Noah said, but he wasn't sure if it would do any good. It was going to take more than a "I'm sorry" to earn her forgiveness.

"Pardon me, Noah," said Meranda Barrett. "Have you seen the waiter with the tray of red wine?"

Noah peered over the crowd to keep an eye out for his wife. He already got in trouble for entering the party with Meranda. He didn't need another strike against him. "Yes, I see him. Let me get you a glass."

After a couple of minutes, Noah returned and handed Meranda the glass. "Here you go." It was known around the campaign office that you had to keep an eye on Meranda's drinking at public events. Some of Tyrone's conservative donors could be wary of donating if they thought her drinking was an "issue."

However, that was no longer his concern. She kicked him off the team.

"Thank you, dear," she said before taking a sip of the

contents. Then, she just walked away.

Noah laughed to himself. Happy to be of service to you, Meranda.

Someone tapped a fork against a glass. "Can I get everyone's attention?! Can I get everyone's attention?!" Everyone looked at Cass who was standing in the middle of the double spiral staircase.

Cass smiled. "Thank you to everyone for coming tonight. I hope that you've enjoyed yourself and had plenty to eat and drink so far."

"I have. Thank you!" someone said loud enough for everyone to hear. The crowd laughed.

"I'm glad to hear it! Well, I'm sure that all of you are wondering why you are here tonight and what the hell *A Celebration of Service* is."

The crowd laughed again as some people nodded their heads in agreement. A Celebration of Service was pretty cryptic. Noah was glad that he wasn't the only one that didn't know what it meant.

"I gathered everyone here to give you some bad news...," Cass continued.

"Awwww...," said some of the guests.

Cass held up his hand. "But, also some good news."

"Yea!" shouted a couple of people and a few clapped. Noah chuckled under his breath. Clearly, more than a few people had enjoyed the open bar a little too much.

"First, the bad news...As all of you know, Tyrone Barrett has served this area in various capacities...first as a member of the school board, then a representative in the North Carolina House...and currently as a North Carolina State Senator. Unfortunately, I am sad to announce that Senator Barrett has decided to not seek re-election."

There were gasps and whispers. People were shocked that Tyrone wasn't running again. Noah already knew Tyrone's decision. What he didn't understand was why Cass was announcing it. From working on Tyrone's campaign, Noah knew that in the past, Cass and his father were generous supporters of Tyrone's political career. However, in recent years, their donations dwindled, and they didn't give any money towards his last re-election campaign.

"So, part of the reason for tonight is to say thank you to Senator Barrett, a man that has worked tirelessly not only on behalf of his district but the great state of North Carolina."

Tyrone, dressed in a black suit with a face somber enough to have at a funeral, walked out of the crowd and stood facing everyone at the foot of the stairs. The room burst into applause. Tyrone smiled and waved, but he didn't say anything.

"And, now for the good news...with the loss of Ty...Senator Barrett in the State Senate next year, we need a strong leader to fill the void and to help take this district to even greater heights. I'm proud to announce that my father, Blake Montgomery, is planning to run for State Senate."

The noise level of the applause was even greater the second time with whoops and whistles thrown in to accentuate the room's excitement of the prospect of Blake Montgomery representing the district. Once again the room burst into applause as Cass' father emerged at the top of the staircase and walked down the stairs to stand next to his son.

What? Now, the picture was clearer. Mr. Montgomery handed the family business over to Cass so that he could run for office. But, how did he know that Tyrone wasn't going to run again. Or, did it even matter?

Noah looked over at Tyrone, standing at the foot of the stairs with a plastic grin on his face, and then up at the Montgomerys beaming above him. There was definitely more to this story.

"Good evening, Noah," said a voice behind him.

Noah turned and saw Jeremiah Walton, the president of Regional Southern Bank, standing behind him. Noah extended his hand. "Good evening, Mr. Walton. I didn't expect to see you here."

"I only live about ten minutes from here. Normally, I don't like to be out so late, but I wanted to be here tonight."

Noah wasn't surprised that Mr. Walton lived out here. He was the founder and president of the largest regional bank in this area. He probably could afford several horse farms. "It's beautiful out there, but it must be quite a drive into downtown every day."

"It is. But, I enjoy the peace and quiet out here. Plus, I'm with my own kind out here."

"Your own kind?" What the....

"Er...er..horse lovers. A lot of horse farms out here."

"Right...horse lovers," said Noah.

"Anyway, I'm glad that I saw you. My assistant is in the process of setting up a meeting, but I might as well tell you now. What do you think about becoming executive vice president?"

Noah almost spit out his soda. Executive vice president? Could Mr. Walton be serious? Noah was the first black senior vice president at the bank. Sure, he wanted the job...had dreamed of having the job...but really didn't think he would get it. Being the only minority in a high profile position had its challenges, and, that was before Dwight smeared his name.

"Did you hear me, Noah?"

"Uh..uh...yes, sir. Yes, sir, I heard you! Of course, I would be...I am interested!"

"Well, that's good to hear. I will have human resources set up a meeting, as well, so we can work out the details." He paused. "And, don't forget to add the next Education Council meeting to your calendar."

"The Education Council? Will you have to miss the next one?" Noah remembered the controversy his presence created at the last meeting. He wasn't ready to relive that drama.

"No, I'll be there. But, you know that there is an open seat on the Education Council...we're hoping that you will fill it."

"Me? On the Education Council?" Was he dreaming? Cass mentioned an open seat was available, but Noah never thought that he would be considered for it.

Mr. Walton chuckled. "Everyone was impressed with your contribution when you attended and think you will be an asset."

Impressed with his contribution? Think he'll be an asset? Noah was confused. He didn't do anything to impress anyone when he attended. He simply followed the instructions that Mr. Walton gave him and voted the way that he was instructed. That was it. Nothing more. Nothing less.

"Now, you are only allowed one opposing vote. And, I think Tyrone and his gang are angling to get Elbert Wilkins the seat. That's not going to happen, but I don't want them to knock you out of the running. So, if you have any influence with Tyrone...."

Wait. Did he have any sway with Tyrone? Didn't Mr. Walton know that Russell Caine was his uncle? Then, Noah thought about it. Who was he fooling? Uncle Russell wouldn't vote for him. Even Mr. Walton knew that.

"Well, do what you can to work on Tyrone. And, keep your nose clean—at least until your seat on the Council is confirmed."

"I will. Thank you, Mr. Walton. Thank you," said Noah trying not to smile too broadly, but he couldn't help it. As Noah watched Mr. Walton walk away he could hardly contain his excitement. He was going to be the executive vice president! And, he never dreamed that he would become an official member of the Education Council.

"Noah, did you hear?" Sahara said practically jumping up and down.

"What Mr. Walton said? Yes, I was standing right there. Can you believe it?"

Sahara looked confused. "Huh? What? No...about Senator Barrett's retirement!"

Huh? "Yes, I heard it." Noah forgot all about that. And, the fact that he never told Sahara about Tyrone's decision.

"Isn't that great news!"

"Why are you so excited? You want Cass' father to be the new senator? How do you even know him?"

"I don't know him. That's not why I'm excited. With Tyrone not running for office, that reduces Meranda's power. I could still have a shot at the presidency."

"I don't understand." Now, Noah looked confused.

Sahara tried to calm down so that she could explain. "Some sorors like having that connection to the State Legislature...not that I think Meranda has leveraged it. However, with Tyrone out of office, I bet I can convince some of the them to vote for me...especially with this!" She held a piece of paper up like it was a prized pig.

"What is that?" Noah leaned closer to get a better look.

"A check...." Sahara handed it to him.

"Is this for real?" asked Noah as he looked at the paper and back at Sahara. "Cass gave you a check for ten thousand dollars for the scholarship?"

Sahara shook her head up and down. "I could just pinch myself! And, it isn't just for the scholarship. It is for *the charity concert* benefiting the scholarship. The event that I organized. They are going to have a difficult time not voting for me when I put this on the table."

Noah looked at the check and then back at her. That was a lot of zeroes for the LUAs to receive from one donor. "I agree."

With her news presented, Sahara moved on. "So, what did Mr. Walton have to say?"

Noah grinned like a Cheshire cat. "You are looking at the new executive vice president at First Southern Bank."

Sahara's eyes opened wide. "I don't believe you! Noah, are you playing?"

He stuck his chest out. "No, I'm not. That's what he told me."

Breaking with her normal decorum at events like this, Sahara grabbed Noah and squeezed him tight. "I am so proud of you. You deserve this."

He did deserve this. However, as he stood in his wife's embrace, he couldn't help but think that this offer had some hidden strings attached. He just hoped that he didn't become so entangled that he couldn't get out.

After a few seconds, Sahara loosened her grip. "We have to say a toast to celebrate."

"Right now?"

Sahara laughed. "Yes. Right now."

Noah flagged down a waiter and took two glasses of wine from his tray. Then, they raised their glasses, surrounded by strangers, in the middle of the Montgomerys' first floor.

"To a wonderful future," said Sahara.

"To a wonderful future," repeated Noah. They clinked their glasses and followed up with a sip of wine.

"Oh, there's Zora. I need to thank her for the generous donation before we leave." Sahara downed the rest of her wine in one big gulp. "See you at home, where I'll give you a real celebration?"

That's right. They drove separate cars. Noah smiled. "Yes, I can't wait for the real celebration."

Sahara laughed and made her way through the waning crowd over to Zora. Noah walked towards the entrance to get his coat. Executive vice president. If he was dreaming, he didn't want anyone to wake him up.

As he stood in line waiting to retrieve his coat, he caught another glimpse of Sahara talking to Zora. His wife's dress hugged all her curves in all the right places. Yes, he was ready to continue the celebration at home. As Noah stood there thinking about all the ways he planned to have his wife, someone bumped into him.

"Oh. Excuse me," said Meranda a little too loudly. "Noah! It's you!"

"Yes, it's me," said Noah. He came in with Meranda so he guessed it made sense that they would leave at the same time.

"I'm not sure where Tyrone is...but he'll need you now, dear. He may have a smile on his face about all this but you know...."

Given that Meranda had requested he not attend meetings with Tyrone, Noah was surprised to hear her say that he should get together with Tyrone. Maybe it was the alcohol talking. Judging by the whiff he got of her breath, it probably was a whole lot of alcohol talking. As they waited for the maid to bring their coats, Noah could tell that Meranda wasn't exactly steady on her feet.

"Meranda, are you okay to drive? I can take you home." Although Noah did not want to ruin the rest of the night and put Sahara in a bad mood, he couldn't let Meranda drive impaired.

"Oh, how sweet of you, dear. I'm alright. Just a little tired."

A little tired...yea, right. He had—

"Noah, thank you so much for coming tonight," said a voice behind him.

Noah turned and saw it was Cass. "Thank you for inviting us. Some big changes ahead for your family."

"Yes, indeed. But, they are exciting changes." Cass paused. "And, what about you? I hear that you have some exciting changes of your own happening."

What changes? He couldn't be talking about—

Cass must have noticed the confused look on Noah's face because he said, "The executive vice president position."

Noah smiled. "Yes, yes. Definitely a good change." Why did Mr. Walton tell Cass? You never knew who was connected in this town...or talking.

"And, it will be great to get a new perspective on the Education Council. I'm doing all that I can to get your nomination confirmed."

Apparently, Mr. Walton and Cass were more intertwined than Noah realized. "Thank you," said Noah. So, Cass wasn't voting for his father-in-law, Mr. Wilkins? Noah knew that Cass and his father-in-law didn't have the best of relationships. Zora's father thought that Cass was an entitled, privileged white boy that had the world handed to him. Maybe he wasn't too far off. "I appreciate the support."

As Cass and Noah said goodbye, Noah realized that Meranda already left. Great. He wanted to make sure that she was okay to drive. He did a quick scan of the crowd and noticed that Sahara was also gone.

With most of the food and booze finished, the crowd had thinned considerably. There were only a few faces, one being Tyrone Barrett, that he recognized. He was speaking to Cass' father and another man so he didn't take Meranda home. And, Tyrone looked uncomfortable, like the last place he wanted to be was there.

One thing was clear. Tyrone was out and apparently, Noah was in. As he walked to his car, Noah couldn't help but feel that all of them were pawns being moved around on a chess board. The only question was who was the chess master.

Noah pulled out of the Montgomery estate and back onto the winding country road. You couldn't pay him to live this far out. Too few houses and no street lights. It was too dark and too spooky—like in that movie, Get Out.

However, in a few seconds, all of that changed. A row of blue flashing lights broke through the darkness down the road. Must have been an accident. As soon as the words came to his mind, he thought of Meranda. Shit. Please don't let that be her. Despite her objections, he planned to drive her home, but she left while he was talking to Cass.

As the cars in front of Noah slowed, he could see that his intuition was right. There was an accident, and by the number of emergency vehicles there, four police cars and ambulance, it was a bad one.

Please, don't let it be Meranda. But, as Noah was about to pass the accident scene, he braced himself to see her car on the side of the road. However, it wasn't Meranda's blue Mercedes that was flipped over lying by a telephone pole. Was that...?

Noah hit the brakes so hard that if a car had been behind him, there would now be two accidents. The car lying on its side, where police and emergency personnel were trying to pry open the door, was a gold Lexus. Sahara had been in an accident.

SIXTEEN

....

SAHARA – 2   MERANDA – 2

Sahara was on top of the world as she walked out of the Montgomerys' house that night! Sure, Senator Barrett's retirement did not guarantee her a win. However, without a doubt, it put a dent in Mrs. Establishment's armor. And, that is all Sahara needed. She was in it to win it. And, with Senator Barrett's retirement and this ten-thousand-dollar check, she may have a fighting chance to win this presidency.

She yawned. She hated driving at night. And, she wasn't familiar with these dark, country roads with all these curves. She glanced at the clock in the car. 10:04 p.m. Hopefully, she would be home in fifteen minutes. Since she could barely keep her eyes open, Noah may have to take a rain check on their celebration.

Another yawn. She looked back to the road and realized that she was drifting towards the shoulder. Wake up, Sahara. Suddenly, something darted out onto the road. She jerked the steering wheel to avoid hitting it. The car skidded, and she turned the wheel hard to correct her mistake. Maybe too hard. The car overcorrected and started spinning.

For a few seconds, everything was peaceful as Sahara swirled around in the metal coffin in the darkness. It was almost like she was in a cocoon. Then, as the seriousness of what was happening soaked in, every nerve in her body jumped into overdrive. Clarissa. Trevor. Noah. They needed her. "Oh, God! I don't want my family to be without me! Jesus, help me!".

The car was now facing in the wrong direction, and Sahara could see headlights coming at her fast. She didn't want to die. Not here. Not now. However, that was not in her control. The car still had momentum and slid on its side. The force was enough to drag the car off the road's shoulder and into a ditch.

Suddenly, everything came to a standstill. Sahara felt woozy. Her head was pounding. Why was it so dark? What was that ringing in her ears? And, who was whimpering?

Sahara wasn't sure how long the silence and the darkness enveloped her in the cocoon, but it felt like forever. Was this it? Was she dead? She sat there in the peace, but then reality came crashing in.

"Don't move ma'am! Help is on the way!" someone yelled.

Were they speaking to her? Why were they yelling? She wasn't deaf. It was just dark. Why was it so dark? Because her eyes were closed. Duh. She just needed to open her eyes and the light would come in.

Sahara slowly opened her eyes, but everything was

spinning. She couldn't focus. And, every fiber of her body was in pain.

"Don't move! Don't move!" the person yelled again.

She wouldn't, because she couldn't. Everything hurt. When Sahara was finally able to see clearly, her eyes almost bulged out of her head. The car was on its side. And, the whimpering was coming from her. She'd been in an accident. Oh, God. Was she dead?

Calm down. Of course not. She could hear the commotion going on outside. People yelling. Lights flashing. Sirens roaring. She was alive. But, her body felt like someone had hit her with a sledgehammer. And, blood. She could taste blood. Oh, God. She was bleeding. Calm down. You're okay. You're okay.

"Ma'am? Are you alright?"

Sahara tried to turn her head to see who was talking to her, but she felt a sharp pain shoot up her neck. "Yes, I think that I'm alright."

"Okay, we are going to open the door and see if we can get you out. Are you comfortable with us doing that?"

"Yes." The last thing she wanted to do was to remain in this car sideways.

Once she gave the okay, she heard the car door being opened and her seat belt unfastened. Someone said, "One...two...three!" Then, she was pulled out of the car.

Out in the cold night air, she stumbled around for a few seconds. She still had trouble focusing her eyes.

Then, she was able to steady herself. She saw the two officers that pulled her out of the car look at each other. "Ma'am, are you alright?"

Didn't they already ask her that? "Yes, but I feel a little woozy." And, she could still taste the blood in her mouth so that wasn't making it any better.

"Ma'am, have you been drinking?" asked one of the officers.

Why wouldn't her eyes stay focused? And, where was her cell phone? She needed to call Noah. "Just a glass of wine...and some champagne. My husband got a promotion." Her head was still pounding. Yes, Noah definitely would have to come get her. Sahara looked at her Lexus laying on its side. There was no way that she could drive that home.

"Ma'am. Do you mind if we give you a field sobriety test?"

Sahara looked at the three, no two, officers. A field sobriety test? Was he serious? She was just in a car accident. Didn't they give those when you were driving drunk? She wasn't even in a car. She was on the side of the road.

"Why would you want to do that, Officer?" she asked.

"We just want to ascertain if you should be driving," said one officer. The other was on the ground looking in her car. Suddenly, he stood up and raised something in the air.

"Are you aware that you have an opened bottle of tequila in your car?"

Sure, she was. It was leftover from the celebration. Zora and Cass hated tequila so Zora gave it to her when she left.

"Ma'am, are you willing to do the field sobriety test?" repeated the officer.

Sahara wasn't sure what was going on, but something wasn't right. The officer's tone went from concerned to suspicious. And, she didn't like it. She really didn't mind taking the test, but something in her gut said not to do it. "No, Officer, I don't want to take the test." The flashing lights from all the police cars were making her head hurt even more. "Can I go home now?"

The officers looked at each other, then one said, "No, we're going to take you downtown."

What did that mean? "Hey! What are you doing?" asked Sahara as the officer pulled Sahara's arms behind her back and put handcuffs on them.

"We're taking you in on a suspected DUI. You have the right to remain silent...."

"What? I'm not drunk! I only had the accident because it's dark and something jumped out..."

"Sahara! Sahara! That's my wife's car!" shouted Noah from the distance.

Sahara tried to yell out to him, but her head was still woozy, and the officer that was shuffling her along was moving pretty quickly. With everything going on, and her head spinning, it was hard to keep up with him.

When they reached the road's shoulder where the police car was parked, Noah yelled, "That's my wife! Where are you taking her? Sahara, are you okay?"

She let out a small, "Yes," before the officer gripped her head and pushed her into the back of the police car. She had never been in a police car in her life. Ever.

"Where are you taking my wife?" shouted Noah. Sahara turned and looked out the back window of the police car. One of the officers on the scene was holding Noah back while another tried to calm him down. Please, God, don't let them do anything to him.

In the front seat, the officer calmly filled out paper work. The car radio crackled with static as the dispatcher gave orders and commands. How did this happen? One minute she was driving home, and the next she was sitting in the back of a police car. Tears rolled down Sahara's cheek.

After what felt like forever, the officer started the car. Sahara looked out the back window again. Noah was still standing there, looking as frustrated and bewildered as she felt. Although the pain in her neck was now unbearable, she continued to watch Noah out the back of the window until he disappeared into the night.

Sahara turned around as the officer raced through the streets of Fairchester. She was cold as she bounced around in the back seat. She had no way to control the amount of air coming from the rolled down window in the front. And, without having a seat belt on, the handcuffs made it difficult to stop herself from moving around so much on hard, leather seats.

She started to recognize the streets and buildings where they were traveling as the landscape shifted from rural to suburban. They were near Trevor's preschool. Suddenly, Sahara's blood ran cold when she saw the police station on the corner. However, the police car didn't stop in front of the police station or drive into the parking lot on the side filled with police cars. Instead, the car went behind the building and drove into what looked like a big warehouse. Once they were safely inside, the giant metal door slammed close. The officer turned the car off and escorted Sahara inside.

District 4. That was on the large sign on the wall. Fairchester Police Department. District 4.

As they walked into the police station, Sahara realized that she had passed this building a million times...Trevor's preschool was a few blocks down the street...but she had never been inside. Until now.

Finally, the police officer removed the handcuffs from her wrists. That was a small relief. There were red ridges where they kept rubbing against her skin.

"Name?" asked a different officer.

"Sahara Kyle." She could hear him typing on the computer.

"Arrested for?"

Sahara paused. Then, she said, "Driving under the influence."

More typing, then the officer took her hand and slid each of her fingers on a fingerprint computer. Sahara watched as the red light flashed indicating that the computer scanned the fingerprint. Zzzip. Zzzip. Zzzip. The sound the computer made was oddly soothing.

After her fingerprints were scanned, Sahara was handed a small board. Kyle, Sahara. And a bunch of numbers.

"Face forward."

Sahara held the board and looked at the camera. She didn't smile.

CLICK!

The flash was so bright that it almost blinded her.

"Turn to the side."

Sahara followed instructions and listened for the sound of the camera taking the picture. She enjoyed taking selfies, but not this time.

She now officially had a mugshot. What if it turned up on one of those websites where they display any and everyone's mugshots for the entire world to see?

Her thoughts were interrupted when the officer yelled, "Strip!"

"Huh?" she blurted out. What did he mean—strip?

He didn't blink an eye as he repeated, "Strip!"

Did they want to perform another search? Did they think that she had a weapon? She was a mother and wife that lived in the suburbs—just a short distance from here. "But, I was already searched when I was...uh...arrested."

"That was a pat down. What we do here is a full body search. To make sure that you aren't attempting to bring any weapons or drugs into the jail. So, STRIP!" A female officer walked in and held her hands up in the air as she put on the white latex gloves...like she was a surgeon about to perform an operation.

She was going to be sick. She stood there in the middle of the large room and kicked off her black heels and slid out of the red dress that she rarely wore even though it was cute because she was an LUA. She wrapped her arms around her back and slowly un-hooked her taupe lace bra. She liked this bra because it gave her breasts just the right lift to counteract breast-feeding two children. And the lace made it sexy but the color meant that it wasn't too sexy.

But, there was nothing remotely sexy about this. Sahara hesitated but the look on the officer's face was not one of lust. More boredom than anything. She gently touched the band of the taupe lace panties that she was wearing. Normally, she wasn't a stickler for having her bra and her underwear match but she thought that after being out tonight and having a few drinks at the par-ty...Clarissa and Trevor would be asleep when she and Noah got home...she thought that she would get lucky. Matching bra and panties seemed appropriate. However, with his bald head, blue eyes, and white skin, this was not the man that she thought would see her in them.

Her breasts jiggled as she slowly slid her panties down to the ground and stepped out of them.

Sahara held her breasts as the officer ran the latex glove over her entire body and touched her in places that she had taken vows that no other man would ever touch. Tears welled up in her eyes, but she willed them back.

Do not cry. Do not cry. Do not cry.

After determining that she was carrying no drugs or weapons in her mouth, vagina, or any other part of her body, the officer instructed her to put her clothes back on. She had never been so humiliated in her life. But she did not cry. She would not give them the satisfaction of having her suffer that indignity and making her cry. She wouldn't do it.

She quickly put her underwear back on and slipped her dress over her head. After she put her shoes on, a woman in scrubs stuck a needle in her arm. When Sahara looked at her quizzically, the woman said, "Blood sample for the dna test."

After her blood was drawn and she had a band-aid on her arm, the officer led her down a hall and to the jail cell. There was a bench, a bed, a toilet, and two other ladies in there. No pillow. No blanket. No phone. No television. This was definitely not the Ritz Carlton.

As she walked into the jail cell, Sahara jumped when she heard the cell door slam behind her. She sat on the bench and avoided looking at her cellmates. No need in making friends. She didn't plan on being there long.

Sahara sat there and tried to gather her thoughts. The clock on the wall above the police officer's desk looked like it read around two twenty in the morning. It was so far away that it was hard to tell, but she couldn't believe that so much time had passed.

Where was Noah? Wasn't she supposed to get a phone call or something? She looked at the black vertical bars. She was now caged like an animal. She couldn't just sit in this cell.

However, that's exactly what she did. Sat in the cell. No phone call. No television. No talking. No Noah.

To pass the time of the night shift, the officers talked about sports, their families, and nothing that mattered. And Sahara sat. Afraid to move. Afraid to talk. Afraid to think.

Hour after hour passed until tiny slivers of the sun shed light on the dank building. Sahara knew that they couldn't hold her forever. She knew that from watching television. She had seen enough legal shows to know that. *Law & Order. The Practice. Boston Legal. L.A. Law.*

However, nothing about tonight was like what she had seen on shows. There was no rapping and rhyming about unfortunate events. No camaraderie and compassion from the officers. Just silence—and loneliness.

"Alright, ladies, it is time for you to be arraigned."

"Can I get my phone call, please?" Sahara asked. She needed to tell Noah where she was. Where she was going. She was sure that he was worried sick.

"After the arraignment," the officer said as he opened the cell door without even bothering to look at Sahara. "Let's go!"

Sahara and the other two women filed out of the cell. As they passed the officer, he quickly bound each of their hands with a white plastic tie. At least these would be easier on her wrists than the metal ones. Then, they were led to a white van in the warehouse where she was originally dropped off. The three of them got into the van, the huge metal door raised, and before she knew it they were driving out of the police station.

She was still under arrest, and she was still restrained. But, it felt good to be out of the police station. There were bars on the tiny window on the van but at least a little sunlight came through. She took a deep breath and felt herself relax a little. Maybe all of this was almost over. Sahara could only hope.

In about fifteen minutes, the van reached the courthouse with its white steps and flags flying high and circled around the back. Sahara and the other women were led out of the van and into the courthouse through the back doors. As she walked down the halls, she saw signs to the juror assembly room.

Not long ago, she was in the same building in her suit as a juror. Now, she had on plastic ties as a defendant. Funny how things had changed.

It was a little after eight when they left the police station this morning so it probably was close to the time that jurors would be reporting. She felt grimy. A night in her clothes without a shower, washing her face or brushing her teeth did not make the best presentation. What if someone saw her? What if someone that she knew was here?

She knew that worrying about someone that she knew seeing her should be the last thing on her mind, but she couldn't help it. She had been arrested. What if she had to go to jail again? What would she tell her children? Noah just received a promotion. And *"Wife of New Education Council member arrested for DUI"* was not the headline that would help his career advancement.

And, she still couldn't escape the thought of the horror of seeing someone that she knew. What if it was an LUA? Or a Belles & Beaus mom? Sahara held her head down and watched her feet as she followed the woman in front of her into the prisoner containment room. When they got into the room, they weren't the only ones in the room. There were other deplorables, and she recognized one of them. It was the white guy that sat next to her in the jury waiting room before being dismissed because he was a felon. He must have recognized her too, because he smiled when she looked in his direction. She didn't smile back. She just sat down on one of the benches.

And, there Sahara waited. And waited. And waited. She was exhausted. The lack of sleep was beginning to catch up with her, and she could no longer fight it. She was afraid to go to sleep but she kept nodding off.

After a while, one by one, the prisoners' names were called and they were escorted out of the room. Bannon. Carson. Chao. Cohn. Conway. DeVos. Flynn. Kelly. Kushner. And, finally Kyle.

Sahara stood up and followed the bailiff into the courtroom. When she saw Noah sitting in the gallery, tears welled up in her eyes. She didn't know that he would be there. He smiled when he saw her and mouthed, "Everything is going to be okay."

She shook her head up and down to let him know that she understood. Everything was going to be okay. Everything was going to be okay. She just had to keep saying it.

"Your honor, can I have a moment to confer with my client?"

"You may, Mr. Smith."

The bailiff led Sahara over to the defendant's table, where Alton was standing. He smiled when he saw her. "Are you alright, Sahara?"

She was wrong. It felt so good to see someone that she knew. "Yes," she whispered. If she could have, she would have hugged him.

"I still can't believe that this town does not have a bail schedule for DUI. I'm sorry that you had to spend the night in jail," said Alton.

"It's okay."

"Are you ready, counselor?" asked the judge.

"Yes, your honor, I am." Alton squeezed Sahara's hand to reassure her.

After some talking back and forth between the judge and the attorneys, the judge asked, "Is the defendant ready to enter a plea?"

Alton guided Sahara to stand up and whispered in her ear.

"Not guilty," Sahara said repeating the words that Alton instructed her to say.

"Is there a request regarding bail?" asked the judge.

"Given the defendant's standing in the community and this being the defendant's first offense, the DA agrees with the defendant's attorney that she should be released on her own recognizance," said the man at the other table.

Sahara held her breath as the judge looked over his reading glasses at Sahara. Finally, he said, "The defendant is released under her own recognizance."

Alton patted Sahara on the back, and the bailiff walked over and removed the plastic ties. Sahara walked away from the defendant's table and into the gallery where Noah immediately took her into his arms and held her tight.

She didn't care that she was in yesterday's clothes or hadn't brushed her teeth or combed her hair. All she knew was that she was free.

That's when it came. Deep, heavy sobs flowed from

her body like a backed up dam. Noah continued to hold her as her chest heaved up and down rapidly. Slowly she felt her heartbeat calm and began to beat to the same rhythm as Noah's.

She opened her eyes and saw Alton standing in the background. She knew that this ordeal was not over and there would be a trial with more visits to the courthouse and more time with a judge and lawyers. But, she would deal with all that when the time came. For now, she was going home. She looked at Alton and whispered, "Thank you."

SEVENTEEN

....

SAHARA – 1   *MERANDA – 2*

O
ne thing was certain. This case could NOT go to trial.

After Sahara and Noah came from the court-house, Sahara kissed her sleeping children and collapsed in bed. She thought after being up all night, she would sleep for days. However, instead of a serene and restful sleep, as the gravity of what happened seeped into her subconscious, Sahara tossed and turned with agitation the entire time.

Sure, she was embarrassed. The fact that Noah watched his wife, the mother of his children, being handcuffed and put in a police car like a common criminal always started the water works. And, thank goodness that Alton was willing to come to court on her behalf, even after she had refused to talk to him at Cass and Zora's party. And, what if someone else was driving by as she was being arrested? She shuddered at the thought.

Yes, she was disappointed in herself. How many times had she heard and preached that people shouldn't drink and drive? How many news reports had she read that stated that even insignificant amounts of alcohol could impair your faculties and reaction time? But, she only had a little to drink at Cass and Zora's party. If that deer hadn't darted out into the street....

And, it was such a great night. The bank president informed Noah about his promotion to executive vice president and being nominated to be a member of the Education Council. What an honor!

Then, Sahara remembered something. What did Jeremiah Walton say to Noah? *Make sure that you keep your nose clean.* Did that go for her, too? Could Noah's new job or council appointment be in jeopardy because of her?

She was so stupid! How could she let this happen?

Noah was so excited about his promotion and after all that he'd been through with the Dwight situation...he deserved this. If she caused Noah to lose out on these opportunities, she would never forgive herself. Never. She had to figure out something.

Sahara threw on her robe and ran downstairs to make some coffee. She needed to come up with a plan. As the coffee brewed, she sat at the kitchen table with a pad of paper and a pencil.

Options?

She traced over the letters to make them stand out. What were her options? In a nutshell, to fight the charges or to not fight. She quickly scribbled both down on the paper.

The path of least resistance was to plead guilty. That way, she avoided a trial and hopefully any press about it. When a DUI arrest made the news in Fairchester, it was always because there was some horrific crash where someone had been hit or killed. Thankfully, no one was hurt, not even her. But, she would have a record if she pled guilty.

And, she would be sentenced. What if she received jail time? Since this was a first offense, she didn't think that she would—but it wasn't up to her. What if some judge wanted to make an example out of her? There was no way that she could be apart from her babies or Noah.

She crossed a line through the first option and looked at the next one. *Fight the charges.* That was easier said than done. Pleading not guilty would mean hoping that the prosecutor couldn't prove his case against her.

She had watched enough crime shows on television to know not to admit guilt that night. She told the officers about the deer darting out into the road and swerving to avoid hitting it. Unfortunately, she also said that she had a glass of wine...and a little champagne...when they asked if she'd been drinking. But, she refused to take the field sobriety test. However, they took a blood sample at the precinct. They would probably test it to see what her blood alcohol level was.

She really had swerved to avoid that deer. And, she knew that a little glass of wine and a sip of champagne certainly didn't make her drunk. She probably was below the legal limit. Probably. With these hips and curves, she had enough going on to absorb that alcohol. There was no way that a couple of drinks put her above the legal limit.

However, what if the blood test proved that she was? Then, all bets were off. Even if the judge didn't give her jail time. If anyone got wind of what happened and that she was guilty of driving under the influence, that could impact Noah's appointment to the Education Council and even his job. Everyone in their social circle enjoyed some wine or a cocktail at least once in a blue moon. But, having a wife convicted of driving under the influence...that was a whole other matter.

And what about the impact on her and the children? Would a DUI conviction put her membership in Belles & Beaus in jeopardy? If not, there was probably some rule against her transporting children. Sorry, I can't drive the children to the museum. I have a DUI on my license. The talk that would generate...Sahara could hear it now.

Even if she was found not guilty, the damage would already be done. Sometimes, even the thought of impropriety was enough for some people. She would be guilty regardless of the final outcome.

There was only one solution. This case could not go to trial.

The detective in her figured the blood sample was the only thing that could prove beyond a shadow of a doubt what her blood alcohol level was. Without that, the district attorney had no case. No case, no trial.

She had to get rid of that blood sample. Maybe Alton could file some motion or something to get it suppressed? But, what would be the cause? Your honor, my client wants you to throw out the blood sample because it may incriminate her. That wasn't going to work.

What if the sample or the test results were lost? That happened all the time on television.

But, this was reality. How could she make that happen? She didn't know anybody at the precinct or the police lab. You needed connections for that. Maybe Senator Barrett....

What was she thinking? Meranda would never let Senator Barrett risk something like that for her. To make that sample disappear, it had to be someone with a lot of power and with a vested interest in her.

Uncle Russell? She wasn't sure that he had the connections, and Noah probably would wait for hell to freeze over before he told Uncle Russell her secret and let him hold it over them.

No. Uncle Russell was not the answer. Someone with clout and a vested interest.

Sahara closed her eyes, and after a minute, let out a long sigh. There was a person. The question was could she bring herself to ask for help.

Her father. Congressman Charles Allymer. He certainly had the connections and the clout. He also had a vested interest—if for no other reason than to keep their connection and his name out of the paper.

Yet, could she bring herself to ask for his help? She hadn't seen him since that Thanksgiving at church. Not a word. He hadn't reached out to her. She hadn't called him.

And, there was the announcement about the other illegitimate daughter. Still no contact. What would she say? How are you? Heard about the second love child.

However, this was a whole other matter. She had to get this case thrown out, if she wanted to protect Noah and her children. There was no other way. Her father was the answer.

But, how would she reach him? Was he in Raleigh or Washington? Sahara walked upstairs and opened her lingerie drawer. The small slip of paper was still there. She gently unrolled the curled note. The phone number written in her mother's handwriting was still there.

Sahara picked up the house phone and slowly dialed each number. What was she going to say? Hey, it's your illegitimate daughter...no, not the one that you claim...the other one. Maybe she could go for the guilt factor and say that the she got arrested for driving under the influence because she was a raging alcoholic stemming from her daddy issues. That would show him.

She put the phone to her ear. The phone rang—and rang. No one picked up. Great. She hung up and called again. Still no answer. This time she got voice mail.

"Hello, this is Charles." His voice, so this was still a valid number. "Please leave a message." What could she say? Daddy, I need you to make this blood sample go away. Call me back!

Sahara hung up when she heard the beep to start her message. She would keep calling. But, what if he never answered?

Suddenly, the doorbell rang. Who could that be? Sahara looked at the clock. It wasn't even noon. She wasn't expecting any visitors. She was tempted to ignore the doorbell, but whomever it was kept ringing it. Sahara sighed and reluctantly returned downstairs to answer the door. It was Emery.

But not, the normal Emery. She didn't look like herself. Bare faced. No makeup. Her always commercial-ready bob was pulled back into a ponytail, and she had on a black jogging suit. Sure, it was Adidas, but Sahara had never seen Emery look so—ordinary.

"Hey, Emery. Is everything okay?" asked Sahara. She called Emery a few times after the charity concert but always got her voice mail. And clearly, she had more pressing problems now.

"Hi, Sahara." Emery walked in and gave Sahara a hug. She held on for a few seconds longer than expected but didn't say anything. Then, she walked to the family room and sat down. "I know that you've called," started Emery.

Sahara nodded her head up and down as she looked

at the clock. She needed to call her father back in a few minutes.

Emery continued, "I just had to get away...after everything that happened at the charity concert. I never thought that it would come to that." She paused. "I guess I never thought anyone would find out."

Sahara never told Emery that she saw her and Alton in the hotel parking garage. Why bother revealing that information now? And clearly, she wasn't the only one that found out about the affair.

"What did Reynard say?" asked Sahara softly. He certainly wasn't a boy scout himself. However, given his reaction, he expected Emery to keep her vows to be faithful.

"He said that he was willing to work it out...to forgive me. He doesn't want our daughter to grow up in a broken home."

Sahara noticed she was bouncing her leg as she looked at the clock again. She put her hand on her knee to stop it.

"The only issue is...," Emery lowered her voice.

Sahara tried to stop looking at the clock. But, she needed to reach her father today. The longer the blood sample was out there, the harder it would be to stop it from moving forward and being used in a trial.

"Riley isn't Reynard's daughter. She's Alton's."

Maybe he was in a meeting or something, and would pick up.... What did she say? Sahara looked at Emery.

"Did you say that Riley is Alton's daughter?"

Emery kept her eyes lowered. "Yes...but he doesn't know. He suspected when he first got to town, but I lied and told him that he wasn't her father."

"Why, Emery? Why?" asked Sahara. All the thoughts about her father and the DUI were out the window. Emery had her undivided attention.

Emery shrugged her shoulders. "It was...the simplest solution. Both now and then. Alton was shipping off for the military, and Reynard was there. I prioritized Riley over me. I didn't choose the man that I wanted, but the life that I wanted for my child.

"And, Reynard loves Riley, and he is the only father that she knows. I never expected to have an affair with Alton—or to fall in love with him."

Or to fall in love with him? Oh boy. This love triangle between Alton, Donna, and Emery was more complicated than Sahara originally thought. And, it sounded like it was only going to get worse.

"So, what are you going to do? I mean how do you think Reynard will handle not being Riley's father."

Emery looked at Sahara. "He won't ever know. I'm not going to tell him...well either of them."

Wait. "You aren't going to let Alton...." Sahara refrained from saying, "...the man that you were having an affair with...." She paused for a second, then continued, "You aren't going to tell Alton or Reynard the truth?"

"No. What good will it do? We're not going to see

each other anymore. Alton will marry Donna, and I will go on with my life with Reynard. End of story."

"I know that you think that you have everything figured out...but think about Riley. Maybe she deserves to know whom her real father is and...."

"You know whom your real father is and that's helped you how?"

Youch. Apparently, she struck a nerve.

Emery stood up. "Trust me. When I was young, I wished that I was somebody else's child. Sometimes, knowing your biological father is overrated."

Sahara was dumbfounded. She didn't know what to say as she followed Emery to the front door.

"Well, I just wanted to say thank you for your concern. I'll be alright," said Emery expressionless.

The mood in the room had shifted. "No problem. I'll talk to you later," said Sahara.

A tight smile came to Emery's lips, but she didn't say anything. And, as Sahara leaned in to hug Emery as they always did when they parted, she saw Emery hesitate for a second. Then, she leaned towards Sahara but remained stiff and cold. Sahara felt like she was hugging a board.

She wasn't sure what just happened, but something changed. However, Sahara couldn't focus on that now. She had her own problems. And like Emery, her children were her priority.

As Sahara closed the door she thought about what

Emery said. *You know whom your real father is and that's helped you how?* Maybe not much in the past, but that was about to change.

Sahara picked up her cell phone and dialed her father's number. No answer. No ring. This time it went straight to voice mail.

She stared at the clock on the wall. She couldn't keep calling his phone like she was a stalker. Especially if it was off. Was he in a meeting? Out of town? She needed to speak to him—even if it was in person. She needed to get this blood sample situation handled.

But, who would know where he was? She certainly didn't, and she doubted if she called his office that they would tell her. His wife, Winnie, probably knew. But, Sahara knew that pigs would fly before Winnie told her where her father was.

But, what about Fallon? Her Belles & Beaus sister. Her half sister. She may be willing to tell Sahara. Maybe. It was worth a try.

She hadn't seen Fallon since that day at the hospital, and then, Fallon took a leave of absence from the Belles & Beaus immediately afterward. Sahara had not reached out to her after she was inducted into Belles & Beaus. After Winnie's behavior, Sahara's plan was to maintain a sort of invisible wall, where Fallon stayed on her side, and Sahara stayed on hers.

And, Fallon was a no-show at cluster, and there paths hadn't crossed anywhere else. Maybe Winnie was wrong. Apparently, Belles & Beaus was big enough for both of them.

But, this was an emergency. Sahara really needed to get in touch with her father. Their father. And, Fallon may know where he is. Ordinarily, she would be happy to keep their unspoken agreement in place, but this was an emergency. Sahara had to call her.

Now that she had the courage to do it, she realized that she didn't have Fallon's phone number. However, Emery did. Maybe she could call and get Fallon's.... Nah. Emery was pretty chilly when she left, so she should give her a minute before she asked for a favor. And, she would want to know why Sahara wanted the number. The fewer people involved in this operation, the better.

An idea popped in her head. The Belles & Beaus online directory. Fallon's number would be in there. Sahara pulled out her laptop and logged on to the directory. She typed in Fallon's name, and her information popped up on the screen. Perfect.

Sahara picked up her cell phone and dialed Fallon's cell phone number. Here goes nothing.

"Hello," said the voice on the other end.

"Hi...Fallon?" said Sahara.

"Yes, this is she." Her voice sounded cheerful but cautious, probably because she didn't recognize the number.

"Hi...." Sahara wished that she had planned what she would say before calling. Now, she would have to wing it. "This is Sahara."

"Oh." Fallon's voice dropped an octave.

Now, Sahara wished she hadn't called. How would Fallon react to Sahara asking for their father's number? Sahara hadn't spoken to Fallon after she found out that Charles Allymer was Sahara's dad, too. She didn't even know how Fallon took the news. For all she knew, Fallon was like her mother and hated her for ruining Fallon's perfect life.

"Hello?" asked Fallon.

"I...um...I was calling to see if you knew where Charles...I mean your...um...our father is. I am trying to get in touch with him."

Now, it was Fallon's turn to hold the phone without saying anything. She probably wanted to know why Sahara wanted to talk to him or was weighing her options. However, after a minute, she said, "I don't know where he is. You should call his chief of staff, Darren."

Chief of staff? "Do you have his number?" Sahara asked quickly.

Another awkward pause. However, like the first time, Fallon chose to give Sahara the information. "The number is 202...."

Sahara breathed a sigh of relief. Fallon spoke so quickly that she wasn't sure that she wrote down the numbers correctly. But, she was not going to ask Fallon to repeat it. "Okay, Thank...." Fallon hung up the phone before Sahara could finish what she was saying.

She pushed her feelings down and tried not to read anything into Fallon's abrupt exit from the phone. The phone number that she had scribbled on the pad was the main task at hand. At least Fallon gave her the chief of staff's number. Sahara hoped it was correct.

She dialed Darren's number, and he picked up on the first ring. "Hello," said a male voice.

What was his last name? Although Sahara never spoke to Darren or even knew that he existed ten minutes ago, calling this stranger was much easier than talking to Fallon. "Hi, Darren. This is Sahara, the congressman's daughter." No need to beat around the bush.

Darren continued without missing a beat. "Good morning, Mrs. Kyle. How may I help you?"

Mrs. Kyle. She said Sahara. He said Mrs. Kyle. He knew her name. He knew whom she was. "Uh...I'm looking for my father." Maybe she was supposed to say Congressman Allymer or something. Darren lowered his voice, "They're at the vacation house...in Wrightsville."

Sahara had no idea whom "they" were, but she played along. She didn't want Darren to clam up before she got the information that she needed. "And, what's the address?"

Five minutes later, she ran up the stairs to get her purse. A taxi was on the way to take her to the rental car center to pick up a car. Maybe this was going to be easier than she thought.

An hour later, Sahara walked out of the rental car center downtown and opened the door to the black Mercedes SE parked in the lot. With no reservation and low inventory, it was either the Mercedes or a red Porsche. Given the circumstances, the Mercedes seemed more appropriate. Armed with the address that she got from Darren and a full tank of gas, Sahara had a three-hour drive ahead of her. She might as well do it in style—after all she was a congressman's daughter.

~~~

Three hours later, the Mercedes drove through the narrow streets of Wrightsville Beach. Two hours from Raleigh, the island was popular with families that liked its proximity to the North Carolina mainland and enjoyed the development and activities that the Outer Banks lacked. Cultured exclusivity.

Sahara looked at the paper with the address that Darren gave her again. It was at the end of the street. As she pulled in front of the three-story elevated house two blocks from the beach, she was sweating—and it wasn't from the heat. Her nerves were creeping up, but she had to do this.

She looked around. She wasn't sure what she expected, but this wasn't it. Secret service? A limousine, maybe? But, this looked like a regular street on a regular day. A few cars in the driveway. A man mowing the lawn. Postal worker delivering the mail.

She took a deep breath and got out of the car. Saying that she didn't have the best relationship with her father was an understatement. But, she really needed this. He may not have been there in the past, but if he got this done....

No more procrastinating. There was no time like the present to find out. She rang the doorbell, held her breath, and listened for footsteps coming to the door. Nothing.

She rang the doorbell again and looked around. There wasn't a car or anything parked outside or in the driveway. Was Darren wrong? Maybe her father wasn't at the vacation house. Or maybe he drove back home already. Sahara prayed that she didn't drive all this way for nothing. She rang the bell one last time.

Finally, there were footsteps. Then, she had a horrible thought. Please don't let it be Winnie. Please don't let it be Winnie.

The door opened slowly. It wasn't Winnie. Thank goodness. Sahara was standing face-to-face with her father, the distinguished Congressman Charles Allymer. The fair complexion and the straight nose placed him in the privileged category. The silver low-cut hair, mustache, and beard marked him as respectable.

"Sahara, I wasn't expecting you." Okay, THAT had to be the understatement of the day. He stood there in the doorway in his robe, even though it was the middle of the day.

"Can I come in?" asked Sahara.

He looked over his shoulder before moving to the side. This was going well.

Sahara stepped inside the foyer. Okay. She just needed to spit it out. "I don't really know where to start...so I won't beat around the bush. I was arrested."

His eyebrows went up. "You were what?" Was that alarm? Embarrassment? Sahara couldn't tell.

"I was arrested for driving under the influence. I don't think that I was really. They only arrested me because I got into an accident."

He crossed his arms. "You were in an accident?" Was he concerned? She hated that she was analyzing his every movement...every word. But, deep down, she was still that little girl looking for Daddy's love.

"A minor one. Well, not really minor. I mean no one was hurt, but the car ended up in a ditch."

Her father was standing there like they were on a television show...like Jim Anderson on *Father Knows Best* or Phillip Banks from *The Fresh Prince*. His arms were crossed, and he had a curious look on his face while his daughter rambled on and made excuses about being caught at her latest antics.

Except this was not a television show. And, the stakes for this mistake were much higher than getting grounded.

She needed to get to the point. "Noah earned a really

big promotion and an appointment to the Education Council. This DUI could hurt him, hurt us. I don't want that to happen. Is there anything that you can do?"

Sahara thought she heard a noise come from one of the rooms. Her father must have heard it too because he looked behind him but then focused back on Sahara.

They stood facing each other without either saying a word. Then, another creak. No wonder these beach areas took such a beating during tropical storms. The houses seemed to shift and creak with even the slightest breeze.

Suddenly, her father said, "I'll see what I can do."

No questions? No brow beating? Sahara hadn't expected it to be so easy, but she knew better than to look a gift horse in the mouth. Instead, she breathed a sigh of relief. "Thank you."

She felt like the occasion called for a hug or something. But, that would be awkward. She couldn't remember hugging her father since she was a child. Plus, he was in his robe...in the middle of the day.

After another awkward few seconds, her father said, "Well...if there's nothing else that you need...I'll start making some phone calls...."

Sahara picked up on his cue. "Yes, of course..." Right, he needed to make phone calls. To help her. She should let him get to it.

Yet, Sahara's feet felt like they were stuck in quicksand as she slowly moved towards the door. She didn't know what more she expected. She should be glad that this was so easy...that he didn't make her grovel. Or worse—said no. Yet, something didn't seem right.

She could hear him shuffling behind her as they walked towards the door. His hand reached for the door knob before she did. Okay.

As Sahara turned to say goodbye, she saw it. On the sleek glass table against the foyer in the wall stood a gold Birkin bag, with its handmade leather and palladium hardware, as proud as a peacock. For a quick second, Sahara envisioned the owner strolling in the front door with her father—laughing at something amusing he said. Ready to begin their beach vacation, she would toss a purse or a clutch casually on the sofa.

But no one, not even Oprah, would toss a Birkin. That handbag was meant to be treasured and not carelessly left just any place. No matter how flirtatious Charles Allymer was or how ready she was to officially begin their rendezvous, the owner would take the time...make the time...to gently put the handbag on the glass table.

Sahara felt a lump form in her throat. She got what she wanted. Her father was going to take care of the DUI, but she knew that she had to ask.

She looked at her father. "Is my mother here?" she almost whispered.

Her father looked confused and his eyes darted around the room. However, as the seconds ticked by,

Sahara knew that whatever came out of his mouth was sure to be a lie. Yet, she asked again, "Is my mother here?"

This time was a little louder. A little stronger. However, why bother asking the question, when she already knew—

"Yes, I'm here," said her mother as she stood in the shadow of the hallway on the other side of the room.

Although it was obvious as her mother wore a black silk robe, Sahara felt that she still had to ask, "What are you doing here, Mother?"

For the first time in her life, Janice Robinson was at a loss for words. She looked at her daughter, then at Charles Allymer, and back at Sahara. "I....I..." She sat down in the chair beside her without finishing.

"She's here visiting me," her father said quickly.

She's here visiting you? Why would she be here visiting you?

The robes. The shifting eyes. Her father's nervous behavior when she arrived. Sahara narrowed her eyes. Everything clicked.

"Are you sleeping with him?" asked Sahara, although she was having difficulty comprehending what she saw. Yes, she asked the question, but she already knew the answer. But, she had to hear the words come from her mother's lips.

Unfortunately, she was not cooperating. Her mother sat in the chair, not saying a word, like she was waiting to see what happened next.

But, Sahara wasn't so easily dissuaded. She strode past her father over to the chair where her mother sat. "Mother, are you having an affair with *him*?"

The word *him* came out as dirty and perverse as whatever brought these two together again. Then, out the corner of her eye, she saw the two lovers exchange glances.

How long had this been going on? Sahara's eyes flew from her mother over to her father and returned. She couldn't believe it. They stood there like this was the most natural thing in the world. Sure, they were embarrassed that they had been caught. But, there was no remorse.

All the heartache. All the lies. And, Winnie. No wonder Winnie went out of her way to keep Sahara out. She wasn't a vestige of an indiscretion of long ago, but a reminder of ongoing disloyalty and disrespect.

Sahara turned and looked at her mother. Although she was afraid of the answer, she asked. "Why, mother? Why?"

Her mother, such a proud woman. Janice Robinson could make anyone think twice about a poor decision with just one look. However, today...right now...on her face was not a look of the prim and proper maven that Sahara knew so well. Instead, she looked defeated as she said, "Because I love him."

However, Sahara wasn't going to let her off that easily. "IF you love him, then why keep him a secret? That's right. Because he's some other woman's husband." Sahara paused thinking back to that conversation that she had with her mother last Thanksgiving. "With all this secrecy, why did you want me to tell Noah?"

Her mother looked at Sahara with tears in her eyes. "Because you needed to." Then, she put her head down. "But, I also wanted to make sure that you didn't know that your father and I were together again...so I stood outside the door to make sure that wasn't part of your revelation."

So, there had been someone outside the door. Someone concerned about her own selfish desires.

Sahara shook her head. "I had it all wrong. Winnie's not the monster, Mother. You are."

EIGHTEEN

....

SAHARA – 0   MERANDA – 2

‖T‖he entire drive home Sahara was so angry. Her mother was having an affair with her father. Correction. Her mother was having an affair with her father again. After all these years.

Sahara had never spoken to her mother like that. But, she couldn't believe that her mother lied to her. Did Winnie know? She had to know.

No wonder she hated Sahara and was so protective of Fallon. She had every right to be. Too bad her own mother didn't feel that way. All the lies over the years. Sahara only told Noah last year whom her father was, and her children still didn't know.

Deep down, Sahara thought that her mother's intentions were from wanting to protect Sahara from backlash and notoriety. Now, she doubted all of that. Her mother didn't lie to protect Sahara. The lies were to protect herself, plain and simple. The idea of her mother's selfishness and duplicity turned Sahara's stomach.

As she pulled into the garage a few hours later, her cell phone rang. It was her mother. She probably figured that she would give Sahara a little time to cool off and then everything would be alright.

Sahara hit the red *Decline* button without a second thought. It was going to take more time than a ride home from Wrightsville Beach before she was ready to talk to her mother.

However, as the days dragged on, Sahara continued to avoid her mother's phone calls and wished that she would hear from a different person, her father. When she told him about her DUI, he said that he would see what he could do. But, what did that mean? And, how would she know when it was done?

She wanted to ask so many questions, but to be honest, she hadn't felt comfortable talking to him. And then, there was the discovery of her parents' affair. The statement sounded so ludicrous that she almost laughed. But, what if the argument with her mother caused her father to change his mind about helping her?

She needed to know what was going on. Right now.

She was walking on egg shells not knowing if he was successful or if her secret would be found out. Could she get her life back? If so, when? When could she breathe?

A few days later, she had her answer. "Sahara? Hi, it's Alton."

She could tell by the tone of his voice that he did not have good news. She took a deep breath before answering. "What's going on, Alton?"

"Well...," Alton started and just stopped. Now, Sahara

was certain. If it was good news, Alton wouldn't have trouble getting out what he wanted to say.

Then, he continued, "I'm not really sure what is going on. I was trying to convince the assistant district attorney to drop the charges, but he cut off communication with me suddenly. My sources in the district attorney's office tell me that district attorney is planning to run for re-election and doesn't want any plea deals or minimum sentence recommendations because he doesn't want to seem soft on crime."

Sahara gulped. No plea deals or minimum sentences? A district attorney wanting to crack down on crime was not what she needed right now. Not at all. It sounded like there could be some serious consequences to this DUI. What if she went to jail?

Tears welled up in Sahara's eyes. She couldn't be away from her babies...from Noah. She just couldn't. She choked back her tears as she asked, "What can I do?"

"Nothing, right now. I'll keep trying to get in touch with the assistant district attorney. I didn't mean to upset you. I just wanted to give you an update."

Sahara wiped away the tears that were streaming down her face. "No, I appreciate you keeping me updated, Alton. Thank you."

Please don't let this be happening. Sahara tried to calm down and not jump to conclusions, but she couldn't help it. She knew that her father being able to do something was a long shot. But, she had wished...had hoped.... But, it seemed like even he couldn't get Sahara out of this mess.

Before, her biggest concern was that people would find out about her arrest or Noah wouldn't get his promotion. Now, it was possible she could face jail time. What was she going to do?

She eyed the refrigerator where she knew there was an unfinished bottle of wine. She shook her head. She couldn't use that to calm her nerves. That was what got her in trouble in the first place.

Sahara paced back and forth. What was she going to do?

Ding, ding, dong.

Sahara looked at the door. She wasn't expecting anyone. And, she was certainly tempted to ignore it. Dara, Dwight, Emery...it seemed like nothing good came of unexpected visits.

What the hell? What else could go wrong?

However, when Sahara caught a glimpse of a blue uniform through side panels of the door, she had second thoughts. She slowly opened the door and breathed a sigh of relief. It was the postman. Alton's phone call really had her spooked. Every uniform looked like a policeman to her now.

"Good afternoon, ma'am. You have some certified mail that you must sign for receipt." He held out his hand and gave her a white envelope and a pen.

She looked at the envelope. The green certified receipt card covered the return address so she couldn't see who sent it. White and flat, there were no telltale signs as to what the envelope contained. But, Sahara was curious. Who needed to send her certified mail?

She quickly signed her name and handed the pen back to the postal worker. In exchange, he handed her a group of envelopes and circulars. "And, here's your regular mail," he said before turning around and walking back to his car to finish his delivery route.

Sahara slowly walked to the kitchen as she opened the non-descript mailing. She tossed the rest of the envelopes on the kitchen counter and pulled the paper out. Her heart skipped a beat when she saw the top of the stationary.

Office of the District Attorney.

What was this? Her hand trembled as she unfolded the rest of the letter.

Dear Mrs. Kyle....

Sahara's eyes narrowed as they danced over the print. Her heart beat faster and faster. This couldn't be right. She just talked to Alton, and he said.... She took a deep breath and tried to calm down. Maybe she read something wrong.

She took another deep breath and exhaled slowly. Just read it again.

Dear, Mrs. Kyle. Regarding People vs. Sahara Kyle Case No. 45374., the district attorney has dropped all charges against you. If there are...

She had read the letter twice, and it said the same thing each time. The district attorney had dropped the charges. The district attorney had dropped the charges.

Sahara was still staring at the paper when her cell phone rang. She answered it without bothering to see who was calling. "Hello?"

"Sahara! I'm glad that I caught you," said Alton excitedly. "You're never going to believe what happened!"

"The district attorney dropped the charges," said Sahara softly. The news was like a sleeping baby. She was afraid that if she rocked the boat in anyway—spoke too loudly or sounded too excited—like a dream, it would go away.

"Yes! Yes! This is great news!" shouted Alton, apparently not having the same fears.

Then, a question popped into her head. "How?"

"Did you say something?" Alton asked.

Sahara didn't mean to rock the boat. "How? How did this happen?"

"Well, that's the craziest thing. Apparently, they can't find your blood test results. First time that I've ever heard of anything like that happening," said Alton.

Sahara let the words settle. They couldn't find the blood test results. Her father. He made a way.

She half listened as Alton rambled on about next steps. All she needed to know was that it didn't include jail time, a record, or anything that would take her away from her family. After a few more minutes of instruction from Alton and then thanking him profusely for his help, Sahara hung up the phone.

And, for the first time in what seemed like forever, Sahara could breathe.

NINETEEN

....

SAHARA – 1   *MERANDA* – 2

As Sahara walked into the Fairchester Economic League building on Monday, there wasn't a cloud in the sky. The sun was shining, and the birds were singing. Today was going to be a good day.

"Sahara, you look pretty. Love that dress on you!" said the receptionist when she got inside the building.

"Thank you!" Sahara said as she gave the blue and gold dress an extra twirl. "Is Glynda in?"

Jonecia looked around. "Yes, but something must be up. She's been locked up in her office since she came in this morning."

"Really?" Sahara wondered what today's drama. She didn't think she could deal with anything else.

She walked to her office, sat down at her desk, and looked around. At that moment, she realized that she really didn't have anything to do. She was caught up on the few projects that she had. She turned on her computer and checked her email. Nothing new there. What was she going to do all day? She just got to work. She couldn't turn around and leave now.

Well...she could always work on the campaign. For some reason, Sahara felt a little funny. But, she really didn't have anything else to do. And, she did have a big check from Cass and Zora. So much had happened since the party at their house that she almost forgot about it. She looked in her purse, and there it was.

But, she wasn't feeling inspired. She sat at her desk poking around until Jonecia stuck her head in Sahara's office and put her out of her misery. "Sahara, we are going to Ale House in Five Points for an early lunch. Want to go?"

She was getting nothing done there, so why not? As usual, the line for the Chinese restaurant next door was out the building. Across the street they saw bulldozers and cranes busy with activity in front of the boarded-up buildings.

The seven-block walk to the Ale House seemed short as the ladies chatted and enjoyed the break from the monotony of the office. When they arrived at the restaurant, they were quickly seated.

"What can I get you to drink?" asked the waitress.

The voice sounded familiar. Sahara looked up from the menu. It was Helena, from Coffee Moms. How many jobs did she have?

"Hi, Sahara! We see each other again," Helena said with a smile.

Sahara felt a little uncomfortable. After they ran into each other at the bridal shop, Helena called her a few times to see if they could get the girls together. However, Sahara never returned her calls.

"Hi, Helena." Since she was with work colleagues, she didn't want to prolong the conversation. "Are there any specials today?"

Helena looked a little surprised at the abrupt change of the conversation. However, she rattled off the restaurant's daily specials and then began to take their drink orders.

It seemed that no one could agree on the what pub fare they wanted to dine on that day—nachos seemed to be in the lead—but what got a unanimous decision was the drinks should have alcohol in them. Sahara guessed when the work at the Fairchester League was slow, a liquid lunch was an accepted thing.

"And for you, Sahara?" asked Helena with her pencil poised to write on the small pad in her hand.

The room seemed to stand still. What was she going to drink? The Strawberry Sunrise, with tequila, blood orange liqueur, fresh squeezed orange juice and fresh strawberry, sounded like a winner. Abbey Creek was on their wine list, and she loved their wines.

Yet, Sahara hesitated. She hadn't had a drink since that night at the Montgomerys' house. But, everyone was drinking. It would seem weird not to. But... "I'll take the Abbey Creek chardonnay."

Helena smiled. "Excellent choice. I'll put your drink orders in and come back and get your entrees."

As soon as Helena walked away, Jonecia asked, "So what's the story with the waitress, Sahara?"

Sahara took a sip of her water and asked, "What do you mean?"

"You know that you are Mrs. LUA, Mrs. Belles & Beaus...I just didn't think that you would know someone that...you know...was a waitress."

"Well, I don't know her *know her*...," said Sahara as she shrugged. "Our children were in playgroup together. That's all. We're not friends or anything."

Helena returned to the table and put the drinks on the table. "Ready to order?" she asked. After taking their orders, she shuffled away from the table.

The conversation quickly turned to office gossip. Who didn't like whom. Who was sleeping with whom. And, who was doing what dirt. Sahara had no idea that so much drama and scandal were going on at the Economic League. Guess that's what happens when you work a flexible schedule.

Suddenly, a picture of Senator Barrett and Meranda was on the television screen. Sahara's eyes immediately became fixated.

"Looks like Senator Barrett is finally retiring," said someone.

Sahara resisted the urge to squeal with glee. Yes! Now that the word was out that Senator Barrett wasn't running for re-election, Meranda lost some of her leverage with the chapter. With no direct connection to the North Carolina Senate, some of Meranda's sparkle with the chapter was sure to dim. And, Sahara still had the check from the Montgomerys. A smile came to her face.

"He's been in office forever. I wonder why he's leaving now."

"Well, whatever the reason. It is about time. Rumors have been swirling around him for years that he was corrupt and taking bribes." Sahara didn't say a word.

"Well, it does seem that North Carolina is booming, even Fairchester, except where black people live."

"That's why we have the Fairchester Economic League."

The whole table burst into laughter. As they finished their entrees, the conversation shifted. "So, what are the chances that we'll have a job this time next year?"

"Honey, I like to gamble, but I don't like those odds."

"What are you talking about?" asked Sahara.

The other ladies exchanged glances as Helena removed their empty plates from the table.

"That's what I always liked about you, Sahara," said Jonecia. "You really are all about the mission of the Fairchester Economic League, not just there for a paycheck."

Sahara wasn't sure about that, but it seemed like a compliment. "Sure, there have been a lot of changes...but you don't think...."

"Well, this isn't my first time at the rodeo, and this is what it looks like when a place is going under. Changes at the top. Little work. Bills mounting. Heck, they're even selling the building."

"Selling the building? There's no *For Sale* sign in the front."

Jonecia rolled her eyes. "This isn't your auntie's house. Give them some credit. It is being shopped around quietly, but it is happening. Trust me. I have a friend that works for B.A. Montgomery Real Estate Services. Don't get it twisted. The sharks are circling."

"I believe you," chimed in Quana. "I've been sending out my resume. I have a couple of interviews next week."

Sharks circling. Interviews. Sahara had no idea.

"Oh, don't look so sad, Sahara. Women like you always come out on top," said Quana.

"Women like me?"

"Sahara, we know that you are here with us but...you know...you're not like us," said Jonecia. "How many times have you sat and had lunch with us?"

"I'm here now."

"But, that's because there was probably literally nothing else for you to do." She paused. "And, even then...you probably had to take a second to think about it.

Sahara looked down remembering that she had paused before accepting their offer to lunch.

"It's okay. We get it. No biggie. We're happy to see a sistah make it," added Quana.

"But, I don't understand. I need this...."

"No, Sahara. You don't need this job. You're like her," said Jonecia.

Everyone's eyes shifted to where she was pointing—the television screen, which again showed a picture of Tyrone and Meranda Barrett.

She was nothing like Meranda. Sahara started to object, but Jonecia continued as they headed towards the door. "Sure, you may need this job to put a little extra cash in your pocket so that you don't have to worry about cash when you hang out with your girls or so you can have a little spending money for vacations and conferences and things like that. But, you don't need this job to survive. We do."

"Bye, ladies," said Helena as she walked to their table to remove the dirty plates and glasses.

Sahara didn't know what to say to Jonecia or Helena. So, she hurried out the door without saying a word.

Thankfully, the walk back to the Fairchester League went quickly. When they returned to the building, they quickly said goodbye and went their separate ways.

"Sahara, can I see you for a minute," asked Mia as Sahara entered the building.

Great. After that lunch, the last person that she wanted to talk to was Mia. "Sure. What's up?"

"I just wanted to give you a heads up. There are some questions about a contract that you signed," said Mia as they got to Sahara's office.

"A contract that I signed?" Sahara looked at the papers that Mia held out. They didn't look familiar, but there was her signature. "I don't remember signing them. But, what's this all about?"

"Well, there was some fraudulent activity on some of the accounts, so we're investigating it. I just wanted to see if you remembered these."

"Fraudulent activity?" Sahara's face went white.

"Yes, fraudulent activity. And, on top of that, the weirdest thing happened. My cousin was in jail last weekend for not paying his child support. Seems there was a Sahara Kyle also being arraigned that morning. It wasn't you, was it? It could make things look worse for you if you already have a record...." She shook her head like she was disappointed.

However, as Mia opened the door to Sahara's office to leave, instead of Mia stepping out, officers with drawn guns stepped in. "Hands up! Hands up! Hands up!" they yelled as they rushed in.

Sahara and Mia immediately complied and threw their hands into the air. Sahara felt like she was going to pee on herself. What was going on? She received the letter saying that the charges had been dropped. Why were the police here? And at her job? And, she was worried about a DUI hearing? This would be all over Fairchester in two minutes.

An officer walked over to Sahara while her hands were in the air and patted her down looking for weapons. Having been through this before, she knew there would be another, more thorough search, at the precinct. Tears welled up in her eyes as she tried to block out the memories of the physical violation by staring at the officer across the room performing the same motions on Mia.

A third officer entered the office and said, "Okay, ma'am. You can put your hands down now."

Mia smirked at Sahara as she lowered her hands.

"NOT YOU!" The third officer quickly shouted while drawing his gun. "Her!" He nodded his head in Sahara's direction with his gun still pointed at Mia.

Startled, Mia slowly raised her hands again, as Sahara lowered hers. A look of disbelief crept onto Mia's face as the officer beside her said, "Mia Johnson, you are under arrest for embezzlement, fraud...."

Sahara slumped in the chair as they led Mia out of the office. Mia was the one under arrest, not her.

There was no work getting done for the rest of the afternoon. However, no one could leave as police officers and members of the State Bureau of Investigation carried boxes of documents and who knows what else out of the building. Sahara had to call Noah and ask him to get the children because there was no way that she could leave in time to get them.

Many of the employees tried to walk casually by where things were being collected in hopes of getting a glimpse of something that could be material for the gossip mill. However, Sahara had heard enough, seen enough, experienced enough that she was content to sit in her office by herself until they got the all clear that they could leave.

As Sahara answered questions and gave her statement, she was in a state of shock. Most people were reluctant to leave whether they were asked to stay or not. Sahara was sure that many were just trying to get the details of everything that happened. But, she wanted no part of it. She just stayed in her office until the officers said that they no longer needed her. Thankfully, by that time, the office was quiet, and the buzzards waiting to pick the remains of the gossip carcass were long gone.

Sahara was exhausted and emotionally drained as she walked down the dark hallway in the Fairchester Economic League in disbelief. As she walked, she saw there was a light coming from Glynda's office. Sahara started to leave without saying anything, but something made her walk to Glynda's office. "Hi, Glynda. You're still here?"

Startled, Glynda looked up from the papers that she was staring at on her desk. "Yes," she replied. Her eyes were somber, and her face looked like she had aged years over the course of the day. "Yes, I'm here. Just going through some of the few documents that the State Bureau of Investigation didn't take."

"Well, I guess you won't be here long, because I'm pretty sure they took just about everything."

Glynda chuckled. "You are right about that. But, I'm glad that you are still here. I would like to talk to you if you have a minute."

Sahara was tired and her body had started to protest the lack of food since lunch. Plus, Noah and the children were waiting for her at home, but she was curious to hear what Glynda had to say. The day's events had certainly provided plenty of material.

Glynda seemed hesitant to speak at first, then she said, "To be honest, I don't know what is going to happen with the agency now. From a political standpoint, the organization was already on shaky ground. But, Mia's embezzlement...that certainly complicates matters even further. I really don't know what will happen."

Sahara wasn't surprised to hear Glynda say that. But she did have one question. "Does anyone know why? Why Mia did it?"

Glynda shook her head. "No, but..." She paused. "I don't know how to tell you this...but Mia set you up to be the scapegoat."

What? She must not have heard Glynda correctly. "I'm sorry. Did you say...?"

Glynda nodded up and down. "Yes, you heard me. If anyone found out about the embezzlement, the paper trail led to you as the thief."

Sahara sat up in the chair and looked at Glynda in disbelief. "Huh? Me? You've got to be kidding me!"

"Unfortunately, I'm not. Your signature was on the papers opening up a second account, and one of the checks put in there was a check from the Marriott that was issued to you."

The check from the Marriott. Sahara had a feeling that the mistake would come back to bite her. "My signature on the papers that opened the account?" That couldn't be right. She always read papers before signing them. There was no way that.... Then, her mind flashed back to the day of her father's news conference. Mia was trying to get her to sign some papers, and she was so distracted that she signed them without reading.

"But, if she left a paper trail leading to me, then how is she in jail and not me?" asked Sahara.

"The Barretts."

"The Barretts?" asked Sahara. What did they have to do with this?

"The discrepancies were found in an audit and brought to the board of directors. However, Senator Barrett insisted that you would never do anything like that and demanded that the auditors dig further. It wasn't until they looked deeper that they realized that it was really Mia and not you."

Sahara stared at Glynda in disbelief.

Glynda cleared her throat. "I'm sure that the truth would have eventually come out...but probably not before your name was dragged through the mud." Glynda sat back in her chair. "You are blessed. In a world full of posers and temperamental people, you have some great friends in Senator and Mrs. Barrett. You really are lucky."

Great friends in Senator and Mrs. Barrett. Sahara

held her head down. She thought about the conversation about the Barretts at lunch—and she didn't say one word in defense of their reputation. The past few months, she had behaved as if the Barretts, specifically Meranda, were Public Enemy Number One. And yet, Senator Barrett was the one that stood up for her, not just her name—but her character.

Sahara felt ashamed of herself. As tears welled up in her eyes, she said, "Thank you, Glynda, for letting me know."

Sahara didn't know what tomorrow held for the Fairchester Economic League, but one thing was certain. She had to talk to Meranda.

~~~

As Sahara pulled up to the Barretts' house, she turned off the radio. The scandal of an arrest at the Fairchester Economic League had replaced the news about Senator Barrett not running for re-election as the top story. She turned off the engine. She just needed a minute of peace and quiet.

She was nervous. Not only had she never shown up to Meranda's house unannounced, she had no idea what she was going to stay. But, the longer she sat there, the more anxious she became. She got out of the car and walked to the front door. She didn't want to lose her nerve.

Ding, ding, dong.

Silence. What if Meranda wasn't home? However, after a few minutes, Sahara heard footsteps approaching the door.

"Hello, Sahara?" said Meranda opening the door slightly. "Is everything alright? I wasn't expecting you."

"Yes, everything is fine, Meranda. I just needed to speak with you for a minute. Is it okay if I come in?"

"Yes, if it's important." Meranda stepped back to let Sahara step inside.

Normally perfectly polished and coifed, Meranda had on a large white robe over pink pajamas. Her honey complexion was missing the light application of makeup that gave Meranda's skin a sun-kissed glow. Still pretty, in its absence, the fine lines and signs of aging were more prominent. But, what caught Sahara off guard was Meranda's hair. Normally, wrapped tight in her signature bun, Sahara couldn't help but stare at the long flowing tresses that went well past Meranda's shoulder. Sahara had never seen Meranda look so...vulnerable.

"Well, I don't want to keep you. I just wanted to let you know that I'm dropping out of the race," said Sahara quickly.

Meranda looked perplexed. "You're not running for president?" She closed her robe tighter. "Why, may I ask?"

Sahara chose her words carefully. "Because I think that you are the president that the chapter needs now."

"I don't understand. You have the new ideas, the large donation from the Montgomerys.... If the election was today, you would probably be the winner. Why would you want to drop out now?"

"Because I don't like what this election is doing to me...to us. All of this—the campaigning, the politicking, the strategizing—it's never been me. If this is what I must do to be president, then I don't want it. Remaining true to whom I am and our friendship means more to me."

"I...I...I don't know what to say."

"Say, that you'll be the president that I know you will be. Look, I was running because I feel that the chapter is in a rut. That we need some new ideas. But, you have great ideas, Meranda. I've seen how you've implemented them in other organizations. I know that you have the ideas and the leadership to take the chapter to the next level—and I am willing to help you in whatever capacity you need me."

"Sahara...I never meant for this...." Meranda looked down on the floor.

"Let's call the last few month water under the bridge."

Meranda shook her head as she dabbed at her eyes. "Yes, yes...I would like that..."

Sahara and Meranda embraced. It felt like a weight had been lifted off Sahara's shoulders. And as Meranda and Sahara's hug came to an end, Sahara said, "Now, I have one little favor to ask of you...."

TWENTY

....

~~SAHARA – 1~~   *MERANDA – 3*
              NOAH – 2

Sahara watched from the other side of the dresser as Noah looked at himself in the mirror. The slim-cut Fitzgerald tuxedo jacket fit his boxer frame like a glove. Noah always complained about the little bit of gray hair that had crept onto his temples, but she felt that it made him look distinguished. His signature glasses, made him look wiser, and were a nice touch.

"What happened to the Armani tuxedo?" asked Sahara.

"I was going to wear it, but in the end, I liked this one better for tonight. I'm going to grab the tickets," Noah said as he walked out the room.

Sahara looked at her rose gold sequined gown in the mirror. She always liked gray and silver—and you could never go wrong with black at a formal event—but for some reason she felt like wearing something a little different, a little bolder. When she saw the eye-catching dress in the window of one of the boutiques in Midtown, she knew that it was perfect.

"Sahara, are you ready? We don't want to be late," Noah said from downstairs.

No, they didn't want to be late. Sahara slid another layer of the mauve lip gloss across her lips.

"Britney, I'm so glad that you're home and able to watch the children," Sahara said as she descended the stairs. "How is college life?"

Britney, their neighbor and a student at Hampton, smiled. "I love it, Mrs. Kyle, but I'm glad to be back home—-and able to watch these two kiddos." Trevor and Clarissa laughed as she tickled them.

"Well, I know they are glad to see you. They missed you." Sahara gave the children a kiss goodbye before following Noah into the garage.

Normally, even though she and Noah had been going for years, her stomach was a ball of nerves and excitement when they left for The Sphinx Masquerade Ball. She always felt the same as she did the first time they attended, in shock and disbelief that they received an invitation.

However, not tonight. As they drove downtown to the Fairchester Convention Center, for some reason Sahara was as cool as a cucumber. When she saw her mother's name pop up on her cell phone, she hit the Decline button. She still wasn't ready.

"We've arrived, my lady." said Noah as he stopped the car at the valet stand, and the valet graciously helped Sahara out of the red BMW. Colored spotlights swirled around the convention center, and Sahara felt like she was at a Hollywood premiere as she and Noah walked the red carpet to the entrance.

Like every year, the lobby was filled with women dressed in beautiful ball gowns and tuxedo-clad men. Everyone wore ornately embellished Venetian masks in keeping with the ball's masquerade theme. Some masks had pearls, others feathers. Some had intricate beading, others simple lace.

Sahara smiled and returned nods as she and Noah walked through the room. They had been to the event and around these people enough times that even behind the masks, many were easily identifiable.

"Good to see you, Brother Noah," said Carl Hopkins, Noah's fraternity brother and Senator Barrett's former campaign advisor. "Or should I say, Sentinel Noah." Noah's face broke into a huge grin. "Congratulations on the appointment to the Education Council," continued Carl Hopkins as he slapped Noah on the shoulder.

"Thank you, Sentinel Carl. I'm looking forward to working with Sentinel Tyrone to get some things done for our HBCUs...."

Oof! Someone bumped Sahara from behind. "Oh, I'm so sorry. I didn't...Oh, it's you, Soror Sahara," said a woman in a large baby blue mask with tall feathers. "It's always so hard to see with this mask on my face."

"Good evening, Soror DeBerry. Is your husband here, also?" said Sahara as she tried to hold back a small chuckle. Soror DeBerry always spent the evening bumping into half of the guest.

"Yes, I was so busy looking for him that I wasn't paying attention to where I was going."

Sahara smiled. 'Well, if I see him, I'll send him in your direction."

"Thank you, dear. And, I must let you know that me and the other Golden Girls...you know that's what the golden sorors in the chapter call ourselves...we hated to hear that you removed your name from the ballot. You would have made a fine president."

"Thank you for your support, Soror DeBerry. It means a lot. And, I am looking forward to helping Soror Meranda in whatever we she needs."

"Hmmph! She may not be a Golden Girl, but she is an oldie...not sure about the goodie part. Well, let me find Horace...." Soror DeBerry teetered off without saying another word.

Carl Hopkins and Noah were still talking when Sahara spotted a woman in a white lace mask making her way through the crowd. It was Glynda Clayton.

They hadn't spoken since the night of Mia's arrest at the Fairchester Economic League. The next morning everyone received a robocall saying that the offices were closed until further notice. The few people at the office that Sahara spoke to were not waiting for the call and already looking for new jobs. With Noah's promotion to executive vice president, Sahara was content to stay at home with the children.

"Hi, Glynda! How are you doing?" said Sahara as she

stopped her and gave her a quick hug.

Glynda seemed startled but returned Sahara's embrace. "Well, it is nice to see you."

Sahara wasn't sure why Glynda seemed so stand-offish. "Any word on when the office is going to open again?" Sahara knew that she should say if...but she wanted to be positive.

Glynda stood there for a second without saying a word. Then, she looked over her shoulder like she wanted to make sure that no one could hear her. Why the need for cloak and dagger act?

"I assumed that you heard," said Glynda once she checked again that no one was within earshot. "The Economic League will re-open in the fall."

How would she have heard? "Why wait to fall? Why not let everyone come back now?" asked Sahara.

"Well, the buildings been sold."

"What do you mean the buildings been sold?" But then, Sahara remembered the conversation at the Ale House. Jonecia said the board was quietly looking for a buyer for the building.

"With everything that is going and the financial issues that the Economic League has, the board of directors thought it best to sell the building," said Glynda.

"Well, that could take a while so why not let everyone come back to work now?" questioned Sahara.

Glynda shook her head. "You misunderstood me. They aren't planning to sell the building. The building has already been sold."

"So quickly? How? To whom?"

"B.A. Montgomery Real Estate Services."

Cass Montgomery's company. Sahara would like to say that she was surprised, but she wasn't. They had bought everything else on the block. Why not the Fairchester Economic League building? She just didn't know why she hadn't seen it sooner. With the scandal at the Economic League, she was sure that he swooped in like a vulture to get that prime real estate in West Village. That was one more notch in his empire's belt.

But, she tried to be optimistic. "Well, with all that has happened, there is no way that the board of directors will leave Mr. Johnson as the executive director, so hopefully, you will get your old job back."

An odd expression came across Glynda's face. "Oh, they aren't planning to leave Frank as the executive director...but I won't get my job back."

"Huh? Well, who will be the new executive director?" No one else was as experienced as Glynda so she had no idea who else would be a consideration.

"Tyrone Barrett," Glynda said matter-of-factly.

"Tyrone Barrett?"

"Yes, I thought you knew. Tyrone Barrett is the new executive director."

That, Sahara had not seen coming. Sure, he wasn't running for re-election so she guessed that this was a way to stay involved in the community. He would definitely help raise the profile of the organization. But, Ty-rone Barrett was the new executive director?

Sahara felt bad for Glynda. She knew that Glynda hated being demoted to deputy executive director and wanted her old title back. However, Sahara knew where her loyalties lay. She agreed to not run for LUA president in exchange for Meranda getting Senator Barrett to shore up the votes that Noah needed to get on the Education Council.

Not only had Meranda upheld her end of the bargain, Senator Barrett was responsible for Noah getting into The Coalition of Sentinels. No, there was no way that she was going to speak against them on this situation. No way.

"Well, I'm sure that everything will work out," Sahara offered.

"I'm sure," said Glynda unconvincingly. "I see one of the human resources manager at MobileComp so let me make my way over there. It was good to see you, Sahara."

"It was nice to see you as well," Sahara added, but Glynda had hurried off. So, Tyrone was going to be the new executive director at the Fairchester Economic League. Interesting.

People were beginning to file into the main hall so Noah and Sahara walked to the other side of the room to the registration table. "Hello...Noah and Sahara Kyle." Noah said to the woman sitting at the registration table.

The woman looked down at the papers in front of her. "Yes...Mr. and Mrs. Noah Kyle. Enjoy your evening." She smiled and handed two place cards to a woman standing behind her. "The hostess will seat you."

The hostess led the way into the convention center's main hall. The decadence of the decorations always took Sahara's breath away. The soft purple lighting in the room danced across the gold metallic linen on the tables. The round lanterns hanging from the ceiling illuminated the long plumes of ostrich feathers in the tall centerpiece vases. Like the lobby, people were networking everywhere. And at the front of the room, the twelve-piece band was playing Jill Scott's *Golden* on the stage.

The Sphinx was one of the premier women's organizations in the country and getting an invitation to the masquerade ball was an achievement within itself. However, they didn't want to stop there. You may have an invitation but the table layout outlined where on the totem pole of the Fairchester elite you fell.

The Sphinx president and chapter officers had tables in the front closest to the band. Then came the tables of the Sphinx chapter members followed by the tables for the other elite organizations—The Coalition of Sentinels, The Shield, Darlings, Marigolds, Gazelles, and Belles & Beaus—followed by the sororities and fraternities. Two community tables were also near the back of the room.

As the hostess started towards the tables, Sahara waved and smiled at people that she knew. They quickly moved past the sororities and fraternities' tables to the rows with the social organizations. As they got closer to the Marigolds' table, Sahara saw Emery and Reynard.

Dressed in a beautiful red sequined gown with a matching beaded mask, Emery looked stunning as always. Sahara thought back to their last conversation on the day that she went to her father's vacation house. Emery hadn't said it but her demeanor told Sahara that their friendship was over. She guessed they would remain cordial...smile when in public, even make small talk...but the sisterhood that they had developed would be no more.

And, Sahara was okay with that. She and Emery had been on every point of the friendship spectrum— friendly at their brief meeting that first night at the Theta's party and then enemies fueled by Rozlyn's lies. Finally, they had been friends, real friends, but that would be no more.

Sahara and Emery smiled politely at each other as the Kyles walked by, but that was it.

"Mr. and Mrs. Kyle," the hostess said, "We are at your table." She handed the place cards to Noah.

Noah Kyle – Table Seventy-three.

Gone was the time that Sahara and Noah weaved through the ballroom like serpents past the tables of the general members of the Sphinx to the front of the room where the chapter president's table was. Ida Wilkins Marsh was still the chapter president of the Fairchester Sphinx, but Noah was offered a seat at the Sentinel table, and although it was further in the back, that's where he wanted to sit.

"Sentinel Noah, it's great to see you and the wife," said Alton when they sat down at the table.

Noah's face broke into a huge grin. "Sentinel Alton...Donna...great to see you, too."

Sahara and Donna looked at each other, rolled their eyes, and suppressed the urge to laugh. Noah and Alton were inducted into The Coalition of Sentinels together, and apparently were getting a kick out of being part of this new brotherhood.

As Noah and Alton became engrossed in their conversation, Sahara turned to Donna. "So, what have you been up to?"

Donna got a sheepish look on her face and then held out her left hand. "Well...."

Sahara looked at the diamond encrusted band nestled below the engagement ring on Donna's finger. "Oh my goodness, did you...."

"Yes, we eloped yesterday. We just decided to go ahead and do it...because I'm pregnant," whispered Donna.

"You're what?" Sahara's eyes opened wide. "Oh my goodness, Donna! I'm so happy for you!"

"I know...," said Donna. "It's not quite how we

planned for things to happen, but we figured that we would go with it." She smiled. "We're hoping for a girl. Alton would love to have a daughter."

Sahara continued to smile but didn't say a word. She would go to her grave with the secret that Alton already had a daughter with Emery. "Well then, I'm going to wish for a happy and healthy baby girl for you." She paused. "So, how was the ceremony?"

"Short and sweet," said Donna still beaming. "Our family was there and then a few friends joined us at a restaurant to celebrate."

Sahara stiffened. She knew that "a few friends" included Tania and would have included her and Noah, especially since Noah and Alton's induction into The Sentinels...but because of what happened she guessed Donna didn't want her there. "I'm glad that everything went well, Donna."

"Thank you," said Donna. "So, what are we going to do about these two newly minted 'line brothers'?"

Sahara laughed. "I know. Sentinel this, and Sentinel that. I wonder how long this phase will last."

"Probably forever," said Donna, as they both laughed. "Quick question. Did Noah get a gift for his sponsor? Alton is still trying to figure out what to get Senator Barrett."

Senator Barrett? "Oh goodness. Now, they have an even tighter bond. Senator Barrett sponsored Noah, too." said Sahara.

Donna got a funny look on her face. "I didn't think members could sponsor more than one person, and Senator Barrett definitely sponsored Alton. Meranda mentioned it at our transitional executive board meeting."

Sahara didn't want to belabor the point and let the conversation move on to another subject. However, as she and Donna discussed the ups and downs of pregnancy, what Donna said remained in the back of Sahara's mind.

"And another thing I don't understand is this constant need to go to the restroom," said Donna. "I'll be back."

Sahara laughed. "I'll come with you." It had been more than a few years since she was pregnant with Trevor, but she remembered the physical manifestations of pregnancy, beyond a large belly, all too well.

As they walked past the throngs of people in the convention center on their way to the restroom, Sahara and Donna chatted like the way they used to. Sahara knew that it could be a long road to getting her friendship with Donna back to where it used to be—but she was willing to try. "I'll wait for you out here," said Sahara when they reached the ladies' room.

As Sahara waited for Donna to return, she people watched in the lobby. There were still so many people mixing and mingling in the lobby. Sahara thought back to the time when she was nervous to be at these events and around these people—her father's world is what she had dubbed it. However, now everything seemed normal, commonplace.

A woman wearing a beautiful green gown with a large pink and green mask caught Sahara's attention. Meranda. Just the person that she wanted to see. Sahara made a beeline in her direction.

"Good evening, Soror Meranda. You look beautiful as always," said Sahara as they exchanged air kisses.

"You look wonderful, too, Soror."

Sahara didn't know how much time she had before Donna returned so she had to be quick. "I just wanted to thank you again for getting Senator Barrett to endorse Noah's appointment to the Education Council. And, Senator Barrett sponsoring Noah into The Coalition of Sentinels was a surprise but a welcomed bonus."

"Sahara, you don't have to thank me. We had a deal, and I upheld my end of the agreement. And, I'm sure Noah will be a valuable asset to the Education Council." Meranda smiled. "And, don't think just because you are not president means that I am going to let you off the hook. We need to get together and figure out what role makes sense for you. I'm not planning to be president forever, you know."

Sahara laughed. "I wouldn't have it any other way. Can we get together next Tuesday?" Sahara saw Donna emerge from the rest room. She needed to head back in that direction.

"It's a date," said Meranda. As Sahara walked away, Meranda added, "And Sahara, Tyrone was Alton's sponsor. He didn't sponsor Noah."

Sahara gave her a quick wave and hurried to Donna's side. "Ready to go back to the table?"

"Yes. But, I'm sure that this evening will be filled with a few return trips to this place."

As Sahara returned to her seat, she couldn't help but think about what Meranda said. *Tyrone was Alton's sponsor. He didn't sponsor Noah.* If Senator Barrett didn't, who did?

A look of horror crept onto Sahara's face. There was only one other person that she knew in The Coalition of Sentinels. Her father. But, he couldn't have. He wouldn't have. Would he?

"May I have this dance, my lady?" asked Noah when they returned to the table.

Noah led the way as they meandered around the tables to the front of the room. Sahara smiled and waved at people she knew. The band started playing an instrumental jazz version of Nicki Minaj's *Moment for Life* as they reached the dance floor, and Noah pulled her into his arms. Sahara tried to get into the groove of the music, but there was something nagging her.

"Noah, do you know who sponsored you in The Sentinels?"

"Yes," he said as he looked loving into her eyes.

Okay, was he going to tell her? "Who?"

"Hal Scott."

Who was that? "Hal Scott?" Sahara asked.

"He's on the board of directors for the Black Achievers. He told me that he thought that I would be an asset to the organization. Why?"

Black Achievers was a program where Noah mentored. She knew that Noah had a tremendous impact on the children there and that many people were impressed with his dedication and hard work. "Oh, no reason."

No reason at all. She had absolutely nothing to do with Noah getting into The Coalition of Sentinels. Nothing at all.

As their bodies moved as one across the dance floor, Sahara rested her head on Noah's shoulder. She thought about Clarissa and Trevor and the life they had built in Fairchester—the friendships they made, the relationships they had lost. The time hadn't been perfect, but it was theirs.

As the band transitioned to Stevie Wonder's *Are You Sure Love Is the Name of The Game*, Sahara knew the answer was a resounding¬ yes.

Thank you for reading my book. If you enjoyed it, please take a moment to leave a review at your favorite retailer. Thank you!

-Shonette Charles

ABOUT THE AUTHOR

Shonette Charles is an active member of Alpha Kappa Alpha Sorority, Incorporated, Jack and Jill of America, Inc., and The Links, Incorporated. Ms. Charles holds degrees from Harvard University and the University of Michigan. A former freelance writer and editor, she resides in Raleigh, North Carolina with her family. Visit her online at www.shonettecharles.com, and check out her blog— Pearls, Poise & Protocol. You can also connect with her on Facebook, Twitter, Instagram, and LinkedIn.

A book club discussion guide for *Winner Takes All* can be found at **www.shonettecharles.com**.

CPSIA information can be obtained
at www.ICGtesting.com
Printed in the USA
LVOW11s0915220617
538962LV00003B/442/P